Longing Lust, and Love

BLACK LESBIAN STORIES

Longing, Lust, and Love

BLACK LESBIAN STORIES

Edited by

Shonia L. Brown

NGHOSI
books

Published in the United States by Nghosi Books
P.O. Box 1908, Stone Mountain, Georgia 30086.
www.nghosibooks.com
Printed in the United States.
Cover design: MarionDesigns
Cover photograph: MarionDesigns
Cover model: Dani Nikole
Text design: MarionDesigns
Logo art: Jon Stemp
First Edition.
ISBN: 0-9785954-0-8

"Longing, Lust, and Love" Poem © 2006 W.L. Tracy appears by permission of the author. "No Frills" Poem © 1999 Torrena "Torri" Dye appears by permission of the author. "Is this Love?" Poem © 2006 April N. Royal appears by permission of the author. "Let Your Fingers Do the Walking" © 1997 Stephani Maari Booker was originally published in *Gay Black Female Magazine* (GBF, 1997), and appears by permission of the author. "Symphony" © 2005 S. Stephens is excerpted from the novel, *Am I My Sister's Keeper?* (iUniverse, 2005), and appears by permission of the author. "Tuesday" © 2004 Trish Carter is excerpted from the novel, *Linger...Lust is Surface* (Gate Way Publishing, 2004), and appears by permission of the author. "Walk Like a Man" © 2006 Laurinda D. Brown is excerpted from the novel, *Walk Like a Man* (Q-Boro Books, 2006), and appears by permission of the author.

TABLE OF CONTENTS

Acknowledgements

In all things that I do, I must acknowledge God's work and purpose moving through me. The idea of this book was conceived in 2004, as a way to share my blessings with other new writers. After promoting my debut novel since 2002, I had contemplated publishing a second novel under my own small print press. The small dividends received from royalty payments from a print-on-demand company coupled with my initially large efforts to market and promote the book, were catalysts to the further development of my own publishing house. I realized very soon that the only luxury of having someone else print your book was the time, money, and energy that was spent in the actual printing process; the rest of the equation that would determine the success of your book, was solely based on your efforts. So Nghosi Books.com was reinvented into a new voice for African-American LGBT literature. As it was originally designed to not only promote my novel but the creative talents of independent artists of all disciplines, so would its new role as a printing house be to promote my books as well as other writers. I thank God for allowing me to see this vision become a reality.

I also have to give thanks to the women in my life who despite my faults, alway see the best that I can be and don't mind putting their money where their mouth is. I thank my partner in love and life, Tracy Dionne Griggs for her endless belief that there is always some good in the bad that we experience in this life. Her love, patience, diligence, faith, kindness, and determination have kept me inspired even when giving up seemed like the best thing to do.

To Dawn Jernigan, I give thanks for her friendship that has felt like a lifetime of laughter, fellowship, tears, and inspiration. She has helped me to see just how valuable my ideas and efforts truly are, and without her financial and physical support, this book would not have been possible.

My idea of friendship has been redefined many times over but I'm glad to say that my friendship and sisterhood with Trinia Clark, Lucelia Flood-Partridge, Sylvia Cordell, Nadestra Benson, and Renita Santos has sustained me through some very difficult times.

A special thank you goes to Trinia and Melvyn Clark for making me the godmother of a handsome baby boy by the name of Hamilton Wesley Augustus Clark.

I'd also like to thank Raye and Diana of Aphrodite's Toy Box for always saying, "Yes," to whatever idea or request I make of them. Without the use of their space, lingerie, ideas, and continuous blessings, the photo shoot for the cover wouldn't have been as fun and engaging! And much thanks goes to cover model Dani Nikole for her beauty, intelligence, kindness, and willingness to withstand long hours under the pressure of delivering fantastic results.

To the 25 contributing writers documented in this anthology, I thank you for sharing your blessings and having the courage to let your voices be heard in a world that would feel more comfortable denying that you truly exist.

Introduction:
Labels Don't Define Me or Do They?

Even though most people detest stereotypes because of their negative connotations, often there is some validity hidden within these labels. In the land of milk and honey, the home of the free, we proclaim, "I gotta be me," and stake our claim on our individuality. Yet, within the characteristics that we think make us so very different, there is at least one underlying similarity. We are all human beings who at one point in time will long for the touch of someone else, will lust over a forbidden desire, and will give our love to another. Whether that other person is the same gender, is not what's most important. Rather, what is important is that we share our love and ourselves with someone else.

This book has been written and published during a time when people will use our sexuality to incite fear and hatred in our hearts, which weren't designed to hate and destroy, but rather to love and procreate. Some people say that is the problem with homosexuality. God didn't intend for men to have sexual relationships with men, or women to have sexual relationships with women; He wanted us to consummate our love with the opposite sex and to procreate. Some ask the question, how can people of the same gender procreate? But I ask the question, how could we not procreate? Not in the most literal sense of the word, do I believe that two men will create a child together although they may be raising children that they have created outside of their union. However, I do believe that as same gender loving (SGL) people, we also have the ability to create new life, new art, new thought, and new culture. I also think that these creations are just as beneficial to the universe as the birth of a new human being. The importance of an SGL person's creation may not be quickly recognized by those individuals who deny our rights to be proud of who we are and to love as they love, but the truth of our contributions is still relevant.

What would we be without the talent of actor, Neil Patrick Harris of *Doogy Houser* fame; the athleticism and showmanship of WNBA player Sheryl Swoopes; the courage of activist, Maya Keyes (daughter of conservative politician, Alan Keyes); the prolific literature of author, James Baldwin; the humor and candor of comediennes, Ellen DeGeneres, Rosie O'Donnell, and Sandra Bernhardt; the infamous strut and model expertise of Ms. J. Alexander of *America's Next Top Model* fame; the activist/folk singer, Joan Baez; the American composer and songwriter, Cole Porter; icon and American popular music singer, Johnny Mathis; acclaimed choreographer, Alvin Ailey; modern classic horror filmmaker, Clive Barker; accomplished actor, Raymon Burr of *Perry Mason* fame; glamorous women's clothing and sharp men's tailoring, and fragrance creators, Dolce & Gabbana; pioneering photojournalist and documentary photographer Frances Benjamin Johnston; and countless others too many to name in this one Introduction (Information derived from http://www.glbtq.com/, an encyclopedia of gay, lesbian, bisexual, transgender & queer cultures).

Even more significant are the creations of the contributing writers of this anthology. Without their abilities to breathe new life into stories of infatuation, desire, and amour, some young, middle aged, or senior woman would have no written account of her own journeys through the sometimes scary, exciting, painful, rewarding life of loving a person of the same sex. Our stories would be hidden and overshadowed by the media's reports of *so called newsworthy* topics like "down low" brothas or straight girls who like to kiss other girls to arouse their boyfriends. Our stories are believed to be non-existent or re-written by a publishing industry that seeks the almighty dollar rather than the truth by disguising straight women's fantasies as lesbian eroticism. But thank God for divine intervention and His ability to grant these 25 writers the ability to tell their stories in their own voices, through their own experiences, within their own community with honesty, integrity, and accuracy. Will you find stories of sex, dildos, vibrators, dykes, bull daggers, femmes, tops, bottoms, aggressive femmes, soft studs, lawyers, doctors, teachers, mothers, grandmothers, daughters, sisters, family? Yes, you will find all of these and much more within *Longing, Lust, and Love: Black Lesbian Stories*. Will you find stories that anyone can identify with no matter what their race, color, religion, sexual orientation, culture? Yes, you will find a story or many stories that anyone can relate to. Will everyone read them? No, in the words of Abraham Lincoln, "You can please some of the people some of the time, but you can't please all of the people all of the time." This book was created for the reader with an open mind and an open heart. It was created for the reader that recognizes there is no right or wrong when love is involved. You are right, I am right, we are ALL just right, when it comes to the rush that we feel at the sight of a potential lover; the passion that grows like a rising flame as our bodies become consumed with a new lover; and the warmth of contentment and familiarity that comes with the comfort of the timeless years with an existing lover. No matter what stage of your relationship you are in, whether it is the longing, lust, or love phase, it is all worth celebrating or reminiscing. The ladies of *Longing, Lust, and Love: Black Lesbian Stories* can't wait to share their stories of celebration and memories with you.

Are these stories similar? Yes, some of them have very similar experiences but then don't we all? Just when we think we've cornered the market on the best sexual experience or romantic encounter, there is always someone else that comes along that either has a very similar story or an even better one, which takes us back to that whole idea of just how much alike we are more than we are different.

I encourage you to enjoy the tales of longing with stories like, *She*. Memory is a bitch when you can't remember the name of the woman you took home the night before. The main character in *She* discovers this when playing the field too long turns into the day when the player gets played. She finally longs to share her heart with another. This theme is carried over into *Heartfelt*, when another player must come to terms with meeting

Ms. Right. Does she turn in her player card for a lifetime with the same woman? When religion and family expectations forces us to remain in silence and deep in the closet, we find that what gives us courage to walk with pride is the chance of redefining what we believe in and what our family looks like. We find that with the women in *Symphony, The Homecoming,* and *Pink Laces*. Religious practices carry over into the story of *Morning Music*, as we discover a woman who longs for the passion of her lover but must abstain during the season of Ramadan. Longing from afar opens the stories of *The 410* and *Pink Laces*, and our stories of this initial phase are culminated with the desire of women who are not only from very different age groups but also of a different race in the *Unspoken*.

Your journey with these prolific writers continues when the heat is turned way up with stories of lust. A vacation or weekend getaway will never be the same when the women of *The Weekend* and *Tuesday* find themselves in for a very long and bumpy ride with girls that can't wait to get next to them. The church picnic is a scene for more than just good soul food and fellowship, as the woman of *Walk Like a Man*, finds herself receiving more than second helpings from Sister Estelle. Following rules seem to be a challenge not only in the church but in the military, as a Private and Drill Sergeant find themselves too close for comfort in *Don't Ask, Don't Tell*. A stud just wants to have fun in *Look at Me When You Come* but with vicarious play comes a price that she might not be willing to pay. Phone sex, instant messaging, and masturbation prevail in *Bringing Up Daddy*, and *Let Your Fingers Do The Walking*. Supernatural forces reveal a deeper lust that promises to be deadly in *Once Bitten*!

This journey culminates with the women who share just how they keep the flames ablaze with stories of love. Love develops within a long-term friendship that is finally consummated in *From Friends to Lovers*. The loss of a potential lover makes room for a lifetime of the perfect love in *Titalyo*. Love split between lovers and their family is expressed in *Nora's*

Lover, Steps Are Made for Climbing, and *Bye, Bye, Beautiful*. Out of sight and out of mind is not the case with the lovers who survive long distance relationships in *Space and Time: Theory of Relativity*, *Love Has Never Felt Like This*, and *The Place for Pride*. Adding spice to their long-term relationship is celebrated in a very special way in *The Birthday Present*.

As I finished reading and editing these stories for publication, sadness consumed me. I found myself missing them like old friends that were no longer a part of my life. I longed to sit with them again and learn more about their characters; I lusted over the images that flickered through my mind of their previous stories; and I loved the fact that they had entered my life, if only for a short period of time. Even as I write this introduction, I look forward to not only revisiting them in my own private time but I, more importantly, am excited about sharing them with you, their new readers, new friends, new family. I hope that you will discover, as I did, that our stories are not so different, but very much the same, as we all take this journey in life, searching, wanting, and achieving the love that God has for all of us. Enjoy your journey and make sure that you share these blessings and more with others.

Shonia L. Brown
P.O. Box 1908
Stone Mountain, GA 30086
www.nghosibooks.com
November 2006

Longing
Phase 1

Longing, Lust, and Love

Our eyes meet,
we exchange glances,
smiles that secrete lust.
We continue other conversations,
frequently making eye contact.
With a bashful flutter of an eyelash
and a knowingly confident smirk,
finally an approach is made.
One brave or maybe over-confident soul
approaches the other.
Exchange of words,
or flirts,
of soft hands stroking one's back
with the tenderness, yet lustful intentions
of a prospective new lover.
Two days later,
there is the first date.
Dinner with a late night stroll in the park,
nothing too intense,
yet with the foreplay of things to come.
We kiss our first kiss on the steps of one's home.
There is heated passion,
so intense, clothes start to drop as the next-door neighbor
walks his dog.
Remembering where we are,
we giggle
that playful, lustful laughter that salivates desire.
The door opens as we rush in fumbling for buttons,
zippers, straps, whatever is bonded must be unleashed,
must be pleasured.
Fingers swarm around bodies once clothed
in fine, alluring attire.
A tongue searches the other's mouth finding a home in a place

of beautiful smiles.
Hands grab at waist, breasts,
buttocks with all knowing desires.
Passion is felt through every hair on every inch of our bodies.
We linger in the scent
of the moment of sexual explosions.
One month later,
we are sharing a bathroom.
Both getting ready for work,
giving each other kisses
of love,
glances of
"Have a good day, Baby."
We go our way with our hearts
stayed on each other throughout the day.
There are e-mails, lunch phone calls, and text messages of
"I Love You"
that keep us content until we see each other again.
That night we share a bed,
giving each other the warm embrace
that confirms we are home.
We snuggle in those embraces
never wanting to part;
treasuring the moments we share
each day,
each night,
in a love that is our own.

She

DaVita Baker

I awakened to the lingering scent of her perfume; it hung in the air heavily. As the fragrance filled my nostrils with sweet memories, the events of last night were slowly coming back to me. I had gone out for an evening on the town wearing my royal blue, silk suit with the matching hat, turned to the back. Scented from head to toe in Dolce Gabbana, I was, as usual, taking no prisoners.

I am what they would call the happily single stud. Me and relationships never clicked. I had only one relationship that I can speak of and that was enough for me to call it quits forever. Women these days wanted too much drama and too much money. I sat down one day and figured out just what it was I wanted from these ladies and came up with one answer, *the punany*. Seriously, it was easier to get and I didn't have to make any commitments. You would be surprised how many females wanted nothing more than a good fuck, period. No ties, no questions, no answers, and no goodbyes…just straight sex.

This night had begun like all the others. I drove to the spot in my 2002 Escalade. It was ivory with custom blue interior. I had The Isley Brothers bumpin' on the stereo as I pulled up to the club. Every head turned in my direction when they heard the sultry bass of *In Between the Sheets*. I parked in my usual spot out front. I was a permanent VIP so parking was not an issue. The line outside of the club was long as usual. I got a few sideway glances as I ducked the velvet rope and walked right in the front door. The music was loud but they were doing a run of old school rap. It was just the kind of music I liked to hear to get my pimp mode pumped up. A few of the regulars came up to me and gave me love. You know how we do, a dap here, a hug there, some slap-me-ups, and what have you. I made it to the bar and ordered my usual, Cognac on the rocks.

I assumed the position and commenced to seek out my prey for the night. As I looked around the room, I became very disinterested. Either the females were busted, broken, or with someone. Not one woman in the place looked like she deserved my time. I strolled to the rear of the bar and figured on getting a table. Since I was VIP, I had a seat automatically. My table was at the corner of the dance floor. As I turned in the direction of where my table should have been, I had to look twice when I noticed a homely looking female sitting in my seat! She wasn't bad looking. She was light skinned with long curly hair. She was wearing a basic low cropped sweater with a basic skirt. No glamour or glitz. No name brand bling on her at all. I did notice she had a small gold heart on a chain around her neck. What stood out even more was that she was at *my table*, in *my seat*. I walked over to the table and cleared my throat.

"How are you doing tonight?" I asked, unsure of how to tell her to move.

"I'm fine." She said, like she was really disinterested and quite bothered by my instrusion.

"My name is Romie. Can I get you something to drink?"

"Hello, Romie. Pleased to meet you. Um, sure…White Zinfandel, please."

I shook my head okay then walked back to the bar. I was trying to come up with a way to break the ice and tell her to get the hell away from my table. I ordered her wine and took it to her.

"Here you go." I said as I set her glass down in front of her.

"Thank you, Romie. I appreciate it."

"Do you mind if I sit down?" I asked abruptly. *I was clearly tripping as to why I was asking to sit at my own table.* Come to think of it, this was the first time I can remember that I have ever had to clear my table. Usually the bouncers protect the VIP tables from unwanted guests. I looked around to see if I could spot any of the bouncers and not one was in sight.

"Sure, I would love the company," she said.

I pulled out a chair and sat down. I glanced over a few times at her while I sat there enjoying my drink. She appeared to be off in another world, completely oblivious to my presence. But there was something about her perfume that intrigued me. Perfume usually gave me insight into the kind of person a woman was but this scent was familiar to me. I recognized the scent of Jasmine with hints of Vanilla and Sandalwood. I tried to recall the fragrance but I couldn't quite place it. It was heavenly, downright mesmerizing. I made a mental note to ask her what it was.

The moments that followed were silent. I drank a couple of more glasses of Cognac and she had one more White Zinfandel. I hadn't realized how much time had passed until I heard, "Last call for alcohol!" I had been at the club for an hour and hadn't done anything but sit at my table with a woman who wasn't giving up any conversation.

Then the DJ made an announcement:

"I have a special request for She...*If Only for One Night.*"

The lights were dimmed and when I looked across the table, she was looking right at me. She got up, came over to me, took my glass, and pulled me to the dance floor. My heart was pounding rapidly. I stood up and she pulled me close to her.

"May I have this dance?" She asked in the sweetest voice I had ever heard.

"Y-yes," I stuttered. My whole pimp game had just fallen on the floor.

She led me further onto the dance floor then turned and faced me. I placed my hands on her waist and looked into her eyes. Lightning shot through my loins as she moved into me and started a slow grind. The scent of her perfume was intoxicating. It swirled around in my head and mingled with the effects of the Cognac. I was spinning. *Damn! My mind was racing and my sex drive was in overload.*

I was totally mind blown. This was usually my move but she had made it. I usually go get the girl and take her to the dance floor but she got me and was no doubt leading this dance. The music was loud in my ears and everyone but the two of us had disappeared. I leaned into her and began reciprocating her moves, giving her what she was giving to me. I couldn't help but to smile, I was so into this. When the song ended, she kissed me on my cheek then softly whispered, "Can I go with you tonight?"

I was shocked! If I had written the next steps in a book, I would have sworn she had read it. I could not believe she had just asked me that...not me...not Romie! I could have given any answer but the one that came forth without being coerced was, "Yes."

My mind was doing weird things and my crotch was throbbing. I wanted her in the worst way. I led her outside to my SUV. She waited quietly while I fumbled with my keys. As I went to open the passenger door, she stopped me.

"Do you mind if I ride in the back?"

"What!" *Why in the hell would she want to ride in the back seat?*

"Romie, I just wanna ride back there. Is it okay?" She asked in a seductive whisper.

I opened the door and hit the unlock button. She went to grab the door handle but I stopped her.

"Will you at least allow me to open the door for you?"

"Of course, I'm sorry." She giggled as she stepped back to allow me to open the door.

I held the door while she climbed in. When she moved

past me, she intentionally brushed her ass against me. *That fragrance. Damn!*

She didn't appear to be drunk. I mean it was a long way up into the seat and she negotiated it perfectly. She sat down and looked at me with those beautiful eyes. I couldn't see them in the club but she had the biggest hazel eyes I had ever seen and a beautiful set of lips. Damn, she was gorgeous!

"Thank you, Romie. You are such a gentleboi."

I smiled at her as I closed the door. I was grinning from ear to ear. My heart was still pounding and my now swollen clit was about to explode against my silk pants! I hurried around the SUV and hopped in, buckled my seatbelt, searched for some mood music, and then prepared to adjust my mirrors before pulling off. *If nothing else, I was a safe driver.* When I looked up in the rearview mirror to make sure everything was alright in the back, I found her sitting in the middle of the seats, completely naked! I started to turn around because my brain could not comprehend what my eyes were seeing but it was as if she could read my mind.

"Romie, don't...just drive."

I started the engine.

"Where do you want me to take you?" I asked, quite curious by now.

"Romie, this is not about where you can take me. This is about where I am gonna take you. But you can drive to your home for starters."

I looked at her through the rearview mirror. She had her legs wide open and she was stroking herself. I heard her say, "your home," and I wanted to ask her why my place and a whole lot of other seemingly meaningless questions. But all of them vanished when I saw her masturbating on the back seat of my Escalade!

"Romie, watch the road dear, we want to get there in one piece." She said as she adjusted herself and leaned backwards just a bit more.

I pulled away from the curb and headed towards my

condo. I didn't dare turn up the radio. I could hear her wetness cooing to me over the soft music coming through the surround sound. The soft slickness in her loins was singing to me. I could hear her beautiful moans. *Damn! Damn! Damn! This shit is NOT happening to me!* Here I am, driving home from the club with this woman masturbating in my back seat. I was so turned on it was hard to concentrate on the road. All I kept thinking was I hope she don't finish before I get her there. I found myself speeding up a bit but she was on it.

"Romie, baby...take your time, there's plenty for you. Don't worry, Boi...I got you."

She purred as she continued her stroking and moaning. I glanced up in the mirror and I could see her breasts. She was fondling one of her nipples. I watched as her hand deftly cupped and softly teased it. She brought her breast to her lips and I damn near ran off the road when she licked her nipple, then sucked on it!

She felt the Escalade shift and slowly looked up at me in the mirror. The look on her face was enough to tell me to keep my eyes and mind on the road. I silently cursed at myself wondering why I had to live so far away from the damn club! I was ready to fuck and this highway was in my way. But as she lovingly played with herself, even smiling to herself, I began to think about all of the women I had had up until now. All of them, save one, were one-night stands. I mean when I went to the club I was looking to fuck...nothing more. I never really had a need to be in a relationship. The one time I did try failed miserably. Not only that but when you fuck them and flee, there are no expectations on either part. She goes her way and I go mine.

But strangely as the thoughts had come to me, I found myself thinking about having a steady woman. Someone who will always be there and someone I can be there for. Maybe I was tired of the pimp life. Maybe I was ready to try it again. *Nah! Shit like this only happens to the playas!* As quickly as I had thought about settling down, I just smiled the thought away. My mind was in a whirlwind as I glanced back up into the rearview mirror. She was still naked but was now looking out of the side window. It looked like she was daydreaming...like she had something real heavy on her mind.

"You okay?" I asked with genuine concern.

"Yes, Romie...I'm fine." She said with a smile. She started twirling her hair in her fingers and I found myself staring at her again. *Damn, she was getting more and more beautiful by the moment.*

After about twenty more minutes, we arrived at the gates to my condo. I pushed my access panel and the gates opened.

"We're here." I said, trying to control the anxiety in my voice.

"Good." She said as she started to put her clothes back on.

I parked in my unit and got out to open her door for her. As she stepped out, her fragrance penetrated my senses. The pounding in my heart became almost deafening as I took her hand and led her to the elevator.

The ride up to my floor was real quiet. She stood there smiling at me, twirling her fingers in her hair. The way I felt, I could have climbed up the side of the building...all eighteen floors! When the door opened, I led her to my entrance. I don't know what I was thinking but I scooped her up and carried her in. She wasn't surprised, in fact, she settled back in my arms as we went in. I sat her on my couch and instinctively hit the remote for the stereo and the fireplace.

"Romie, turn the music off, please."

I did what she asked. The fireplace was still roaring with a romantic overtone. I went over to the bar to pour us both a glass of wine. When I went back to the couch, there she was...naked. I watched as the light of the fire danced in her most secret places.

"Thank you, Romie. Now, sit down." She said as she took her glass from me and set it on the coffee table.

As soon as I sat down, she was on me. I was scarcely able to set my own glass down before she straddled my legs and brought her lips to mine. The kiss that she gave me was unlike any I had ever felt. Her tongue danced inside of my mouth, finding and caressing mine. She kissed me deeper than I had ever known. Slowly, she began to unbutton my shirt. The heat that was building inside of me was at a point of pain. I needed her. I wanted her and for the first time, I felt myself actually wanting to beg her to taste me. To kiss me there, like she had kissed my mouth. I reached for her.

"Quiet, Boi, I got you." She whispered as she sucked and teased my nipples. I gave into her…to her passions and to mine.

She continued downward, placing kisses in places that had never been kissed quite like that. As she was moving, I was slowly coming out of my clothes. Once I was naked, she laid me down and straddled me. Our bodies were closer than skin now. I could feel every part of her body pressing against every part of my body. I felt her begin a slow seductive grind, the same one I had experienced on the dance floor but this time it was enhanced by her wetness and mine. I reached for her again and she didn't stop me.

"Now, Romie…now. Love me now." She said, her voice barely escaping between the rise and fall of our bodies grinding together.

I rolled over on top of her and paused. She was beautiful. She looked into my eyes and smiled. I slowly began to kiss her, to touch her, and caress her. I began to make love to her. I wasn't fucking and I wasn't playing. I wanted her to feel the emotions inside of me, especially the ones that I had kept hidden. I wanted to caress each and every part of her body, and shower her with kisses. For the first time in many years, I wanted to make love to a woman, completely. I wanted to show her the woman I really was, not some lesbo club pimp or some unfeeling dyke. I wanted to tell her my real name. I wanted to actually have a conversation with her about a future. I wanted to wake up to her and do it all over again.

And I did just that. I made love to her like I had no tomorrow. We spent hours making love in all sorts of ways. Kissing and touching, feeling and tasting, each and every part of our bodies. She was no stranger to this as she gave me what I gave her and then some. We never spoke though. Not one word. We didn't need words because our bodies spoke in tongues for us. It was beautiful. The last thing I remember was her lying on my chest gently massaging my breasts. I kept kissing her on her forehead and stroking her hair. Still no words, just the flickering of the dying fire, her breathing and mine. My body was spent. *Hell it all felt like one big orgasm because she was relentless in her hunger, just as I was.*

I must have drifted off sometime in the early morning. When I woke up, I could hear the shower. I smiled. *Damn. Was I dreaming? Was this real?* I just spent an incredible night with an incredible woman. I looked over to where she had been. The sheets were neatly pulled up and the pillows were straightened. *Oh, I am loving this! She is a neat freak just like me.* I laid there and listened to the shower, wondering what body part she was washing now. I had so much to say to her. I wanted to keep her… for real. I wanted a relationship and I wanted her in the worst way. Forget about my player days and settle down, maybe have a kid or too. I wanted to find out what her interests were and where she wanted to go in life. I wanted to know if she wanted me like I wanted her. I wanted to know what her favorite color was, or her favorite flower, her favorite song, or her favorite movie. I wanted to know every little thing about her.

I leaned over the bed and started to call her name. I paused. *Oh no. Oh no! Shit! Damn! What was her name?* I had been so wrapped up that I never even asked her name. I felt embarrassed. I could not believe I had made love to this woman and I didn't even know her name. As I sat there, I caught the lingering scent of her perfume, which hung heavily in the air. I remembered now, Jasmine with hints of Vanilla and Sandalwood. I inhaled slowly. Yes, that heavenly seductive scent. I sat there and smiled, recalling the night's events. I could not wait to have her in my arms again. I wanted to hold her and tell her all that I had been thinking.

Then I realized that she had been taking an awfully long

shower. In fact, she had been in there for quite some time. I got up, put on my robe, and walked into the bathroom. There was no steam. I went over to the shower and found that the cold water was the only faucet turned on. I got a sinking feeling in the pit of my stomach. I looked around the bathroom and nothing had been disturbed. What in the hell was going on?

I hurried out into the living room and the fireplace had been turned off. The couch pillows were placed neatly back on the couches and there was a single glass of wine on the table. I walked over to it and picked it up. The glass was still a bit chilled. A piece of paper with a note on it was on the table next to where the glass was. My heart started pounding and confusion was setting in. I took a big swig of the wine and read the note:

Romie,

By now you have figured out that I am gone. Enjoy the wine, I chilled it for you. My dear Boi, last night was phenomenal. I knew that it would be like that. I know you are wondering who I am and what is going on. See, most people don't understand their role in life. You thought yours was to seduce women for your pleasure, then leave them with no emotional recourse. This wasn't about a fuck, Romie. This was about showing you that this life is not a playground and if a woman gives her body to you, it is special. Not something to be bragged about or thrown about. Remember that perfume? No, of course you don't. See I was wearing it when I met you two years ago. Yes, I was one of your first sexcapades. You found me, and fucked me, and then you left me. What you didn't know was that you were my first. The first woman to ever touch me. So even though you thought you were just fucking me then fleeing, you happened to be the best thing to ever happen to me. I didn't know what love was but I fell in love with you that night...

I sat down hard on the couch. I felt a single tear fall down my face. I realized what I had done, what I had been doing, and now I was feeling it. I took another swig of the wine then read on:

*I never recovered from that. I never trusted another woman.
I became like you. I didn't want to feel, just wanted to fuck...
finding any willing Boi and getting myself off. But as time went
on, I knew I had to settle things with you. What you do from here
on is your choice. For the record? Last night was different than
the first. You made love to me last night. But you have a long way
to go Romie, because you still don't know my name.
Always,
She*

As the sun continued to rise in the sky, I sat there and absorbed what she had said to me. Every now and then, the emotions won out and I found myself weeping uncontrollably. I realized that I had to change. I understood what I had been doing to women all of these years. But on that night, she had shown me what I wanted, and what I needed in my life. I was tired of playing but I had never known the cost at which I had played. I kept coming back around to the fact that I still didn't know her name and I hadn't even taken the time to ask her.

Heartfelt
Nikki Rose

Sirens hollered, horns honked, and tires screeched. I loved the hustle and bustle of the Big Apple. Sometimes I really believed that I could taste, even smell the scent of New York City. But I don't know what compels me to take that crowded, dirty ass subway. I pushed my way through people, dashed into the all mirrored, high rise building, and hit the button for the elevator. I gazed at my watch and ignored the snickers of the slow pokes who got in my way. I'm just a stickler for time. Luckily, I made it before the meeting started. I nestled in a big, cushioned, high back chair, and unloaded my paperwork and laptop onto the long oval-shaped table.

My colleagues were all men whose piercing eyes monitored my every move as I got up, strutted across the room, and served myself a bottled water and bagel with honey almond cream cheese. I sat back down and smirked without shame as they continued to stare. When people see me they do a double take, because first of all, I'm striking. Not that I look like some gorgeous model or actress or somethin' but I just carry myself with a lot of pride and confidence, and I'm always ready to handle my *business.*

When I was younger, my dad used to say that I intimidated people, especially men and that I'd never get married because I was too aggressive. But I don't care if it were Usher or Denzel Washington, I ain't sleepin' with no man. I don't dress to impress them and neither did I ever care to marry one. I wear my hair in thin braids all going back into a long ponytail midway down my back, my make-up lightly applied to accent my natural attractive features --- a little lipstick with the eyebrows arched, and my manicure is styled for short nails if you know what I mean! I'm happy with who I am. No matter what anyone says, men, women, straight, lesbian, or, bisexual…they've all wanted to do me even if it were only to advance their careers. But I'm a no-frills-business-always-on-my-mind kind of person; and when it comes to business, I don't mix it with sex. Most refer to me as a hard nose or shall I say the word for it in today's society is *bitch*. Hardly ever am I seen without some kind of a brief or attaché case because my career is my life and baby, I've come a long way. I mean a really long way to get to where I am today.

It all started right out of high school when I decided to put this little female group together. I dressed them, booked them, and sold their CDs from the trunk of my car all with my own money. The reason I own it all now is because I promised myself that I wouldn't have to pay anything back if I didn't borrow it. Through my career I've been exposed to a lot; and I'm so grateful because I've been able to travel all over the world more than just once. So when the Music Administrators entered the office and took their respective seats and opened the meeting announcing me as keynote speaker, decision-maker, and founder of the company, mouths dropped to the floor. I'm the most respected music producer in the business and in this line of work, I'm not supposed to make it this far and become successful as an out lesbian.

When the daylong meeting had ended, it was well after dinner but I stayed anyway to answer questions and exchange business cards to kill the time. I was accustomed to drowning myself in work in hopes of not letting the relationship I was currently in take precedent over my work. The most ironic aspect of my life is that from all of my travels and experiences with my work being the forefront of my life, relationships have taken a back seat and now I'm suffering from it. With all of the escapades I'd been through, it seemed that they only wanted me for my fame and money. In turn I took them for granted as well and lost my belief in love. I've had so many one-night stands and fast relationships that I kinda' lost focus of all the reasons I'd enjoyed about being with a woman. So, I decided to stay behind and chat with a young intern who had been getting good reviews from the staff.

"So, Jerod, that's your name, right?" I asked as I flipped through his personnel file and resume.

"Yes, Jerod McNeal." He graciously shook my hand.

"How do you like what you've seen about our company so far? I heard some good things about you." I said as I checked him out from head to toe.

He had the perfect look for what we wanted for our company, almost model-like with a square jaw, smooth shaven skin, and coal black, wavy hair that was cropped close. He kind of reminded me of a choir boy dressed in a neutral colored suit that wasn't flamboyant with a simple tie and plain white shirt.

"Yes, sure, very well." He smiled with all straight pearly whites glowing.

He had the biggest brown eyes I'd ever seen and such a bubbly personality. I sensed that he was family. *Gaydar*, I guess one would call it.

"You have the kind of energy we want to represent our company."

I was so impressed with him that I just let him know right then and there.

"The only drawback I would have is that you're a bit younger than you appear."

"Don't let my age be a drawback. I have a proven track record that I can handle any kind of pressure." Jerod went on a serious rampage to sell himself.

The kid's got guts. "Okay, okay, you've got the position, but you and me...we're going to work closely together, so I'll be checking out your work."

"Thank you so much. I'll do my very best for you and the company." Jerod promised then hugged me.

He gathered up his papers, notes, and pens, and shoved

them into his briefcase. "I promise. You won't be disappointed. I can't wait to get together and start on the new singing group!" He shouted as he disappeared into the copy room.

I was still sitting at the conference table shuffling papers and sipping coffee while Jerod muttered something from the back. He was a joy to be around with all of that young energy. His excitement and enthusiasm even cheered me up and took my mind off of myself. As Jerod continued to yell from the back, there was a faint knock on the office door.

"Excuse me. I'm looking for Jerod."

"He...uh. You want Jerod?" I stuttered at the sight of such a beautiful woman, who almost rendered me speechless. She resembled Jerod but with longer hair, full soft lips, and big brown bedroom eyes.

"Hey, sis, you're here early." Jerod said as he walked over to his sister and lightly kissed her on the cheek. "I see you two have met."

"You have a sister?" I said in awe. I did a terrible job of hiding my ignorance.

"No, we haven't met," his sister interrupted.

"Well, let me introduce myself..." I said oblivious to her harsh reaction.

"I know who you are. I've heard a lot about you from my younger brother, here."

"Yeah, sis, and I got the job!"

"Good, lil' brotha. I'm so happy for you, see, I told ya' you could do it."

"Okay then, my pleasure too..." I mumbled.

"Oh, I'm sorry, Taris, this is my sister," Jerod politely introduced. "Kai please meet and *be nice* to my boss, Taris."

"Hello," Kai held out her hand. "Nice to meet you," she said dryly.

"The pleasure's all mine," I smiled happily.

"Jerod, are we ready to go?"

"I guess so."

"Good, come on then, I'm running late."

"My, it's chilly in here. Maybe I need to turn on some heat?"

"You won't have to, I'm leaving."

"Nice meeting you too."

"Likewise," Kai frowned. I must have sat at that table for a good twenty minutes after they left, mesmerized by the gift that the angels had graced me with. But how did I manage to bomb out the way I did and what had I done wrong? I just needed to know how to have that woman in my life.

My prayers were answered a few weeks later. It was on a gorgeous sunny day, one of the first days I'd had time off in about nine months. I rewarded myself with this time because my camp and I were going to be on a fearless mission to promote our next venture, non-stop. So dressed down but accompanied by my attaché case, two-way, cell phone, and a couple of other gadgets that I can't live without, I was armed for my chill out day. I had been to several bookstores in the Village and then I ended up at one of the local eateries. I hadn't eaten all day and I was starved and ready to chow down on my veggie burger with sprouts, tomatoes, Swiss cheese, avocados, and mayonnaise with coleslaw. As I was checking out some of my new material, a friend of mine who was a waitress was having a hard time convincing a couple of patrons to try their famous meatless burgers and used me as an advertisement to sell the customers. When I looked up and saw who they were, Jerod was already headed towards my table.

"Hey, it's Taris, my boss," he yelled with excitement.

I wiped my mouth with my handkerchief and stood to meet his peeps.

"Hello everyone, this is a very nice place and I do recommend the veggie burger. Also, there's plenty of room here at my table, why don't you all join me."

"I didn't know we were eating in?" Kai said, coming in from the parking meter.

"Oh, hello, Kai, how are you?"

"Fair…"

"That's good," I mumbled.

"Oh, Dahlin' we're not in a hurry, sure we'll have a seat."

"Cashmere, is that you?" I recognized one of my longtime friends who I used to party with at one of the local underground clubs. "How ya doin'…you're still lookin' as *fly* as ever."

"Honey, this Drag Queen is going to continue looking good."

We all laughed as everyone took seats. Kai sat as far away from me as possible. And before we knew it, an hour had passed and we were all having fun enjoying pleasant conversation.

"Kai, you hardly touched your food." I knew it would eat her up just to acknowledge me…and she didn't.

"Don't mind her," Jerod said. "She'll be alright."

"Jerod, you know I have an appointment…are we ready to go now?" Kai said as she rolled her eyes and looked at her watch.

"Okay, I guess we should be going," Jerod conceded.

"Good," Kai said. "I've been *ready* since we got here."

"Didn't mean to bore you," I said sarcastically. I could tell that her digs were meant for me personally and she was beginning to put me on edge.

"Seeing that we both feel the same way, I hope we don't cross each other's paths too soon." Kai smirked.

Even though her tone was cold as ice, I couldn't help imagining that there was heat between us; and my fantasies quickly transformed to images of licking my tongue between the little slit between her healthy breasts that sat up with pride.

"See ya tomorrow, Taris." Jerod said, interrupting my dreams with a warm hug. "Don't let my sister get you down it has nothing to do with you," he whispered in my ear.

"Thanks," I smiled. All I could do was watch her happy booty sway as she left the café. I had no idea what was going on with me. The more she resisted, the more I wanted her. When I first saw Kai, I knew that there was something different about her. I felt an irresistible attraction but I was beginning to feel it was one sided. I was beginning to lose faith and I didn't want to get wrapped up in some fantasy. So I promised myself that I would let it go and just concentrate on my work for right now. Jerod and I had been working late nights for the past several months. We had to get this new group together to go on tour by fall and that was only a month and a half away. We got a lot done but it was time to call it a night because we had to meet with the publishers first thing in the morning, so I decided to let everyone go home. As usual, Jerod and I were the last to leave. I knew that Kai would come to pick him up as she always did each night. I also knew that I was the last person in the world she wanted to make conversation with. So I decided to let Jerod go early as well.

"Hey, didn't you say you had a date tonight?"

"Man, I'm enjoying work so much that I almost forgot." He said with his usual bright white smile. "Can you handle it from here?"

"Sure, I can wrap it up."

"I could stay a bit longer?"

"No, I'm sure, you go and enjoy your date, just don't hurt him, and be careful in this awful weather."

"Okay, then. I'm out." Jerod said then waved goodbye as he got on the elevator. I dreaded going home because I wanted to take my mind off the fact that it was one of those times I'd go home to a lonely bed. It had been raining off and on all day but it started to really pour down like cats and dogs. So I made my way to the coat closet in the back to find the umbrella.

"Anyone here, hello…is there anyone here?"

"Uh, yes, just a moment." I shouted back.

"Jerod? Where are you?"

"Just a moment!" I yelled back, louder than before, and stumbled to the main office with my umbrella and trench coat all twisted together. I didn't even realize that it was Kai standing in the doorway drenched from the rain. She stood there looking like a helpless little Angel in a skintight black silk dress that fit like a wet T-shirt. Her hair had lost all of its curls and dangled past her shoulders dripping with water because the umbrella she was holding was torn from the wind and rain.

"I'm looking for Jerod...ha chew," she sneezed.

"Bless you! Come on in..."

"Thanks but I'm dripping wet. Jerod told me to meet him here so that I could get a ride home."

"He left here in a very good mood, I'd say about ten minutes ago?"

"So, if my irresponsible brother has already left then that means that I'll have to wait for him to come back up here to pick me up...who knows what time I'll get home in this sloppy rain? I should have never let him take the car."

"Well, I'd hate to be the bearer of more bad news, but I don't thing he's coming back."

"No? Why not!"

I could tell that she wasn't in a very good mood and being that I'm one of her least favorite people, I didn't want to piss her off anymore than what she already was. "Well, I let him go a little early because he had a date."

"Oh, shit! That's right. It's going to take me all night to get home if I have to get on that subway and then catch a cab the rest of the way in this weather. Oh, fuck!"

"I can give you a ride." I said, as sincere as a heart attack.

"You don't even know where I live...it could be way in Brooklyn or somewhere."

I could care less what side of the globe she lived on, I just wanted to get her *mean butt* home.

"It doesn't matter, I mean, I have a car and you need a ride...period."

"And what makes you think that I'd trust you?"

"Well, I do know your brother. I mean, we've been partners on this project for months now. I mean, if you're that apprehensive, you can call your folks and let them know that you'll be riding with me."

She was beginning to piss me off again because I had no idea why she disliked me so much. But somehow, I could tell that she'd been hurt badly by someone very special in her life and that I was getting the wrath of that anger.

"Well, I appreciate your offer but I'm not sure. But... maybe I could call home and at least let my mother know how I'll be getting home."

"It would be my pleasure." I smiled half-heartedly. "Here, you can use my cell and that way you can give your folks my number."

She hesitated then took my cell and made the call. *I thought I would die from holding my breath.*

"Okay, Taris, I'm ready to go. And thank you so much."

"It's no problem, it's late and rainy, so I just want to make sure you make it home safely. So where do you live?"

"I have a place here in the city that's being renovated but for now, I stay with my family in Queens."

"Well, I guess we should be heading out. My car is in the garage below, are you ready?"

"Yes."

We were both frozen in time for a moment, then I smiled and then she smiled.

It was raining so hard and the traffic was terribly backed up that we couldn't even go as far as a couple of blocks before standing still for at least fifteen minutes; and I could tell that Kai was getting restless.

"Wow, at this rate it'll take forever to get to my place."

"I'll do my best to get you there."

"Maybe I should just stay at a hotel or something here in the city."

"Well, I live nearby, we can just go to my place and wait until the rain slacks up then we can try a bit later. How does that sound?"

"Ha chew!"

"Bless you!"

"I think that's a good idea...ha chew!"

"We'll be there in five minutes. I'm just afraid that sneeze is going to turn into a cold."

"I'm getting the chills," she said as her teeth chattered.

"When we get to my place, you can change into something

dry."

"Okay…ha chew!"

As I promised, the ride to my place wasn't very long, which was a good thing because Kai's sneezes were getting more persistent. "We're here!"

"Ha chew…ha chew!"

I hurried her into my apartment in hopes that the warmth of the place would quiet the cold and protect her from the onslaught of the rain. I grabbed a blanket that I had left on my sofa and offered it to her.

"Here, let me wrap this blanket around you so that you can keep warm."

"Thanks, that's better."

"Man, you're shivering." I didn't like to see her this way but it was nice having my arms around her. She was like an innocent little lamb that I so much wanted to protect.

I walked her towards the guest room so that she could get out of those wet clothes. "You can use this bathroom to take a nice hot shower. I'm sure there's something in the closet that'll fit you. I think there's a size three in there," I teased.

"I'm a size seven with some booty."

"Um, huh…I can see that!" I laughed and went to the kitchen to put on a pot of tea while sorting through the mail and listening to phone messages.

"Am I interrupting anything?" When I glanced up and saw Kai, she was the perfect picture of an Angel.

"No…no, not at all. Here sit down. I have your tea ready."

She gingerly took a sip. "Mmm, it's just right."

"The weatherman said that the storm's not going to let up for about another hour or so…"

"This is a nice place you have here and…thanks, for the dry clothes."

"You look cute in that little jogger."

Kai smiled and took another sip of tea. I could tell that I'd embarrassed her.

"I've got some movie rentals…"

"Oh really?"

"Yeah, come on, let's get comfy in the TV room." I suggested.

She followed me and sat right next to me.

"Oh, man, your feet are cold."

"I know, I forgot to put on socks?'

"Here, cover them with this blanket."

I dimmed the lights and Kai got comfortable tucked under the blanket. Then to my surprise, she got even more comfortable under my arm and laid her head on my shoulder. My heart pounded so hard that I was embarrassed. I knew she could feel it.

"Do I make you nervous?" Kai asked.

I was surprised. It was the first time she'd ever attempted having a conversation with me.

"Not nervous."

"Then what are you feeling?"

"I'm wondering if…"

"Yes, I've been with women before, and yes, I'm a lesbian."

"Wow, you're good!"

"And I know that you're a lesbian and currently not involved."

"Jerod?"

"Yes, he talks about you all the time, and I mean *all the time!*"

"Then why were you so mean towards me?"

"Because he told me about all the women who threw themselves at you and that you had your pick of anyone of them whenever you wanted. He brags on you constantly and cherishes the ground you walk on. *Taris says this and Taris did that.* I got so sick and tired of hearing about his heroine that I thought you had brainwashed the poor boy."

"Jerod's one of the best interns our company's ever had and we've got big plans for him."

"And of course I got kind of jealous when he'd tell me

about the times you two would hang out...and he'd tell me of all the female friends you had. I mean, he didn't do it on purpose, we're just close and he confided in me."

"But I'm single by choice. Anybody can have someone sexually but what's important to me is that the woman in my life knows how to stimulate my mind. Now, in the business that I'm in, I always meet men who are business minded or intelligent but I want a woman like that; a woman who isn't afraid to be herself and who hasn't sold her femininity."

"Oh, really?" Kai asked softly.

"Yeah." I said with my full attention on her perfectly shaped lips.

She nervously crossed her legs and turned back to the movie. I touched her delicate hand, raised it to my lips and kissed it. I could tell she liked it because she smiled, even though she tried to ignore me. I pulled her close.

"Come over here, I wanna get to know you better."

"I know but..."

Her words were silenced when I turned her face towards me, inhaling the scent of her soft breath, and cautiously covering her lips with mine. I felt her lips tremble as I caressed her face and neck. Slowly, I moved my hand down towards her...

"Wait, stop...please," Kai said, pulling away. "I don't think, I mean, it's too soon."

"What's too soon?" I asked feeling confused.

Kai straightened her hair and pulled herself together as she got up from the sofa without saying a word and headed towards the door.

"Wait, where are you going?"

"Look!" Kai said in a harsh tone. When she sharply turned around her eyes were cold and squinted, the soft smile was gone and *bam* the old personality was back.

"I don't want to lead you on and...I'm not ready for this yet!"

"Wait a minute, hold up...and slow down. I'm sorry. I didn't mean to rush you into anything." I said and quickly walked over to comfort her. "Now, maybe things just happened the way they did and I will even admit, it was kind of fast…but we can just take it slow because I really do enjoy your company."

"You do?"

"Yes, beautiful." I just stood there and held her in my arms with no strings attached. "Now, come on, sit back down… and let's finish this movie."

"Okay…I'd like that." Kai said shyly becoming more at ease.

I pointed the remote to the DVD player, clicked on the movie, and got comfortable.

"See, look, this is my favorite part of the movie." I said, throwing popcorn in my mouth. "Watch what he does here."

"Oh, yeah, what's going to happen?" Kai smiled then leaned her head back on my shoulder and snuggled up under my arm again.

It was like the whole time I'd try to get close to Kai was like getting to know a sculptured ice figure, heartless. But now I could see there was a lovely human soul, a precious gem right in the center that had truly been hurt and it was going to take patience for me to get to the core. But like the old saying goes… *anything worth having is worth waiting for!*

Symphony
S. Stephens

I'd already figured out what I was going to tell my family before I opened the door. Mother was cleaning the kitchen and Dad and Lynn were watching TV. I walked in and said, as if I was a ringmaster at a circus, "Family, I have some wonderful news. Gather around, I have some really wonderful news!"

Dad had this bewildered look on his face; Lynn appeared unconcerned. Mother came out of the kitchen with this nervous smile on her face. As everyone walked into the family room, I picked up the remote control and turned the TV off. I told Mother to have a seat then shouted, "I'm getting married! Gray and I are getting married!"

There was total silence for about ten seconds.

"When did this happen?" Mother finally asked.

"Well, we talked about it a few days ago and we realized we loved each other and we want to be together forever."

"A few days ago? It took you a few days to tell us the news?"

"I just wanted to be sure."

Dad looked as if he'd just won the lotto. "Congratulations dear, I'm very proud and happy for you. Gray seems like a good man." He stood and gave me a hug.

"Thanks Dad, he is great." I said with a smile.

Mother and Lynn were still looking at me in amazement.

Lynn said, "Are you sure? You just met him. Doesn't he

live in Virginia? Will he be moving to Miami?"

"Yes, I'm sure, and I didn't just meet him. More than likely I'll be moving to Virginia. He's really settled with his job and hopes to start his own business soon. And besides, I can teach anywhere if that's what I decide to do."

"I'm happy for you, Elise, if that's what you want to do." Lynn eventually said with a smirk on her face.

Mother asked, "When's the big day?"

"Well, we haven't decided on that yet but I'll be going to see him for a few days to meet the rest of his family and talk about dates."

Mother gave me a big hug. "I love you, Elise, and all I ever wanted for you was happiness. I can't wait to share the moment with you."

Yeah, right. What she really meant was all I ever wanted for you was happiness as long as it's not with a woman. But I always understood my Mother's fears.

With my voice cracking I said, "I know, Mother, I know." Then I said, "Look, I'm going to hang out with some friends tonight. I'll see you all tomorrow." Before Mother could ask with whom, I was halfway to my room.

I couldn't wait to take a shower. The shower was my sanctuary. I could go in and pretend to be anything I wanted to be and could easily talk myself through any scenario. And right now, I was pretending to be Cinderella awaiting my Prince Charming. I took a twenty-minute shower and felt like a dried prune when I got out. All I could think about was how happy I'd made my parents and the proud looks on their faces. I saw in their eyes that we could finally put all this *gay stuff* behind us. The relief on their faces was something I'd never forget. I'd done what I thought I'd never be able to do: make them proud that I was their daughter. I was so relieved and couldn't wait to talk to Gray.

As I was going through my closet looking for something to wear to the club, the phone rang.

"Hi, Elise."

"Hey, Gray, how are you?"

"I'm doing good but missing you, baby."

"I miss you too. Guess what?"

"What?"

"I told my folks about us getting married."

"So you didn't change your mind. I wish I could've been there. What did they say?"

"Of course I didn't change my mind. They were ecstatic, and so am I."

"I can't wait to see you. Are you still coming up on Wednesday?"

"Yes, I am. My flight gets in at eight. Is that okay?"

"That's fine. I have a few surprises planned and I can't wait to introduce you to my family. My father's flying up and a few of my buddies will be here too."

"Well, I can't wait to meet them."

"Okay, Elise, let me get going and I'll talk to you later."

"Bye, Grayson."

"Talk to you later, honey."

A part of me was really looking forward to meeting Gray's mother and spending time with her. I'd never felt so good. Just maybe I could change this life of mine. THANK YOU, GOD! I'M READY!

But as for tonight, I was going to be around some great folks who helped me to survive this far. I was determined to have a ball with that "family" tonight. I'd decided to wear my black jeans, a black low-cut fitted shirt, and my heels. I wanted to look good on my way out of the life.

It was about midnight as I pulled into Carmen's driveway. I didn't even have to look around because it was so late and I knew it was safe. Carmen met me at the door and we were off.

"Hey, girl, what's up?" I said in the car.

"Nothing. I'm really glad you decided to hang out tonight. Sorry for my stuff earlier. I think what you're doing is crazy and I don't want to see you get hurt or anyone else. But we've been girls for a long time so whatever you want to do, be happy. Now, understand this is pre-alcohol talk, and as you know, before the night is over I'll be acting up about how wrong this is all over again."

We both laughed and I said, "I know you have my best interest in mind and I appreciate that."

I turned up the music in the car and we talked and laughed and before we knew it, we were at The Waterfront. It was packed. It took fifteen minutes to find parking and the line to get in was wrapped around the place. As we got out of the car and walked through the parking lot, we saw Iran and some of the guys. Donna and some of the others were already in line. We started hugging as if we hadn't just spent time together a few hours ago. As always with Iran, we went straight to the front of the line. He whispered something in the bouncer's ear and we were in. Iran was the man. He had the connections and we all tailgated in behind him.

The place was hopping with people of all different shapes, sizes, and ethnicities. And the eye candy was out tonight. The place was jammed packed because it was finals night. The Waterfront had a female impersonation contest each week and the last Friday of each month the final contest would be held with a cash reward. It was so entertaining to see the Patti LaBelles, Donna Summers, Jennifer Holidays, and Gloria Gaynors perform. It was standing room only.

We made our way to the bar and ordered our usual margaritas. As I looked around, I saw a few faces I hadn't seen in years and many I hadn't seen since I quit going to the clubs. Folks were dancing and having a ball. It felt so good because I could be me. If I wanted to flirt, hug, kiss, or hold someone, it was all good. That's why I loved it so much and cautiously I was feeling right at home.

Before I could finish my drink another one was coming my way. Donna grabbed my hand and said, "Let's go baby, one last dance."

We went to the dance floor and danced for five straight songs. I was feeling it. While we were on the floor a few girls tried to make their way over but Donna and Iran were having none of it. They were running major interference for me. After two more songs I was exhausted and left the floor to get some water. I spotted Carmen at the bar and went over to where she and some people were standing.

"Hey, Elise." Carmen said with her drink up in the air. "Let me introduce you to some kids I met at a party a few weeks back. This is Richard, Ashley, and Symphony."

"Don't ask," said Symphony. "My father was a musician and we were all named after something musical."

She was gorgeous. Five foot nine with long brownish-red hair, beautiful light brown eyes, and dimples that made her smile astounding. My mouth hung open. She had on a black dress that stuck like glue. Someone looking that good could only be about games, drugs, or had boyfriend/husband issues. And besides, I was done with the gay life. So I quickly gathered myself and said hello to her and everyone else.

Carmen said, "We're celebrating Elise's...uh...let's just say going away."

"Oh, are you leaving town?" Symphony asked.

"I guess you can say that."

"Well, good luck, girl."

Carmen, Richard, and Ashley headed to the dance floor. As I stood next to that woman, my heart began to pound. She was absolutely flawless.

"So, is your job relocating?" She asked.

"Not exactly..."

"I'm sorry. I don't mean to pry, just wondering why anyone would want to leave Miami."

"I'm getting married," I blurted.

"Oh, a commitment ceremony."

"No, I'm marrying a man."

"Oh, I see. Well congratulations and best of luck."

"Thanks. The kids wanted to bring me out for old times' sake."

"Well, let me buy you a congratulatory drink."

"Thanks, you don't have to."

There was something about her that was different. She seemed so genuine. The whole time we were talking she was looking me straight in my eyes, as if she was looking through me, watching my heart beat out of control. All of a sudden I didn't know what to do or how to act. I felt as if I was a thirteen-year-old girl with a crush. This couldn't be happening. A voice within me said, "Come on, Elise, get it together, regroup."

"No, I insist. It's not a big deal."

"Okay, if you insist, I'll have a margarita."

"So, Elise, is it? How long have you been engaged?"

I smiled, embarrassed, "Well, for a couple of days."

"Oh, I see."

"You must think I'm some kind of mixed nuts."

"Why would I think that?"

"Here I am, soon to be married and in a gay nightclub."

"I can think of a lot of other things that would make you mixed nuts besides hanging out at a gay club. Look sweetie, I don't judge people. You do what you have to do in this life and be happy, cause tomorrow isn't promised."

"Thanks, Symphony, I needed to hear that."

"Hey, let's go out back. I can hardly hear myself think in here," Symphony said.

"Okay."

She grabbed my hand and led the way to the back of the club and out the door. We sat on the patio and I had the opportunity to see her without the artificial lighting. She was truly gorgeous. It's not like I'd never seen a beautiful woman before. In Miami they were everywhere. There was just something about Ms. Symphony that made me feel all warm inside. I asked her how long she had been in the life.

"Not long, I've only had one relationship with a woman but I do believe I was born gay. I can honestly say I've never been attracted to or slept with a man. But I'd been doing what I was told to do and trying to fit in, now that's over. I'm out to my family and anyone else who cares. I'm not sure if that answers your question."

"Well, yes and no."

"What don't you understand, Elise?"

"You mean, you just woke up one day and said, *I'm going to tell my folks I'm a lesbian?*"

"That's about right. After my first relationship with this girl went south, I was devastated. I told my mother what I was going through. Told her I felt that even at an early age I was different. My dad died around the same time I was going through it with that relationship. So I never considered not telling my mother. She was all I had and besides, we're very close."

"So she embraced you with open arms?"

"Absolutely not!" She laughed. "Let's just say she learned to live with it. She told me on a regular basis she didn't like the idea that I slept with women and do what we do."

"And your response?"

"I told her I don't sleep with just any woman and that I was sure that she and my dad's relationship wasn't defined by sex. I told her I love another human being like myself and I'm not a whore. I don't sleep around. I'm the girl you raised to be a woman and one day I'll find the woman I'll love and spend the rest of my life with, just as you and Dad did until his death."

"You see, Elise, this club thing is new to me. I haven't been out much but I've got a good idea what it's all about. It's my outlet. I love to dance and see my sisters and brothers having a good time together. This is who I am and I love being around *family.* There's nothing like it. People dancing and feeling free and being who they are for one night in one place…that's better than any high any drug can provide."

I just sat in awe of her. I was thinking Carmen had set this up and that Symphony couldn't be real. This woman was perfect and I knew perfection didn't exist, so something was definitely up.

So I asked sarcastically, "How did your father feel about his baby girl being a dyke?"

"First of all, to me, the word *dyke* is a derogatory term

and it doesn't describe me. As for my dad, he worked so hard to keep us fed and clothed that we never really spent a lot of time together. He died a very strong and proud man and the topic of my sex life never came up. But if he was alive today he'd know." She paused. "Look, I'm in my last year of school. I'm studying Political Science and French. My plan is to set the world on fire. By the time I leave this earth people will remember Symphony Graves. I don't have a lot of time because of school, so when I do get a chance to get out, I make the best of it. You seem like a real nice person. Maybe we can keep in contact and have lunch sometime…no strings attached. I respect where you are in your life."

Symphony's intellect made her appear even more attractive than her looks; and she was serious about who she was. She was the person I wanted to be. Everything inside me began to twist and turn and I had a knot in my throat the size of a tennis ball. I felt as if I couldn't swallow. A part of me wanted to get up and walk away and never look back. But I asked myself, do I run away from every gay woman I come in contact with? I needed to deal with this. I knew what I was doing was right, despite Symphony making perfect sense with her life. My life was different. I knew I didn't have the courage to love a woman, my family, my God, and myself as one. None of the pieces fit for me. But with Gray, the picture was perfect. I knew I could fall in love with him. After all, he was as great as Symphony and he loved me.

I hesitated before speaking, then I told her, "Lunch would be fine."

"Good. Here's my number, call me whenever." Then she said, "Let me get you back to your party."

We walked back inside the club. I was still in shock; I'd never met anyone like her. She actually gave a damn about her life and the state of this life. She didn't just exist, she was living! I was envious. Thank God she didn't try and press me because I'm not sure I could've resisted. I was sure I'd be safe here because there was no love at the clubs, just games.

Symphony told me to tell Carmen and the gang goodnight. She said, "I hope to hear from you soon or at least get an invite to the wedding." She smiled and walked off into a cloud of smoke.

I looked for Carmen on the crowded dance floor. We danced to a few more songs and laughed all night. I was having a ball, yet Symphony never left my mind.

The Homecoming
Tawanna Sullivan

It had taken eleven years but hell had finally frozen over. It was death that brought Melanie back to the cobblestone driveway of 735 Munson Lane. Not twenty-four hours ago she had watched her mother's coffin being lowered into the ground.

The stubborn pride that had helped the matriarch raise three children on her own kept her from going to the doctor until the pain became unbearable. Left unchecked, cancer had ravished her body.

Melanie leaned against the steering wheel and watched a slug struggling across the sidewalk. *What am I doing here?* The prodigal daughter hadn't expected to be included in the will, much less to inherit the house she had been banished from.

A car pulled up next door and a gorgeous brown-skinned woman emerged from the driver's side. After a brief struggle, she managed to lift a couple of grocery bags out of the backseat. With her hands full, she couldn't close the door and seemed reluctant to use her khaki clad hips. Her grip loosened on one of the bags and it started to slip.

Happy for the distraction, Melanie seized the opportunity to be neighborly. "Hey, let me give you a hand." She sprinted across the lawn and took one of the bags.

"Thanks, Melanie." The woman shut the door with her now free hand. She ran her fingers through the sandy-brown locks that framed her face. "You probably don't remember me. It's Wanda."

"Wanda Andrews?" *No way*. Melanie thought as she followed her up to the porch. This curvaceous beauty was a far cry from the shy, little girl who wore over-starched dresses and patent leather shoes.

"Wow, I can't believe it. It's been almost twelve years."

"Are you still living in New York?" Wanda hesitated at the front door and decided to settle into one of the lawn chairs instead.

Hoping none of the groceries were perishable, Melanie followed her lead and sat in the swing suspended from the awning. The cushion was thin and the rusty hinges cried as she sunk into them.

"No, my wallet couldn't take it. I moved to Delaware a few years ago."

"Sorry about your mother. How have you been holding up?"

"It was a shock but I'm okay."

"How long are you staying?"

"I'm not sure. Mama left the house to me."

"Are you serious?" Her eyes danced with delight but Wanda suppressed her smile. "How did your sister take it?"

"It was the first time I've ever seen Gloria speechless. It lasted all of thirty seconds. She began talking about home inspections and how much she expected from the sale."

"You're going to sell the house?"

"Probably. There's nothing really here for me."

Suddenly, the front door jerked open. Her wig slightly askew, the elder Andrews pressed her nose into the screen door.

"I thought I heard voices out here. Wanda, why didn't you let me know you were back?"

Wanda shifted uncomfortably. "Ma, we didn't want to disturb your afternoon nap."

Motioning towards Melanie, Mrs. Andrews lowered her voice. "Who's this? One of your friends?"

"No, Ma. Remember Melanie from next door?"

Melanie smiled. "How are you doing, Ms. Andrews?"

"Can't move around like I used to but I can't complain. You Vicky's youngest, right? The one who got grown and ran away?"

Ran away? "Well, I…"

"You look pretty good for living out in the street. How many babies you got?"

Now, Melanie understood why she hadn't been invited in.

"None."

The older woman looked unconvinced.

"I lived with my brother for a few months and got a college scholarship that let me move on campus."

"Well, you should thank God for that. Maybe you can talk some sense into this one."

"Ma!"

"Got a little education and she think she grown."

Wanda jumped to her feet. "Ma, Melanie just stopped by to help me with the groceries. She has to get back next door to help Gloria pack some things."

Huh? Melanie thought. A look from Wanda told her to keep quiet.

"Vicky ain't been in the ground long enough to get cold yet and y'all picking over her stuff like vultures. Wanda, don't you let that happen to me when I die. You watch Hattie Mae around my jewelry." She clicked her false teeth in disapproval. "Hmph, that fiend is liable to take the gold tooth out of my head."

"It was good seeing you again." Wanda gave Melanie a quick hug. "Run before she starts asking more questions," she whispered.

The scent of lavender engulfed her and Melanie thought she was going to melt in Wanda's arms. She reluctantly let go.

"Come over if you get a chance. It would be nice to catch up on old times."

"I'd like that."

Melanie held the screen door open while Wanda took the bags into the house. "Nice seeing you again, Mrs. Andrews." The old lady slammed the door without looking back.

Wanda had been a nice little detour but it was time to face the inevitable. Melanie stepped over the thin rain that separated their porches. She took a deep breath, unlocked the front door, and went inside.

The odor of stale cigarettes and beer greeted her in the foyer. It was dark but she easily navigated around the end tables and chairs to the picture window. Pulling back the heavy drapes flooded the room with sunlight. Almost nothing had changed. Melanie felt like she had stepped back in time.

Victoria could never bring herself to throw anything away, so the living room was cramped with furniture. The end tables had a new coat of varnish but one of the St. Bernard lamps had lost its paw. A newer television sat atop a broken, antiquated floor model. Bric-a-brac shelves were nearly overflowing with papers and trinkets. Half-empty cups and paper plates were strewn across the sofa and tables. The gathering may have started somberly but had probably ended in family reunion mode. Once the alcohol had started flowing, they probably stopped crying and started trading scandals and secrets.

Melanie wasn't in any of the photos that lined the faux fireplace mantle. It was likely that she had been exorcised from the family album too. She was a phantom confined to the realm of family gossip. Closing her eyes, Melanie took stock of her feelings. She thought returning would stir up old pain and rage. It was a relief to know her fears were unfounded. There was no anger, just sadness.

Continuing into the dining room, she realized the china closet was empty. The only dishes left were in a box on the table. Next to it was a list of furniture and household items Gloria had claimed as her own. *Damn.* Melanie turned toward the kitchen but the bag of garbage sitting in the entryway was an ominous sign. The last thing she wanted to confront was a sink full of dishes. As if to save her from the dilemma, the doorbell rang.

Wanda was leaning over one of the dehydrated plants giving Melanie a full view of her assets when she opened the door. Her neighbor had certainly filled out nicely.

"My mother cultivated killing plants into a high art form."

"With a little loving care anything can be revived." Wanda straightened up and brushed the dirt from her hands. "I hope this isn't a bad time?"

"Oh, no. Please, come in."

Wanda walked in leaving the scent of lavender in her wake. Melanie quickly cleared the sofa of debris. She hoped the dark patches on the cushions were part of the design and not a sticky spill.

"I have to warn you, this place is like an exterminator's wet dream."

"Don't worry about it. Housekeeping is the last thing that should be on your mind."

When Melanie sat down next to her, she could have sworn Wanda edged a little closer.

"You know, I was pretty impressed with you back there. When we were kids, you couldn't tell a lie to save your life."

"I didn't know any better back then. As soon as you were out of earshot, she told me to find out who was getting your mother's housedresses."

"Your momma is a trip. You still live next door?"

"I live in Washington Village. It's just far enough to keep her from just dropping by unannounced."

"I'd offer you refreshment but I don't trust anything in that refrigerator. Have you had lunch? I can order us something from Loon Ye. They are still in business right?"

"About three years ago Loon Ye changed from a carry out to a real sit-down restaurant. He bought out the stores next to him…"

"The cleaners and the thrift store?"

"Yeah. It's now called Shanghai Delight. The food is the same but now you are paying for ambiance."

"Sounds like property values have gone up. That's why Gloria is in such a hurry to put a for sale sign on the lawn."

"All of this just got sprung on you. How are you really handling it?"

"Honestly? I'm not sure. We still weren't on speaking terms when she passed, so there is this weird aura of unfinished business. On the other hand, if she were still alive, I couldn't imagine us reconciling anytime soon. She...we...were a little too stubborn for that."

"Maybe leaving you the house was her way of welcoming you back home."

"Part of me really wants to believe that. But it's more likely she did it to get back at Gloria." Melanie took a deep breath and shook her head. "How could it have been so easy for her to expel me from her life?"

Wanda put a reassuring hand on her shoulder. "I don't think it was easy but she was too proud to admit she was wrong."

"I want to be over it and I'm fine most of the time. It's not as sharp as it used to be but the pain is still there."

"There's something I need to tell you." Wanda tensed up and pulled away.

The sudden change in tone put Melanie on guard. "What's that?"

"It's my fault you got thrown out."

"What are you talking about?"

"I told your mother that you liked girls. I was jealous of all the attention you were giving Lisa."

"Lisa Jenkins?" Melanie's mind flashed back to the athletic girl she had been infatuated with for a summer.

"I had no idea she would disown you. I'm sorry."

"Listen, it wasn't your fault. I left her a thousand clues, so the confrontation would have happened anyway. Kicking me out of the house was her choice. Nobody else can take responsibility for that."

"I thought Ms. Vicky would make you come back to church and we could sit together like we used to."

"So, you had a crush on me, huh? I had no idea you felt that way. Good thing, too. I probably would have ended up hurting your feelings anyway."

"You think so?"

"I was a bundle of hormones ready to do anything with any girl. On top of that, I didn't even know how to kiss. Thankfully, I've learned a few things since then."

"Have you?"

Before Melanie could offer a demonstration, her cell phone rang. She rolled her eyes when the number appeared on screen. "Hold on." Putting a hand over the phone, she whispered, "It's Gloria."

Wanda's lips brushed against her ear. "Are you hungry?"

Melanie tried to calm the flurry of butterflies in her stomach. "Ravenous."

"Good, I'll make a reservation at Shanghai Delight." Wanda settled back and whipped out her own phone.

Melanie turned her attention back to her sister. "What's up, Gloria? Cancel it. I'm not ready to meet with a realtor yet." Her fingertips traced the outer curve of Wanda's thigh. "I'm going to stick around for a little while and see what develops."

Pink Laces
Musezette Charles

My bus passes by Tabitha's house each morning but it does not stop there. Her father drives her to school everyday, so the Tall Boys can't get to her. She'll be waiting for me as usual by the lion at the top of the steps. I hope she brought the cigarettes and some cookies to eat in homeroom. I know she talks to those Black Barbie Dolls before I get here everyday; talking about cute boys and their fast bikes and shiny cars. Those same girls always ask her why she hangs out with a *girl like me*.

Sometimes I think that "**T**" may really be one of them; longing for pompoms, proms, and Tall Boys. Sometimes I want to long for those things too but they just don't matter to me the way they do to her. I guess I have to give David an answer about the prom soon. My mom says I have to go. I picture that other *flicted* boy with the big head and the little ears in my mind. He'll probably still be standing over her when my bus pulls up; talking about absolutely nothing, leaning against the light post, saying all kinds of stupid shit.

I try to guess what she's going to wear to school everyday and wear something to match. I usually get it right, except when she wears one of those Tall Boy's jackets and her tight black jeans. I know she doesn't do it to spite me. Come to think of it, I'm not sure if she thinks about me at all.

The bus pulls up in front of the school but she's not sitting on the wall. The Pretty Girls are sitting on the benches pointing at magazine photos. I walk inside the school and peek in the bathroom; maybe she slipped inside to take off the black church stockings her mom sometimes makes her wear. I walk back outside and sit next to the lion on the other side of the steps; maybe I'll hide behind the lion and play a trick on her. I'm having a mini nicotine fit and a feeling I can't name yet. One day I will be able to name this feeling all too well. I can see the parking lot much better from this side of the steps. Now I'll have plenty of time to hide when her dad's car pulls up.

I hear the Tall Boy's with the big head and the little ears, motorcycle coming down the street. At least I got here first today. Now I can save her from having to hear all of his stupid bullshit. She always manages to make herself laugh at his ignorant jokes; referring metaphorically to his dick like he's a fucking comedian. He screeches into the lot and revs up the engine one last time. This is how he announces his arrival to the other Tall Boys and Pretty Girls. Then I see "T" get out of one of the Black Barbie Doll's car. She walks up to the Tall Boy and stands on her tiptoes to kiss him.

I walk inside to take my seat for homeroom. I stare at the door for what seems like an eternity hoping desperately that my eyes had betrayed me. I imagine she will walk through the door wearing a different outfit. Not wearing her white mini skirt and pink and black Pumas with the pink laces; the same outfit I saw that girl wearing who kissed the Tall Boy on the bike.

As the door swings open, David walks through and sits behind me. He seems upset that I haven't given him an answer about the prom yet. "T" walks in and sits on the other side of the room so I can talk to David first. As he taps me on the shoulder, I look at her thinking that we need to talk *now*. She motions to me that she will tell me everything later. I tell David yes but I don't ever remember turning around. I don't remember taking my eyes off of her brown crossed legs and those pink laces.

Morning Music
Tonya Parker

I feel her stir next to me. Her flat bottom bumps my fuller one with the soft thump of a drum. Just the cue I have been waiting for. I turn over and slide my Jill Scott leg over her Tina Turner one. Different sizes, both with unique sounds—one soft and silky, the other powerful and frenzied.

Then I glide my arm underneath hers and fill my palm with her warm breast, caressing gently. Perfect harmony. I take my free hand and wind it in her hair, massaging the scalp beneath the soft tangle of her African and Arab roots. I tug gently on the strands. Her body starts to hum.

I burrow my face in the hollow of her neck, inhaling that heady scent of coconut and orange blossom that she ritually uses, intermingling with the yet faint perfume of our more natural juices. I roll her over and nestle closer. As her desire-filled eyes meet mine, notes form in my head, sounds escape from my lips, *sotto voce*.

I revel in the feel of her fullness, the expanse of velvety skin awakening under my slow ministrations. I tease her nipples, feeling them grow with my touch. I gently scratch and then stroke her back, gripping more firmly as her muscles contract. When my teeth find the taught tendons straining on the side of her neck, her contralto moans vibrate throughout the air.

Our full mouths find each other in a clash of lips and tongues as my hand moves between us, leisurely seeking lower, adding urgency, and then stroking gently again. My finger transforms into a bow, strumming the Stradivarius of her clit, the perfect accompaniment to our powerful duet—the rising crescendo of her familiar throb, singing with my quick and ready wetness. My body trembles as it anticipates our grand finale.

The corner of my eye catches dawning light peeping though the curtains. Sunrise, usually my favorite time of the day; the ideal audience for when I compose my best music. Today, an unwelcome voyeur for its too early arrival!

Our morning has been perfect thus far—no discordant notes to mar the beauty of our melodic lovemaking. The rise and fall of the rhythm languidly winding its way to the deliciously anticipated climax. Oh, God how I want to hurry up and complete our concerto; experience the thunderous applause and melt in the afterglow of fawning adoration.

No. Rushing would defeat the whole purpose of our artistry. Not wanting to give up so easily, I consider performing solo, pleasuring myself in order to pay homage to this magnificent build-up.

With love and frustration, I gaze into the eyes of my partner composer and know a solo performance is not in today's program. I will have to hold this note until sundown for our complete, collaborative performance. At that time, her fast will be broken and she will again be hungry for song.

I pray that I get used to postponing morning music during the season of Ramadan.

The 4:10
Nik Nicholson

"I gotchu Ma." She champions in a raspy voice, while clinching my lower right leg playfully, pulling me seriously.

Sitting on the edge of her seat, grasping my attention, we're eye to eye, she sustains me. Anchoring herself, she counters the constant motion of the train and shifting bodies against us. Sliding her hand further between my lower thighs, pressing her bare fingertips against the back of my right thigh and knee, I breathe deeply for composure. Then cupping my kneecap with her other hand, we're braced opposition. I am somewhere between arousal and fear. The train is hot and crowded. I can't zone out. The bar I'm clinching isn't enough for relief, relief from her action, or my involuntary reaction. I need space to brace myself against the dense motions of the train. I need relief from her intrusive but welcomed hands.

Moments like these, I wonder if I'll ever feel like an adult, instead of nervously needing seclusion. Still, I have learned to mask my uncertainty, shock, and attraction with disgust. I've learned to mask my attraction from the years of denial before acceptance and coming out. I stand stern. I am so stern, I am afraid it may discourage her from holding me. I am composed confusion. All at once, I want her to hold me and let go too. I'm trying to ignore her devilish grin, when she shakes me a bit, forcing me to acknowledge her there, us here. In this moment, all my elusive behavior is futile and my hard exterior is transparent. Opportunities I never had courage to act on are tangible. Motionless, I am bound by uncertainty.

I'm wearing a skirt. I never wear skirts. I've fantasized about getting rid of them. Freedom, igniting an impulsive frenzy, I gathered them together in a bag with the intention of giving them away. Then it occurred to me, what if I needed a skirt for some event where the decorum demanded skirts? So they sat for months threatened to be donated until today. Today I woke up fierce! I'm dressed better than I have been in weeks, months. I spent time putting on lotion to buttery perfection, scenting my neck and wrists. Felt so energized and sexy, I even braided down the dreads framing my face and put on a bit of makeup. All day I projected power. Wondered how I became someone else, without a hint. Being dressed up renders me naked apprehended in her perception.

This has been going on for awhile. Me wanting her and hating that I didn't have the nerve to pursue. I've seen her more times than I would like to admit without speaking. Five days a week I catch the 4:10. Three or four days in a lucky week, I run into her. Once I felt her eyes on me and we exchanged a long glance. Intimidated, I evaded connecting. Since then I have been intrigued by her. Thoroughly consumed, I bring a book on the train for the eight minute ride. Never do I accomplish any reading but I achieve the goal, not to reflect her eyes. I contemplate her low curly cut, dark brown skin, and dark gums framing perfect white teeth. A wide grin that thins full dark lips, savored and relished when she smiles or laughs.

I made all kinds of excuses trying to rationalize my silence. What if she already has a woman? That would be terribly embarrassing to initiate conversation, only to make the rest of the rides home uncomfortable. Or the best one, I put the feminist hat on and got angry because she looks masculine, knowing that's the very reason that I like her. Gender roles are "social constructs," social constructs I want to defy but I'm defied by my own attractions.

I'm weary of extreme women: women who dress like

men or Barbie. I am not ultra feminine or ultra masculine, I just am. I never wanted to be the man nor did I want to be Susie-homemaker. I'm frustrated by expectations, superficial expectations that strike me as ironic after suffering painful journeys to acknowledging our truth. Her appearance is extreme. She wears men's long sleeved collared shirts, large jeans, a large faced watch, and matching boots. If not for the softness of her face and the warmth of her smile, it might have been difficult to tell she is a woman. Her posture and gestures are consistent with her appearance. I feel oppressed by extreme women; their expectations have made me feel vulnerable.

I know that the vulnerability is only a manifestation of inadequacy; and as I stand here, now, with her hands wrapped around my leg, my fierceness is strangled. I am overwhelmed with feelings of inadequacy. This morning, this skirt was *all* me. Now, I wish I had chosen big pants and a big shirt. This outfit may insinuate I'll bare children when all I want to do is get grocery and rub feet. I feel she thinks I need her protection because I am wearing heels. I am enraged by her assumption that I *need her* in order to stand, considering I've been on a crowded train before!

The train comes to the transfer stop, people crowd off. I'm mustering all my strength to address this presumptuous fool!

"Excuse me," I say calmly, pulling from her grasp. She tugs a little, then smiles letting go. All in one smooth swoop, she stands against me, her torso against mine. She is a bit taller than me even in these heels. Placing her palm on my abdomen, she applies firm pressure, forcing me back gently, like we are doing a two-step, staring in my eyes unflinching. The imprint of her hand's warmth grows wings. Fluttering wild in my womb, its movements become liquid anticipation escaping my fevered hollowness. I am consumed and brave, leaning towards her to show my appreciation when she turns her back on me, giving attention to the man sitting on the inside seat. She is letting him out. I am beside myself with shame. It's as if she has called me out and when I finally come, she's gone.

I take the inside seat across the aisle from her and hold my bag in my lap like a pillow. It supports my stern look and helps mask infatuation…uncertainty. The doors close, the train feels nearly empty. I'm concentrating on the view outside the window, on people going to other destinations. I try to imagine where they're going. I am trying to forget I am here…she is here.

"What is your name? I see you almost every day and I've never asked your name."

"Bianca." I answer without breaking focus on the tunnel walls.

"Boy, you hard," she muses then continues. "Well anyway, I'm Sharon." She announces not discouraged by my aloofness. Now the walls are passing so fast it is black outside and her image behind me leaning on the edge of her seat is profound. She's cocky. I like that.

"Where you work at?" She persists not needing my encouragement to make conversation.

"The hospital." I drop softly as if I am between thoughts.

"Are you going to look at me?" Her reflection is suddenly illuminated.

"I can see you," escapes me.

"I know." She admits locking eyes with me in the window.

She has been watching me all along, it's frightening. Before she was looking back, I had lost myself in her reflection. Her admission is sobering. My stop is coming, assuring refuge. I commit to catching later trains for the next few weeks. I need to miss this intensity. I need to forget. I stir mobilizing myself.

"You don't have any questions for me?" She pleads playfully.

In response, I stand and smile a shy good-bye.

"Can I call you?" She throws out the hook. I feel obligated to bite. I'm concluding why she can't call. Perfect, the train doors threaten to close.

"Yeah, it would be cool, but I gotta go, this is my stop."

"That's no problem." She heralds leaping to her feet, ushering my paralyzed figure off.

"This time of day, I won't be able to get your number before the next train comes along." I tell her my number, staring at her hands as she thumbs it in her cell.

"What number is this?" She asserts.

"Huh?" I puzzle shyly.

"What number is this: cell, house, work?"

"House," I resolve.

"Bianca. I am going to call you."

I don't recognize the number. I don't answer. She leaves a message with her number. I replay it repeatedly. Two days later, she calls again. This is the final call she announces, she is not into harassing beautiful women. Cowardly, I don't answer. Instead, I write her number on a scrap of paper and erase her messages. Transferring the number from bag to bag and place to place, I misplace it. Relieved when I find it, I write it down several times so that I might know where it can be found at all times. I start my attempts to call her. First, I dial the first three numbers, then six, but not seven. I think about what to say. I don't catch the 4:10. Our meeting was awkward before, now it'd be unbearable.

Saturday after napping all day, I dial the six numbers I know by hard, seventh one too. When it finally rings, it screams annoyingly like an alarm clock. Grateful when her answering service comes on, I practice a message while her greeting plays.

BEEP

"Sharon, this is Bianca. I apologize for not calling sooner. I misplaced your number. Today, I came across it and…"

BEEEEP!

"Bianca." Her voice sang deeper than before, deeper than imagined or suggested on the train. "It's good to hear from you. I haven't seen you on the train. I thought you were avoiding me."

"No, I...I...had misplaced your number." I stammer finding it harder lying to her, rather than a machine.

"Imma go ahead and cut to the chase, 'cause I can already see where this is going. Don't forget, I am a woman too. I'm not into playing games. Cool?"

Half heartedly I become defensive, "I'm not play..."

"Don't explain," she interrupts. "Don't start off lying to me either. You are hot, I'm interested. I want to hang out. I'm not doing anything today, are you?"

"No."

"You bi, curious, or trying to find yourself? Cause I want a hard-core dyke."

"I'm a lesbian."

"Good, when you coming over here or you want me over there?" Her question sounds like a command. I'm startled and ignited by her intensity. *Am I playing games?*

"I need an answer, so I can prepare for you?"

"You offering to cook?" I'm smiling in the phone.

"I could. So my place it is," she concludes. "Where do you live?" She demands a response then gives such precise directions. I've already figured out the best route to her, having never been in or around the area.

"How long will it take you to get dressed?"

"Forty-five minutes," I respond instinctively, on auto pilot now.

"Good. You should be knocking on my door in an hour and a half?"

There is a long uncomfortable silence. I don't know if her last comment is a question or another command.

"You aight?" She inquires softly.

"Nervous," I admit.

"That's a good thing." Her voice smiles seductively. "See you when you get here."

I take a hot shower, shaving and trimming everything. Paying close attention to the intricate folds of my valley, I wash

it several times. I don't plan to have sex but I feel sexy when
I'm ready. I decide to wear something comfortable, simple,
distracting, and summery. Another skirt, this time it's khaki
colored linen, this time it's longer. Spaghetti strapped tank, no
bra. I let my dreads hang, little lip gloss, skin flawless. I spray a
little citrus scent on before I get my things together. Before I go
out the door, I spray it above my head then the exit underneath.

The anticipation has grown to an ache inside. I feel it
intensify with each step towards her house. It's hard admitting
that I like being commanded, I like being obedient. I like her
calling me on my shit. Maybe this is what I've been waiting on,
someone who knows what they want and maybe, what I want
too.

Sharon answers the door dressed more casual than I have
seen her. Wearing an orange "A" shirt and tan cargo pants, it's
clear she works out. She has defined collar bones and chiseled
arms. She immediately grabs my hands, evaluating me. I wait
anxiously on her approval. She pulls me in a full embrace
exhaling in my ear, "You look beautiful."

Then kissing my neck as she holds me, she says, "Thank
you for coming."

She pulls me to her living room and orders me, "Sit
here, I'll be right back." A few moments later she calls from the
kitchen, "Wine or homemade lemonade?" I choose lemonade
above my better judgment. Now I can't excuse any bad behavior
with, "Wow, I did that? I was so drunk."

There are small plates on the coffee table, paper towels,
and a folded towel. First she returns with our drinks and places
them on coasters. Then again wearing an oven-mitt, holding
a large plate warning it's hot and then places it on the towel.
Finally, she joins me on the green velvety couch.

"You want to watch a movie or just talk?"

"Movie." She never asks what movie I want to watch,
although I see she has a large library around her television.
There is already one in the DVD player. The trailers start to
play. She sits on the other end of the couch and starts to make a

small plate. I lean in to do the same.

"Nah, I got you. Just relax."

She smiles then places the plate back on the table. Paper towel in hand, she reaches for my ankles, sliding my shoes off. Then lifts both my feet and turns my entire body towards her. Before I realize it, she has parted my legs. Startled, I press my skirt down between my legs to keep from showing my panties. She is tickled by the response but not interrupted. She scoots into me, placing a leg behind her back, the other on her lap. Pushing my skirt up my thighs until she is snuggly between my legs, she reaches for the plate then turns to me nonchalantly, "Mind if I feed you?"

I can't respond. I just smile nervously. She tastes the small wrap first, testing it. Then blows it cool and offers it to me. She stares into my eyes when I take a bite.

"It's good." I praise her and she seems to know.

"What is it?" I chew and fan her hand to give me another bite.

She is so pleased. After she gives me another bite, she gives me a quick kiss. I feel her aggression ease. She puts more on the plate, paper towel underneath, tells me what I am eating, and offers me the plate. Moving the coffee table closer, she asks if I can reach my drink. After I nod yes, we eat in silence. When I am done, I reach to put the plate on the table but she takes it and does it for me. I don't know what to do with my hands. I fold them across my stomach and get lost in the television. I don't know what I am watching, I don't ask. Her eyes trail from the television to me.

Her hand rubs my leg on her lap, first my calf then my knee. Each time she crosses over my knee, she stops a little further up my thigh. Her glances are long and languid. I rest in them, feeling a little more comfortable about her staring at me. Now at the top of my thigh, she searches my eyes for cues while examining the skirt bunched between us. Running her fingers along its hem then trailing to my eyes. My heart drums and it feels as though I've just come back from a run. She leans into me brushing her nose against mine, then her face. I feel the skirt move, her fingertips on my panty line, waiting. A moan escapes me, which she accepts as an invitation. She kisses my lips hello, then deeply. I waver. Her fingers trace my panty line. Finally lifting my panty line, she touches the center of my panties, moaning.

"You are so wet." Smelling my wet yearning, I want her to touch me. I scoot towards her finger and try to force her hand but she pulls away smiling.

"Let's go upstairs."

I drag behind her stiffly. After the zeal is broken, I remember I don't fuck on first dates. I remember I don't know who she is. I remember I don't have casual sex. She ignores my reluctance, pushing me down on the bed, landing on me, picking up where we left off, rubbing on top of my panties, grinding. I am so hot and saturated I could cry. *What the hell am I doing here? I don't even know this bitch's last name!* Still my hips are responding to every thrust. When she buries her face in my neck, my nipples are in painful knots. All of a sudden my shirt is over my head and she is soothing them with her warm mouth. Agonizing, moaning, I beg her to do something to relieve the heat growing beneath my skin.

I snatch her shirt off then unhook her bra. She is kissing me slowly moving down my body, her breast trailing ahead. I am fucking crying. I want it so bad and am so afraid of the consequences I can barely breathe, but I can't stop. I'm grinding against her, her hand on top of my panties. One finger, again at the crease of my thigh and insides, tracing my panty lines, I feel my panties move. The back of her hand is in my wetness, rising up my body. With her tongue inside my mouth, her finger slips inside me. Eyeing me, she pulls it out and tastes it then kisses me savagely before moving down my body again. Kissing my thighs and the back of my knees, hands caressing everything, I grab her head.

"Do it," I moan.

She enjoys torturing me by only kissing the creases,

tracing my outer lips with her tongue. I squirm trying to get her mouth to the void but she refuses. Then kissing it lightly, she observes my reaction. Her hand unveils it completely; she gives it one long lick. I jerk impulsively. She likes that and does it repeatedly until I can't take it anymore. Then she envelops it with her lips. Her mouth is firm, her tongue steady and concentrated. It feels so good but I move away not sure that I'm able to take it. She clinches my thighs in her arms snatching me back to her mouth. My heart beats so fast and hard it feels like my tonsils are thumping in my throat. She moans too, slipping her fingers inside, my hips respond impulsively. Trembling I can't control it, my body responds erratically. Still, I hear the movement of her hand against fluid gravity. The rhythm is hypnotizing. I become fragile stone, struck profoundly I feel the cracks spread through my flesh, and I crumble. When she rises, she is careful not to interrupt the feeling, kissing my stomach on the way to my mouth. I breathe deeply, slowly grasping the moment. I don't know how much time has elapsed when she sits back on her calves, analyzing me.

"You want some more or are you too sensitive?" She offers a real question I can respond to.

Contemplating the question stirs a deeper need. I don't say a word instead I run my hand over her bare thigh. Then she pulls *it* from the drawer beneath the night stand. Snatching me towards her, resting on her calves, knees to my buttocks, I examine it, while she rips open a condom with her teeth. It's dark black, about 6 inches. My walls are aching for it, something more than fingers, something more than her tongue. Rolling the condom on, she places her hand beside my head bracing herself then holds her strap with the other. I rub my face against her muscular forearm and moan.

"Give it to me."

I can feel the head of it, like an extension of her body searching for my entrance. She is gentle and with one small thrust the tip is in. Observing me, she gages my reaction. I'm aware it's been a minute since I was penetrated.

"Don't tense up." She orders then muffles my moans with kisses and my scent.

I rub my clit, attempting to quell the pain.

"That's it baby." She agrees, teasing my opening with just the tip.

I clench my breast, her back, the sheets, and my hair. Before I know it, she is inside, deep inside, stroking. I am holding on to her butt when she moves my right leg to her shoulder, burying her shoulder in the back of my knee.

"Remember to relax." She whispers between kisses.

"Just let go. It's okay," she promises.

I am in tears, clinging to her, surrendering, moving instinctively. Each movement surges through my pussy to my feet, stomach, arms, and head. It's like the dream I've had of falling, except I can feel the bed beneath. I am so weightless. I float forever it seems, moaning, and breathless into paralyzing eruptions.

Unspoken
Yakiri Truth

She couldn't sleep again. She couldn't get Darin off of her mind. Couldn't stop thinking about their last conversation and the conversation before that. She was haunted by every letter she had ever received. Every word Darin had ever written to her. She lay in bed watching the little blue ant she had downloaded from the Internet dance across the monitor. Her eyes were heavy and her body was tired. Yet, still she was unable to sleep. She couldn't sleep until she talked to Darin. Not until they said goodnight. Her eyes fastened on the monitor, watching the dancing blue ant. They followed its fast movements from one end of the screen to the other. She smiled then yawned. Tried to keep her eyes on the ant, pretending his performance was interesting enough to keep her awake. Sleep began to overtake her…softly…gently.

Darin rushed through the door of the small apartment. Paid the babysitter, escorted her to the front door, walked through the house, then checked the back door and windows to make certain they were all locked. Tip-toed into Chrissie's room who had fallen asleep with her thumb in her mouth and was snoring as loud as a sixty-year-old man who worked on the river. Ran upstairs and turned on the computer to discover that Carly was online!

[DARIN] Hey. How was your day?

The loud chime that came from her computer's speakers nearly scared Carly half-to-death! Her eyes opened immediately. She sat-up in bed, holding her chest.

Darin waited. There was no response.

[DARIN] You there?

The chime sounded again. It was Darin. Darin was on-line!

Hurriedly, Carly climbed out of bed and rushed to the computer.

[CARLY] Hey. My day was fine…long. What about yours?

[DARIN] Same. Glad to be home. Hate working this late. I'd rather be home with Chrissie.

[CARLY] Know the feeling unfortunately. Glad I got off at five. Prefer to kiss Haley goodnight *before* she goes to bed, not after.

Both stopped typing for a moment.

[DARIN] We still on for tomorrow?

Carly hesitated. The invitation was unexpected; meeting an online buddy face-to-face…Darin was supposed to be a fantasy, nothing more, just someone to chat with. She never expected to feel so…so…attracted…so…attached.

Darin sat quietly waiting for a reply.

[DARIN] It's okay to be nervous Carly. I'm nervous too. Still wanna meet though. Wanna see who I've been talking to; see what you look like. Look into your eyes. Get to know you face-to-face. See where this could go.

Carly blushed. *Where could it go?* She wondered about the possibility of their conversation, their connection becoming more stable, stronger. The possibility of rushing home to *see* Darin rather than chat on the computer. There was no question that there was already something special between them. Meeting could only intensify things. They had been chatting for three months. It was time to take things to the next level and if that meant meeting face-to-face for the first time…*I'll be there.*

They chatted for an hour about their plans. Meet in the French Quarter. Watch the sunset over the Mississippi River.

Have dinner. See where the rest of the evening would take them. They decided not to bring their children, since it was their first meeting.

[DARIN] Don't chicken-out on me Carly and don't be late.

[CARLY] LOL. I won't, I promise.

There was something about the summer months that seemed to transform the French Quarter into one of the most beautiful places on earth, especially in the evening. New Orleans in the evening...it seemed as if the city would come alive. As if it had its own heartbeat and danced to the rhythm of the saxophonist who played on the street corner. Creole-style cooking filled the air. Empty shells from crawfish tails covered the sidewalks. Would-be Jazz musicians and thirteen-year-old tap dancers stood at every corner.

Restaurants, shops, and bars stretched from Canal Street and went on for miles. Tourists were everywhere, requesting directions to the Flea Market, the Saint Louis Cathedral, and even the gay-side of town. Guttersnipes sat beside cardboard boxes begging for money, while the rest of the homeless lay across park benches asleep.

In the midst of it all was Carly, seated at a small round table, sipping a cup of coffee, waiting for Darin to arrive. Laughing quietly as she watched beggars and drunks piss on the sidewalks, while offended tourists pass by, too fascinated to turn away. She thought to herself that even they seemed to add to the beauty, the grace that made the French Quarter fascinating, and made her proud to call New Orleans her home.

She looked around. Darin would be wearing a blue shirt, black jeans, and tennis shoes. Darin was Black. Stood about six feet tall, had brown hair, brown eyes, and was about five minutes before being late.

Carly's eyes scanned the sidewalks. She stared at the brick buildings that were more than a century old. She watched as frustrated drivers honked their horns at horse-drawn carriages, slowly trotting through the French Quarter. Fascinated tourists stopped, stared, and pointed at each one. Her eyes scanned the café. Every table except hers held a plate with at least three deep-fried donuts covered in confectionate sugar. Though tempted, she decided to wait for Darin before ordering anything other than coffee.

Finishing her drink, she scanned the café again. She saw no one matching Darin's description but Darin saw her... approached her slowly, quietly from behind. Couldn't see Carly's face, but knew the brunette with the long, straight hair was Carly. She was wearing a blue t-shirt and black jeans with tennis shoes also, which was the attire they agreed upon the night before. She was sitting but Darin could tell she was about five feet, seven inches tall. She was slender and tanned.

Standing behind her, Darin leaned in and whispered, "Hey."

Carly sat straight in her chair and turned to see the person behind the voice.

"Hello." Confusion showed on both of their faces. "Can I help you with something?"

"I'm sorry, I thought you were someone else." Darin stared at the young woman for a moment. Her attire matched. She fit the description Carly gave of herself but she couldn't be Carly. Darin turned to walk away, hesitated, turned again, and asked, "By any chance, is your name Carly?"

Carly hesitated, not certain if she wanted to respond. "I'm sorry, do I know you?"

"No, you can't be Carly?" The stranger asked again. "Carly, as in Karlee822@lycocity.com? Are you *that* Carly?"

Carly was confused and suddenly felt nervous. Who was this person that was questioning her? How would anyone know her name, her screen name, her e-mail address? Carly tried to remain calm. She smiled slightly and asked, "Who wants to know?"

"You're Carly Newman?"

Frustrated, Carly responded to the stranger's question. "Yes. Now who are you?

Anger showed on the stranger's face. "I'm Darin."

Shock riddled through her veins. "Darin?" *This person couldn't be Darin!* Not the woman who was questioning her; standing in front of her in a blue t-shirt and black jeans. It had to be a mistake. *"You're* Darin?"

Darin sat in the chair beside Carly. Leaned close and asked, "How old are you?"

"How old am I? How old are you?"

"Keep your voice down," Darin snapped. "I don't want anyone to call the police because they think I'm on a date with a juvenile." Darin grabbed her arm and pulled her even closer. "Why didn't you tell me you were a teenager?"

"A teenager? Why didn't you tell me you were a woman? What in the hell is a woman doing with a name like Darin anyway? That's a man's name."

"Darin is a unisex name and I didn't name myself, Carly. My mother named me after my father."

"Like I said," Carly responded smugly, "a man's name. Why in the hell didn't you tell me you were a woman?"

"Why in the hell didn't you tell me you were a child? I would have never…"

"A child?" Carly's face turned bright red.

"Yes, a child. That's exactly what you are. Is this how you get your kicks little girl?"

"Whoa…wait-a-minute!" Carly's voice elevated. "Let's get one thing straight *lady*, you IM'd me! You asked me out. And when I said no, *you* talked me into it!"

Darin could only sit quietly. Carly was right. Three months ago, they met in a chat room. She had signed on under the name DodiMac. She saw the name Karlee822 and…

That's a cute name, she typed, is it your real name or just a screen name?

Thanks, Carly responded, yes it's my real name, except its spelled Carly. What about you? Is DodiMac short for something or did you make it up?

Actually it's short for Darin
McCallister.
Carly Newman, nice to meet you.

Five minutes later, they were in a private chat room. A few days later, when Carly logged on again, she had an invitation to be added to *DodiMac's* buddy list. They chatted almost every night. Found that they had a lot in common. Both were New Orleans' natives. Both liked football. Italian food. Swimming. Lived in Mid-City. Hated the President's views on economics and social issues.

"You lied to me though. You said that you had a child that you were raising alone. You said you had your own apartment, a car, and that you worked in an office."

"That's not a lie. None of that is a lie. My daughter's name is Haley...she's three. My mother kicked me out when I got pregnant. I lived with my boyfriend and his parents until he decided that he wasn't ready for fatherhood. They threw me out before Haley was born. I've been on my own ever since. My first apartment was owned by a slumlord in Uptown. I moved to Mid-City after Haley was born."

Listening to Carly explain her life reminded Darin of the reasons she thought Carly was an adult. Although they had only talked in the chat room, there was something about her conversation that made her sound so mature, intelligent, and determined to succeed. "What did you do with Haley while you were in school?"

"A friend of mine dropped out of school after she got pregnant. She doesn't work and lives in the projects. She kept Haley for me while I was in school and at work. She still watches her for me. That's where she is tonight. Now that she's three, I'm going to put her in a pre-school. I'm just waiting for the summer to end." She paused. "Why didn't you tell me you were a woman?"

Darin smiled then chuckled softly. "I didn't know you thought that I was a man."

Carly rolled her eyes. "You said your name was Darin."

"It is."

"Darin is a man's name."

"Darin is a unisex name."

"You had to know that I thought you were a man."

"I could argue the same thing about you being an adult. And actually, the thought never crossed my mind. I just assumed you knew whom you were talking to. Obviously, I was mistaken. We both were."

Both sat quietly for a moment, staring into each other's eyes. Darin smiled. Carly blushed then leaned forward. Her voice was low, "So, I'm here. You're here. What happens now?"

Darin frowned, uncertain how to answer Carly's question. She stared at Carly's face. Noticing everything about her green eyes, her freckles, her pink lips, her rosy cheeks, she was beautiful. She was breathtaking. But she was only eighteen. That was a line Darin would not cross. "Nothing," she responded. Her smile faded into a frown. "Nothing could happen, even if we wanted it to. I'm gay and you're straight. I'm an adult and you're a child."

"Stop calling me a child." Carly's face began to turn red again. "I am eighteen-years-old but I have lived on my own since I was fifteen. I have a three-year-old daughter that I am raising by myself."

"Having a baby doesn't make you an adult Carly. Being eighteen doesn't make you one either. I could take you inside of a bar but I couldn't buy you a drink."

Carly's eyes narrowed. Her voice was low and firm. "You tell me what makes me an adult then…age? I have taken on more responsibilities than half the so-called *adults* I've come in contact with. Name one thing you have that I don't! Not an apartment, because I have that. Not a car, I have that too."

"How about a high school diploma?"

The smug look on Darin's face infuriated Carly but she took a deep breath and kept talking. "Actually, I graduated from high school in May. And since I work for one of the top mortgage companies in the U.S., it's possible that I already make more money than you." Leaning forward she continued, "And while we're on the subject of my age, my birthday *is* tomorrow." She sat back in her chair, smiled, and said, "Anything else?"

Darin sat silently. She smiled and nodded her head as if to say, touché. "Happy birthday!"

"Thank you."

Darin lowered her head, her smile faded. "This can't happen, Carly."

Carly sat straight in her chair again. "This *won't* happen," she snapped, "but it's only because you can't see past my age and I can't see past your gender."

"Excuse me?"

"You heard me. Just like you're not interested in dating a *teenager*, I'm not interested in dating a *woman*. I won't raise my daughter that way. I don't want her to think that it's okay for two women to..."

"Wait just one damn minute!" It was Darin's eyes that narrowed. Darin's face that turned red. Darin's voice that spoke in a low-firm tone. "What the hell do you mean? You don't want your daughter to think that it's okay for two women to do what?"

Carly was silent.

"Let me tell you something. This wasn't some big decision that I made or some sort of experiment that I'm trying out just to see if I like it. This is who I am. I didn't have a choice in the matter, Carly. I didn't choose to be a lesbian. And I will not sit here and be insulted by some narrow-minded, judgmental..."

"*Narrow-minded?* Judgmental!"

"Yes...yes...yes!"

"Okay, this conversation is going nowhere. I'm gonna just go ahead and leave."

"I think that might be best." Darin grabbed her purse and watched as Carly stood. They turned and exited the café, both walking in the same direction.

"Are you following me now?" Carly turned to face Darin

who had been walking close behind her.

Darin could see the anger and hurt in her eyes. Her disappointment was written all over her face. She could tell that Carly felt misled; that she was hoping for more to come out of their meeting face-to-face. She was probably hoping to find a husband, a man to father her daughter. She probably never expected to meet a woman ten years older than she was. She began to realize everything that she had said to insult Carly... calling her a child, a little girl, accusing her of lying; and she had never acknowledged all that Carly had overcome in her young life: homelessness; single motherhood; obtaining her high school diploma, her career, her goals.

"My car is parked a few blocks up." She pointed in the direction they were walking. "You know how hard it is to find a parking spot in the French Quarter."

Carly lowered her head then turned away. She glanced back at Darin who had already begun to walk towards her. They walked side-by-side quietly. The awkwardness of their meeting loomed over them like a dark cloud.

"You never showed me a picture of Haley." Darin spoke to break the silence.

Carly smiled and opened her purse. She looked in her wallet and removed a photograph of a little girl with milky-white skin, dark hair, wide green eyes, and freckles. "That's my girl."

"Oh, she's beautiful!"

"Thanks."

They passed the restaurant where they had planned to eat. Both heads turned at the sound of the live Jazz band playing. The smell of pasta and seafood seeped through the open doors.

Carly stopped walking. Darin turned to face her. "I'm hungry."

Darin smiled. "Me too." She looked at the restaurant and sighed, "So close." She sighed again then looked at Carly who was looking at the ground. "Sure is a shame that we might end up eating burgers and fries or leftovers tonight." She looked at the restaurant again, "I would hate to have to go home and cook."

"You…" Carly hesitated. *What the hell, she thought.* "You promised to take me to dinner."

Darin laughed. "Well, as long as you don't mind having dinner with a woman?"

Carly's eyes rose slowly, her voice was almost a whisper. "I don't mind," she said. Her mouth curved into a small smile. "As long as you don't mind having dinner with a…what was that you called me…little girl?"

"Not at all."

Both laughed. Together they walked into the restaurant. They apologized for their insults; discussed their personal lives; and talked about their love lives (or lack thereof). They talked about Haley and Chrissie; and showed as many pictures as they could find in their purses. Then came the questions…

"So where's Chrissie's dad?

Darin rolled her eyes, "Oh, girl who knows? I heard about a year ago that he was headed to Chicago but he's probably living around the corner with some woman who pays all his bills and lets him smack her around every now and again."

"He was abusive?"

"Not really. He tried but when he saw that I would fight him back, he backed down. He never stopped bracing up to me. I got sick of threatening to chop his balls off, so I threw him out. I was still pregnant. He's never seen Chrissie."

"Haley has never met her father either." Carly paused. "So let me ask you something…how can you be gay and three years ago you were in a four year relationship with a man?"

She smiled. "I used to swing both ways. Before him, I was with a woman. When we broke-up, I met him and he seemed cool. He had a reputation for intimidating his women but I didn't find out about that until after we had been together for a while. I wasn't afraid of him and I didn't think he'd ever hit me. So I stayed with him."

"So he's gonna be your last man?"

"He was, yes. But I've only casually dated after we broke-up. Nothing serious." Her eyes fixed on Carly. "I guess

I just haven't found the right person yet."

Carly couldn't help blushing. Neither could Darin. They felt it again, the attraction, the connection they felt when they were chatting online.

They finished dinner, paid the check, and left the restaurant. They walked along the Moonwalk, discussed their careers, shared their goals, and secrets. And when they were ready to leave, laughed at how close they had accidentally parked to one another.

"So, I had rented some movies, bought all of this popcorn, and sent Haley to sleep at a friend's house because I thought that you might have been coming over tonight." Carly was blushing when she admitted that she had planned to invite Darin to her house.

"Well, I actually don't have anything else to do. Chrissie is with my mother, so I don't have to rush home to relieve a baby sitter or anything." She saw the hesitation on Carly's face. "We could just hang-out. I'm having fun with you. And honestly, I'm not ready for the evening to end."

Carly blushed again. "Yeah, me neither." Carly said the words as if she were surprised. She looked at Darin and smiled. *I can't believe I'm doing this.* She thought as she opened her car door and said, "Follow me."

They pulled into the driveway of the townhouse Carly had lived in since she was sixteen-years-old. Locked their car doors. Carly showed Darin into the living room and invited her to have a seat. She offered Darin a soft drink. The first movie was in the DVD player, a horror, then a comedy, then a drama. Then...

Somehow between the screams and laughter during the horror film, Darin found herself in Carly's in arms. How they ended-up holding hands during the comedy was uncertain. Neither of them knew who looked into whose eyes first but something happened while they were watching the final movie, a drama that neither of them could explain....

"It's midnight," Darrin whispered.

Carly blushed, sat her soft drink on the coffee table.

"Happy birthday," Darin whispered.

"Thanks," Carly replied.

They kissed, softly, sensuously, as if the only lips they were ever meant to kiss were each other's. Carly had never known a kiss could be so passionate, so inviting. She couldn't stop herself. Her will, her mind, all of her senses betrayed her. She felt her body lean backwards, her back rested against the seat of the sofa. Darin climbed on top of her. Her lips never parted with Darin's lips. Her arms never released Darin's body.

Darin told herself that she couldn't…wouldn't…it was wrong…wasn't it? But something happened when their eyes met. Those green eyes seemed to set Darin on fire. Like Carly, she couldn't help herself. Couldn't stop herself. She had to kiss her lips. She had to run her fingers through Carly's dark hair. She needed to feel Carly's body next to hers. Touch her softness. Taste the sweetness of her. Plant soft kisses on her neck and face, as she lost all sense of time and space in Carly's embrace.

Carly felt it too, the fire, the heat. She felt the intense desire that burned between them. Their hands grabbed at each other's clothes. Snatching. Pulling. Untying. Unbuckling. Removing. Merging. Like poetry, their bodies moved. Eyes closed. Legs wrapped around one another's thighs. Sweating. Clawing. Holding onto one another. Both tasting a forbidden fruit with flavor so sweet, neither of them could turn it away. They exploded in each other's arms, together, in perfect unison. Clinging to each other as they lost themselves in a whirlwind of pleasure.

The room became silent. The world stopped spinning. As their bodies stilled, reality came crashing down around them. Their eyes opened. They looked in one another's arms, at one another's bodies. Realized the lines they had crossed: Darin had been with a teenager; Carly had been with a woman. They moved to separate ends of the sofa. Both grabbed their clothes and quickly, quietly tried to cover themselves. They searched for words…excuses…explanations but neither could find justification for what had happened between them.

They sat, quietly, staring at one another. Darin's eyes gazing at Carly's milky white skin. Carly's eyes raking over Darin's golden brown body. Darin didn't want to leave. Carly wanted her to stay. Both were too afraid, too ashamed to admit the truth. So, they admitted the obvious...

"Carly," Darin said quietly, "you...you're still a teenager."

"And you're a woman," was all Carly replied.

She turned her head and listened as Darin walked out the door and left.

Lust
Phase 2

No Frills

I usually don't do bars,
so when I walked into this place
my expectations
were few.
Thought I'd get my dance on,
do a tequila shot or three
and go home.
I saw you sitting here
alone
and I do like the way that skirt rides up on your thigh.
The way it hugs your ass when you cross your legs,
exposing long, shapely limbs, that extend up to
heaven.
Understand, I'm not one to waste my time or my words
so, I hope you appreciate my honesty.
Excuse me, baby gurl,
I didn't ask for your name.
I don't need to know your name.
Pardon me, sweet lady,
you didn't get my name 'cause I didn't give it to you.
It's irrelevant and no, I don't want or need your number
and I'm not givin' you mine .
I just wanna fuck you!
You look shocked.
Have I offended?
Forgive my being so forward but I'm not one to waste my
words or my time.
I saw you sitting here alone , fine as hell, and I'm truly likin'
the way your breasts
rise and fall beneath that sheer silk blouse.
Damn, you look good!
I don't want to know, nor do I care what you do for a living.
Don't wanna hear about degrees you have or have not.

Don't care what books you've read or what movies you've
seen.
I just wanna stroke that ass,
caress your breasts,
your. . .
I just wanna fuck you!
Is that surprise I see on your pretty face…are you disgusted?
Please forgive my bluntness; I simply care not to waste my
words or my time.
I saw you sitting here alone with those big beautiful eyes and
those full burgundy painted lips.
I like the way your locs brush your shoulder and your back.
You smell so good.
What was that darling?
No, I don't wanna know how you spend your free time.
Don't wanna wine and dine you.
Don't want you to wine and dine me.
Just wanna kiss you,
feel your tongue in my throat,
mine in yours.
Kiss your navel, your inner thighs. . .
may I. . . fuck you?
You seem a little agitated, are you curious?
I am.
You will forgive a sista for speakin' true won't you?
I just don't want to waste my time or my words.
You were sitting here alone wearin' the hell out of those
pumps!
Hold up Boo, I ain't interested in your dreams or your aspira-
tions;
I don't wanna hear about past love; and
don't care what kind of music you listen to.
I couldn't care less what sign you were born under,
'cause hell, I ain't tryin' to get to know you.
I don't care if I ever see you again
after tonight.

Let me explore your body, inside and out, feel you rake those pretty acrylics across my back,
make you cum.
I just wanna fuck you!
You look a little conflicted, are you intrigued?
I am.
Excuse a sista for speaking her mind
but let's not waste our time or our words.
You see, I don't wanna to know what your favorite color is 'cause there will be
no cute little color-coordinated tokens of affection exchanged.
Do you talk, sing, scream, or mumble incoherent phrases and exclamations when you fuck?
Or do you sigh and moan and make those exotic animal noises?
I don't care if you love your mother and
don't care if she loves you.
Do you like it slow and easy or do you like it straight up jungle monkey love?
Because I aim to please... may I fuck you?
You appear somewhat perplexed, are you aroused?
I am.
So, I'm sure you'll forgive my boldness, as I said before, I ain't down for
frivolous waste of time or words.
You were sitting here alone watching me want you, knowing that I want you.
So let's cut the bullshit, let's forgo the small talk, avoid the emotional clutter, and
cut straight to the chase.
Ah . . . there you go . . . take my hand and we'll take our leave.
After tonight, if we should see each other again, we'll nod, smile, and say hello.
With no strings, no baggage, and no heartaches, we'll continue on our separate ways,
with our separate lives.
Still strangers, we'll remember the night we shared.

We'll remember the night
we simply . . . fucked.

The Weekend
Chanda Rae

Nicole had anticipated her trip to the city all month long. She could barely contain herself on the airplane thinking about Rae's tongue sliding in and out of her anxious pussy. *I want her so badly.* She thought as she sighed aloud. This would be their very first time together.

Nicole had moved away years prior to meeting Rae to pursue a career in theater. Funny how the entire time they lived in the same city they had never crossed each other's paths. It didn't matter though. She was more than willing to hop on a plane to get what was about to be the most incredible sex she had ever had. She began to squeeze her beautiful mocha colored brown legs together as she glanced down at the note Rae had delivered the day before with one beautiful long stem rose.

The note read...

I'm having a limo pick you up from the airport. Something will be waiting for you in the back seat.

Rae was so full of surprises that Nicole couldn't imagine what could possibly be waiting in the limo but she knew it would be something incredibly sweet. As the plane landed, she began to throb even more. The driver of the Bentley limo smiled widely as if she already knew who Nicole was. Yes, Rae had asked that a very sexy female limo driver be the one who brought Nicole to her.

"Hello, Nicole. I was told to welcome you to your

fantasy."

Nicole sat down in the back seat and found two bottles of champagne. One bottle was empty except for a note inside of it. The other was chilled to perfection so she poured herself a glass and pulled the note out of the second bottle.

The note read...

The door is unlocked. Come into the bathroom once you get here. Don't talk, not until I say that it's okay.

Unable to contain herself any longer, Nicole pulled her skirt up slightly, pulled her now wet panties to the side, and began rubbing her swollen clitoris. Her nipples were erect and begging for some attention, so with her other hand she lifted her blouse and rubbed them in a slow circular motion. Just as she felt herself about to explode, she opened her eyes slightly and saw that she was nearing Rae's house.

She quickly tried to gather her composure. Beads of perspiration covered her forehead and her legs felt weak as the car stopped. As she waited for the driver to open her door, she noticed that rose petals filled the driveway leading to the front door. The driver escorted her to the door and smiled widely as she turned to leave.

Nicole slowly opened the door as instructed and found that the living room was filled with candles burning, soft music playing, and a trail of rose petals leading to the bathroom. She heard water running but didn't speak as instructed. As she entered the bathroom she saw Rae standing in the shower covered in slippery suds. Rae looked at Nicole intensely but didn't say a word. She began seductively rubbing the soap around her chocolate nipples. She leaned against the wall of the shower and let the water spray her body completely. Never taking her eyes off Nicole, she began stroking her own clitoris. Nicole couldn't take it any longer. She got in the shower fully dressed.

Rae kissed her passionately while ripping her clothes off. In minutes their bodies were fully exposed to each other. Rae pushed Nicole against the wall as if to arrest her. As she pressed herself against Nicole's ass, she pushed Nicole's legs apart with her feet. Nicole could feel Rae's clitoris throbbing against her ass and began to moan uncontrollably. Rae ran her tongue up and down her back. Nicole was on fire and Rae was feeling the heat. She grabbed Nicole around the waist and dropped to her knees, kissing each of Nicole's cheeks then flicking her tongue between them. Nicole turned the water off as if signaling she couldn't wait any longer.

Nicole lay on her back as Rae hungrily sucked her nipples. She placed Nicole's legs on her shoulders rocking her slowly but her wet mouth never left Nicole's breasts. The only sounds heard were that of Nicole's moans and the smacking sounds of her pussy. With her free hand, Rae inserted her finger slowly in and out, rubbing Nicole's own juices over her clitoris. Rae moaned as Nicole's tight pussy gripped her fingers as if she wanted more. Rae's mouth began to water as she licked and sucked at Nicole's beautiful body until she was finally face to face with the clit that had been calling her name all day. She licked it slowly savoring every moment. She moaned at the sweet taste that was driving her wild. Rae wanted more. She placed Nicole's feet on her shoulders to gain full exposure and started darting her long tongue in and out of Nicole's wet pussy.

She stopped suddenly and looked up at Nicole and said, "Tell me what you want."

Nicole reached down with both hands and pulled her lips apart and whispered, "Please make me cum...please."

Rae placed her lips on Nicole's clit and began to suck slowly. She felt it grow in her mouth as Nicole thrust her hips against her face.

"Rae fuck me, baby. Yes baby...fuck me with your tongue," she whispered.

The thrusts grew faster as Nicole's body started to tremble. Rae became so excited that she started to stroke her own clitoris in anticipation of Nicole's explosion. She darted her tongue in and out of Nicole and with each thrust of Nicole's hips, Rae's tongue went further inside of her.

Nicole raised her head slightly from the bath pillow. The

sight of Rae's hot mouth all over her pussy and Rae tugging at her own clit sent her over the edge. The smacking sounds of her own pussy were now driving her wild.

She whispered, "Suck harder baby...I'm cumming."

Before the words could leave her mouth, she began to cum over and over and over. Rae's mouth never left her hot pussy and the sensation of Nicole's juices all over her made her cum as well. Nicole's thrusts became slower but she still playfully rubbed her pussy across Rae's lips.

Rae looked up at her seductively and whispered, "Welcome to paradise, baby."

Tuesday
Trish Carter

Before Lena knew it, the sun was peeking through the thin curtains to announce that it was morning. The invasion of the sunlight didn't bother her because she was so used to getting up early even though there were times that she wished she could sleep longer. It would have been nice to wake up next to BJ. The last time she had felt BJ's body, it had felt as soft as a baby's bottom! Holding BJ close was like cuddling with the favorite teddy bear she'd had as a child.

I think I'll make some breakfast. Quietly, she opened the door to BJ's room. BJ was still sleeping like a baby. Lena contemplated getting into bed with her and waking her up with kisses over her entire body, but of course, she chickened out and shut the door. *Let's see what's in the pantry.* She smiled with delight as she discovered turkey sausage, eggs, and grits. She decided to include French toast on their breakfast menu for two. As she cracked open the eggs and prepared her French toast mixture, she wondered what it would be like to have BJ in her life all of the time.

She is caring, extremely funny, and has an IQ over 30! Some of the people I've dated had no conversation, no money, too many kids, and just couldn't bring it to the table like I require. That kind of stuff just turns me off. On the other hand, BJ and I have a lot in common, we're both talkers, strong spiritually, affectionate, love family, and most importantly, we can both bring the finances to the table. I know we can learn from each other on so many different levels. I do know that she stresses being one who wants to be in that two percent that owns 90% of the wealth in America and doesn't mind working for it and neither do I.

Hmm, Mrs. Lena Walker-Jordan...Mrs. Jordan, I like that, either way it sounds good. Listen to me! We've spent one night together after not seeing each other in three years and I'm marrying us off. I may not even like her after spending our vacation together. Go ahead Lena, feel your head to see if you have a fever! All this jumping the gun. Lesbians! Obviously, I'm crazy. First of all, I'm not a lesbian; I'm a bisexual bitch. Relationships are great for the first two months and then you start to recognize the issues and then the honeymoon is over.

Stop being a pessimist, everybody in the world is dysfunctional! If I keep telling myself that, I'll be okay. But damn, she's different; I feel as if I've loved her from the moment we met.

I remember when BJ walked through the door of Evonne and Shirl's apartment. She was so attractive with her hair slicked back and waved (before she had twists), wearing wide leg jeans, square-toed boots, and a cute beat up pin-striped wool blazer. We flirted with each other on the DL (down low). More on a subconscious level because we both had lovers and our friends knew it. So, I decided to play it cool and so did she, besides there were friends around that were cool with my lover. I remember her saying to me while in mid sentence, "You have nice lips." I damn near choked! That BJ always catches me off guard.

The scent of breakfast woke BJ. *Was Juan here cooking? Did he forget that I told him I would cook this morning? Oh well, it smelled good anyway.* BJ was glad that Juan was there. She had a slight hangover from drinking all day yesterday and didn't feel much like cooking anyway. When BJ rose out of bed and swung her legs to the side of the bed, a vibrator fell to the floor. BJ picked up her reliable bed mate and placed it under her pillow. *Thanks for last night.*

BJ wondered if Lena was up. The thought provoked her

to look in on her. She walked to Lena's room and found the door slightly ajar. Slowly and quietly, she opened it.

"Lena, are you up?"

With a puzzled and sleepy look still on BJ's face, she walked past the living room, following the smell of sausage and some warm, sweet aroma. There stood Lena, beautiful as ever, cooking her baby some breakfast. At least that's what BJ wished.

"Good morning, Lena." BJ said, startling Lena from behind and pulling her into an embrace.

"You scared the shit out of me."

"Sorry."

"Good morning. Did you sleep well?" Lena maneuvered away from BJ's closeness.

"Like a rock," BJ smirked.

"Yea, I looked in on you." Lena said softly.

"You did? That was sweet."

"So, are you hungry?"

"Very."

"Good. I made turkey sausage, eggs, grits, and French toast. Hope you like it."

"Well, I don't eat French toast but I'll have a little grits. Do you have cheese in anything?"

"No."

"Good, 'cause I don't like cheese in my eggs or grits."

"Picky bitch, aren't you?"

"Yes, very…when it comes to food but you'll learn that."

"Oh, I will? You're that sure, huh?"

"Absolutely," BJ smiled.

"You think that smile will get you anything, don't you?"

"Sometimes."

"We'll see. Why don't you take your tired ass over there and set the table?"

BJ looked at Lena with hesitation, then conceded and walked over and set the table like she had ordered her to do. Lena fixed their plates and brought them to the table. She was wearing a burgundy silk robe that stopped just above the knees. Her robe was opened, revealing a matching camisole with shorts. Her hair was pinned up, some of it draped just above her eyebrows. *Sexy ass!* BJ smiled at her own private thoughts.

BJ said grace that morning adding a special silent prayer to the Lord for allowing her to spend another day with this beautiful woman.

"So what do you want to get into today, BJ?" Lena asked as she nibbled daintily on her food.

"I'd like to spend a few hours on the beach getting a tan."

"You are a little light around the gills," Lena observed humorously.

"You noticed, huh?"

"Okay, BJ, the beach is fine. I'll pack a lunch with drinks."

"We won't need that stuff; they'll bring us whatever we want, except herb."

"Cool."

"I have plenty of smoke. I always come packed."

"I'm sure you do, pothead."

"Look who's talking. You probably smuggled a pound on the plane and got caught but because you have a frequent flyer pass and a get out of jail free card (Diplomatic immunity), they let you go," BJ teased.

Lena even had to laugh at that. "Keep digging a hole, BJ, because that'll be the only one you'll be able to get into."

"Yeah, okay. I heard that one before and I still got wet."

They laughed in unison.

After breakfast, Lena jumped in the shower. BJ called Tony to let him know he wouldn't be needed until later in the afternoon. Then she paged Juan to let him know that she needed him to fix lunch and clean the villa. As BJ walked towards her room, Lena sauntered out of the bathroom.

"It's time to get your funky ass in the shower BJ."

"What? I stink?" BJ asked while sniffing under her armpits.

"Badly!"

"Yeah, okay, that's why you went in first."

Lena went into her room and closed the door again. BJ heard her laughing.

"Smart ass," BJ yelled.

After getting out of the shower, BJ put on some suntan lotion, actually a lot of lotion. She needed some color badly. She put on her yellow and orange two-piece bathing suit and her pullover net top that draped past her thighs.

"Are you ready, Lena?" BJ yelled from her bedroom.

"Yes, in a minute."

BJ walked into the living room, rolled a couple of joints, put them in her beach bag and yelled to Lena to grab a couple of long towels from the closet. When Lena walked into the room, she was wearing a white bathing robe with a hood and beach sandals.

"Hope you have a bathing suit on under that?"

"Of course."

They walked out onto the deck and down onto the beach. They could already feel the island heat penetrating their skin, almost to a point of cooking.

"It's supposed to get up to 90 degrees today, Lena," BJ reported.

"It feels like it's in the 90's already and it's only 11:00 in the morning."

"My guess is that it's in the mid 80's already."

"You're probably right. Hey, here's a good spot," Lena pointed.

They parked themselves about thirty feet from the beautiful turquoise water. The warm, fine grained, oatmeal colored sand felt good between their toes. The few dark twigs that were scattered along the shoreline and sand looked like pieces of sculpture. Maybe they were just broken tree branches but BJ marveled over the fact that everything looked like works of art. They sat down and got comfortable on the full-length beach chairs. Immediately, a waiter from the hotel came over.

"Can I get you ladies an umbrella or something to drink?"

"I'd like an umbrella and a Pina Colada," Lena said.

"I'll have a Margarita." BJ said as she reached in her bag and pulled out a CD player and headphones.

"So, Lena, are you going to let me see your bathing suit?" BJ asked as she peered over her sunglasses.

"When I'm ready to go into the water, thank you very much," Lena teased.

"You're killing me here." BJ whined with a strong New York accent.

"Oh, stop it. Shit, I forgot to put sunblock on. Do you have any?"

"Yes." BJ handed Lena the bag.

"Good, I'm glad you remembered."

She unsnapped her robe and let it fall to the chair. But she wouldn't get up to remove it completely. BJ listened to her music and pretended not to notice but out of the corner of her eyes, she watched Lena rub the lotion onto her legs.

"BJ?"

"Yes?"

"Would you please put some on my back?"

Show Time! "Sure." BJ smirked joyously.

Lena's bathing suit was a white one piece that crisscrossed in the front, holding each breast in separate cups. The sides were a net material, which turned into a quarter of an inch thick band that went down the split of her, disappearing. Taking a deep breath, BJ tried to concentrate on putting the lotion on Lena's back even though she desperately wanted to follow the floss leading to *dat ass!*

"Your drinks, ladies."

Damn, he messed up my groove! BJ stopped rubbing and reached into the bag to get money to tip him. After taking a sip, BJ sat back, put her headphones on and continued to listen to Meshell Ndegeocello's *Rush Over* off the *Love Jones'* soundtrack. BJ reached back into her bag and pulled out her relaxing tool, the best weed she could get her hands on from this very beautiful island. She twirled the fat spliff under her nose, took a deep breath of the herb, the sea and the suntan lotion still on her fingers, and relaxed. After her initial puff, she admired the sights around her. She was really groovin. Lena got up and headed towards the water.

Oh, my God! Her booty sucked that string in like it was a suction cup. Actually, a person sucking on a spaghetti noodle was more like it. Her butt cheeks were so tight and air lifted that she must do at least, what 800 squats a day! Damn, I wish I wasn't lazy when it came to working out! BJ buzzed.

She watched Lena play in the water. It was definitely inviting. Before she could get up to join her, Lena motioned her towards the water with her pointer finger. BJ became so excited that when she jumped up, she almost tipped over her chair. Embarrassment crept over her. Bloopers seemed to be the story of BJ's life but the 78-degree water felt like a soft, smooth milk bath and that made it all good.

"The water is great," Lena said. "Come and play with me."

As BJ's body adjusted to the sudden change in temperature, she swam towards Lena.

"Would you like to go out into the deep part?"

"Hell, no!" BJ answered quickly. *She was high but she wasn't fucked up!*

"Come on. I'll take you. I won't let you go."

"Okay, I guess. I'll try anything once."

"Hold onto my shoulders."

"From the front or back?"

"Front. I want to see your face when I leave you out here."

"Fuck that! I'll meet you back on the sand." BJ turned to swim away but Lena grabbed her suit bottom and pulled her back.

"You do need some sun, you're light around the crack," she laughed. "Come on, I'm just kidding, I'll never let you go."

"I hope not."

They went further out into the tropical water. She and Lena were the only ones out there.

"Isn't it wonderful?"

It seemed like they were far out into the water but their

feet were still touching the bottom. BJ removed one hand from Lena's shoulder and stopped her from going any further by cupping her hand inadvertently between her legs. BJ's hand moved from front to back, rubbing Lena with the same motion of the ocean currents. She could feel Lena's clit swell through the thong bathing suit. This turned BJ on. Lena began to relax and move closer to BJ. She placed her arms around BJ's neck and they began kissing like two young kids who were kissing for the first time. Waiting for something to happen, BJ figured Lena wouldn't mind if she went inside. She slid her long middle finger inside Lena and made her rise up on her toes. As she weakened and gave into BJ, Lena's head dropped onto BJ's shoulder.

From the thrusting of BJ's finger, Lena's insides began to catch on fire and BJ knew she had her. Lena defiantly pulled away but BJ wrapped her arm around Lena's waist and firmly pulled her back into her arms, thrusting quicker. A moaning sound came from Lena, then she slapped BJ's face and pulled away again. This time she managed to break away.

"Shit, BJ! I told you I was going to make you wait."

Lena swam back to shore and BJ followed. She sat on her beach chair and dried off a little. When BJ walked up to the chairs, Lena had a pissed look on her face.

"So, Lena, you wanna tell me what that was all about? It did feel good, didn't it?" BJ smirked. "Are you mad at me because it felt good or because you weren't inside of me?"

"Fuck you, BJ! I'm controlling this shit!"

"Oh, I see now. You want to be in control of this situation and your emotions. Well, get over it sweetie. One thing I've learned is that we don't have as much control as we would all like to have. You have to learn to go with the flow. Enjoy each moment and you'll be fine." BJ said indignantly.

"BJ, you're full of shit! You'll say anything to get some pussy."

BJ laughed. "Lena, really! Pussy is a dime a dozen. I don't even have to say anything and women will give it up."

"You're such an arrogant bitch!"

"And your point is?"

Lena rolled her eyes and stuck up her middle finger.

"I see you're having a lot of hand problems today."

They busted into hysterical laughter. This lightened the conversation, which helped Lena get over what had happened and move on.

"For real though, what's up with that smacking shit?"

"Enjoy the moment. Isn't that what your smart ass was preaching about a few seconds ago?"

Lena went over to BJ's chair, straddled her, and took BJ's face in her hands.

"I'm sorry. Did I hurt the Boo Boo? Maybe you can go and find some of those dime a dozen girls to make it feel all better." Lena playfully kissed BJ then dismounted and returned to her own beach chair.

They talked a little while longer about Lena's busy schedule and her not being able to play or hang out often. Finally, Lena apologized for slapping BJ, promising she would make it up to her. Of course, BJ forgave her even though she was never mad.

"Let me know when you're ready to go back. I can stay on the beach all day." BJ closed her eyes and relaxed as Lena sipped on her second Pina Colada. The beach started to get crowded as the day went on. BJ and Lena engaged in small talk while they people watched.

"Am I dark yet?"

"Actually, you look dirty," Lena joked.

"Good, that means that my tan is going to look great."

A few hours later, they packed up their things and went back to the villa. Juan finished cleaning up the kitchen after creating irresistible Caesar salads for them.

"Hello, ladies."

"Hi, Juan. How are you today?" Lena asked.

"Couldn't be better. How was the beach?"

"Wonderful," they said in unison.

"BJ, you look like you got a tan."

"I did. When I get out of the shower, my tan is going to look fierce!"

As Lena waited for BJ to get out of the shower, she relaxed and poured herself some water and put in a CD that accompanied the moment. She smiled as she passed the terrace window where the breeze billowed lightly through the sheer curtains. She had to admit she was feeling good being there with BJ, the wonderful island, and good people.

"So, Juan, have you lived on the island all your life?"

"No, I came here with my mother when I was a young boy."

"Where are you from?"

"Puerto Rico."

"Obviously, you love it here."

"I do. To me, it is truly home. Mr. Albert has always treated me good. I am blessed and thankful."

Lena smiled. "So, what do you do for fun?"

"My favorite thing is scuba diving. I teach a couple of days a week."

"You're an instructor?"

"Yes."

"I've always wanted to learn how to dive."

"You and BJ should come to the north side where I teach and I'll give you guy's lessons."

"Great. Are you working tomorrow?"

"Yes, between 3 and 5 o'clock."

"Sounds good. I'll talk to BJ about it."

"You should check out the submarine tour; it's really incredible."

"Oh maybe we'll do that today."

"A lot of tourists also rent mopeds to get around the island. They're fun to ride."

"I'm sure Brazil has tons of plans for us. Well it was nice talking to you, Juan. I need to get myself ready. Will you be here all day?"

"I'm not sure what BJ has planned for me."

BJ finished her shower, dried off, wrapped herself in

the towel and headed towards her room. Lena must be in her room because her door wasn't open enough for BJ to peek in. She shrugged her shoulder and went into her own room. As she began dressing, there was a knock on the door.

"BJ, it's Lena."

"Come in."

BJ moisturized her body with a peach body lotion. She stood with one leg on the bed in only a towel wrapped around her waist. Lena walked in, closed the door, and stared at BJ.

"I just came to see what your tan looked like without the bathing suit."

BJ confidently stood straight up, turned towards Lena, and untied the towel. Lena admired that BJ was definitely golden all over except for her V and the areas surrounding her breasts.

"Beautiful, isn't it?" BJ said in a sexy, cocky tone.

"Does it taste as good as it looks?"

"You'll have to see for yourself."

Lena walked towards BJ, stood very close, and looked into her eyes. With her middle finger, she slid it from the part between BJ's outlet and her clit, straight up into her own mouth.

"Mmmmm!" She purred as she turned and walked out the door.

BJ trembled with fever wanting desperately to continue what Lena started. After regaining her composure, she threw on a pair of ripped shorts, a light blue and white cut off sleeveless top, and a matching pair of Nikes. She blotted sensitive spots with Synful oil and beat her face (applied makeup) as the final sign that BJ was ready for the day.

Walk Like A Man
Laurinda D. Brown

The first time I lied naked with a woman, I was nervous but anxious to get it on. I had no idea what we were supposed to do. All I knew was that my vagina was throbbing fiercely and she, in her nude state, looked so good to me. But hell, she had the same thing I had and I felt, since she was older, she would give me some direction. As I sat waiting for her to make her move, she was lying there waiting for me to make mine. So I kissed her. It was a passionate kiss, full of tongue and juice; there was no way that this could be what gay sex was all about. She kept whispering for me to stick my dick in her. *What dick?*

In my youthful innocence and desperately not wanting her to stop kissing me, I slowly slid my fingers between her legs and into her. She started moaning. *Oh that dick.* I quickly found out that I could imitate a man's thrust with just my fingers. She wiggled on my index and forefingers like a big worm and I, amazed with this newfound pleasure, because it did feel quite nice, moved my lips from hers and redirected my passion to her breasts. Caressing them with my lips, I did to her what I knew had felt good to me whenever a man had sucked my nipples. She moaned some more and before I knew it, she had an orgasm. *What about me?*

As she lied there stretched out on her mother's bed, I watched her chest rise and fall while in her sudden slumber. Her nipples were still erect. She seemed comfortable. I, believing I had done my part, rolled over into a fetal position and covered myself with a blanket. *What about me?* Maybe an hour or so later, after I was no longer aroused, I felt a kiss on my neck. It was soft and gentle, wet and tender. The kisses continued down my spine, along my thighs, and ended at the tip of my toes.

Rolling me over, she moved her lips up the front of my calves and spread open my legs. Her kisses, now longer and more succulent, generated this vibration in my lower abdomen that I'd never felt before. My eyes fixated on her slender body as it slithered toward me; my body watered as she drew near. Anticipating her lips touching my private button, I jerked away and told her that I wanted to stop. I couldn't envision getting any pleasure for someone pulling and tugging on that thing between my legs. Sitting in a huge wet spot created by my own moisture, I knew I wasn't ready for that kind of sex. I wasn't seeking my own gratification that night. I was merely satisfied with knowing I could get a woman off just like a man could but with no dick.

After that experience, I went back to dating men feeling that there was no substitute for a stiff hard one. As long as there was no woman with a big booty and voluptuous breasts in front of me, I was fine. But then, on a hot summer's day at the church picnic, there was Estelle.

At 22, I had dumped my boyfriend because I felt no emotional bond to him. Don't get me wrong, he was a sweetheart, but he wasn't meant for me. He loved it when I wore those tight skirts to work with my high heels and silk panty hose. Every Friday when I got my hair done, he would sit in his car and read a book while he waited for me. On his paydays, he would go to Macy*s and ask the beauty consultant for advice on new fragrances and after hours of testing new scents until he'd chosen one, he'd get me the largest bottle. No matter how many times we had sex I found myself imagining a woman touching me and kissing me instead of him. I was turned off by the scent of his cologne, for I found myself actually wanting to smell, well, ME! After two years of faking it, I'd had enough. Now back to Estelle.

The picnic was fun as usual with lots of barbecue and watermelon. I wore a baseball cap, some denim shorts, a white wife-beater, and a pair of Timberlands, since I thought I might be running around in the dirt with the kids. I had on makeup and earrings but if you asked me, I did look a little tomboyish. In the 90-degree heat though, it was all about comfort and I wasn't even going to wear my nice tennis shoes out there in all that dirt. Besides, none of my coworkers were going to be there, so I just chilled.

Estelle was the daughter of one of the associate ministers and she was a firecracker. BAM! BAM! BAM! She had ass in all the right places, and titties that made her V-neck tank top scoop into a C. I'd seen her before but not like this. When I went over to the grill to get some ribs from her, Estelle, eight years my senior, flashed that gorgeous smile.

"Hey, Pumpkin. How many bones you want?" She asked.

Something that simple made me giddy. I started laughing and told her I'd take four of them with a hamburger.

"Hungry, are we?"

As I stood there holding my plate and having no regard for the flies, I tried to keep from drooling.

"Yes, I'm starving. Been waiting all day to get over here."

Now why did I feel like a man trying to pick up this woman? Why did I feel like I'd just said the dumbest thing I'd ever thought of in my life?

Estelle, watching me as closely as I'd been watching her, grinned and said, "Well, come see me a little later and I'll have something else for you."

Hmphf! You better believe my ass was right back over there after everyone else had left. Throughout the afternoon, I'd found every reason in the world to go back over to the grill. Estelle, putting her mark on me by rubbing up against me or by winking at me every time she caught me staring, seemed to feel my passion.

While she put the last of the food in the back of the car, I walked over and asked, "Now what is it that you have for me?"

I leaned against the hood and folded my arms. I saw her smiling as she closed the back passenger door.

"You know, you would come over here after I packed all the food in the trunk. All the meat's down at the bottom. Just like a man coming over here after all the work's been done." She chuckled. She came and joined me against the car.

"That's not a fair comment. I was picking up the trash to help you out so you wouldn't have to be here for a long time."

"I'm just kidding, Levia."

Estelle, who knew me from when she used to be my Vacation Bible School teacher, moved closer to me where our arms were now touching.

"I know you were helping and I appreciate that. Since it's getting dark, why don't you come over to the house and help me unload this stuff? That is, unless you have plans?"

I didn't want her to think that I didn't have a life, nor did I want to lose this golden opportunity.

"Sure, I'll come over to help you."

Now, at this point, you, the reader, are probably anticipating this hot, steamy love scene with Estelle and me. Well, you're right! There was a hot, steamy love scene, but I'm not going to share it with you. I will say that our lovemaking was one of the most intense events of my life but during the whole thing, I found myself wanting to be a man with this huge dick planted inside her nature. I was on top of her, like my boyfriend had been on top of me, working it and stroking it like a champ. And when I came, the muscles in my back tensed up as I released myself in her. That whole night I felt this powerful aura about myself that I'd never felt before. Resting between Estelle's legs, embracing her torso, I tickled her breasts with my tongue. She begged for me to enter her again, and I did but now with two fingers, try three.

The butt of dawn caught me racing through the streets trying to make it home to get ready for work. And then it hit me. I had spent an entire night with a woman consumed with the idea of me being a man; the idea of me having a dick; the idea of me fucking her with something that God didn't give me. The irony of the whole thing is that I felt like I had one; I felt that shit like that was real!

I went into the house and took a quick bubble bath and afterwards, I sprayed myself with some perfume. I put on my tightest skirt and my highest heels and strutted myself back out to the car with my face beat. On the way to work, I thought about my new sexual freedom and quietly laughed to myself. I checked my lipstick and got my purse from the backseat. On the outside I walked on the tips of my toes bouncing my hair side to side. I looked every bit of a lady, but on the inside, I walked like a man.

Don't Ask, Don't Tell
Claudia Moss

Rita pulled on her thigh-high, black boots with the pointy toes and pencil heels then stepped back from the wide bathroom mirror to assess her appearance. She turned sideways and struck a pose; there was no cause for the mirror to testify, she knew she was phyne. She let her gaze photograph her sugar-baby reflection. Succulent tits stood at shotgun attention. Rounded belly sat above the curly, black coochie hairs. Tapered thighs, firm, defined, and strong, were something to write the White House about. They could squeeze the hell outta anyone who thought they could control her shit, as if she wasn't running her own show. The only person who could run Rita Florentina Whitlow's show was the one woman Rita was dressing for right now.

Rita got hot watching her own body work moves she'd learned from her dancer girlfriends. *If she could bend herself with pretzel ease, she'd kiss her own self.* Rita laughed at her own private disclosure. For all the front of her did to wreak havoc in her mirror, her back was cinematography. She did a sexy two-step to music inside her head. Winding her middle in a circular motion, she turned slowly, neck craned to peep over one shoulder. What she saw made her reach back and palm herself with adoring, *I-can't-believe-this-is-all-mine* strokes. Basketballs. That's how Dodie, her last boyfriend had described them. Rita laughed and jiggled her awe-inspiring booty. It was chiseled like she lived on the Stairmaster. She bent forward, leaning against the bathroom wall. The word "Bitch" in glittering rhinestones glowed across the top of her black thongs.

No wonder Dodie acted a fool when Rita cut him off. She pulled Dodie's *fuck card* without an option for renewal the day she decided to go monogamous. Though Dodie was a cutie, he bored Rita…pitifully. Rita was a hard-loving sistah who required a harder-loving lover and the lady Rita cherished now was a dissertation in hard loving. Just thinking about her made Rita's butt bounce and wiggle from side to side.

Rita finished putting on her make-up, clipped a sparkling rhinestone belly chain about her waist, pulled on a trench coat, and high heeled it out the door. Not one for air conditioning, she pressed a button on the driver's door of her gold '96 XL Jaguar and breathed in the electric crispness of the spring wind. Usually, when she got hot and bothered and had a few minutes to spare, Rita would take matters into her own hands. Then again, when she was lowdown hot all up in the coochie, break-her-back hot, she found her way across town to a woman she'd loved for 5 years.

The wind was alive with whispers that year in 2001 but the only whisper Rita paid any attention to murmured, "Don't ask, don't tell." The only time she connected any real meaning to it was the first time she ever eye-wrestled a woman and lost. Rita was 20 years old and the baby girl of her family. She'd gone into the military to find herself, to stand on her own, and to not have to depend on her sisters. The product of a Puerto Rican mother and a Black Mississippi, blues-singing father, folks used to say that with such an attractive combination of genes, Rita ought to be in the movies or on magazine covers. Instead, she was standing at attention under an unapologetic sun taking commands, assembling weapons, and chipping her nails. Yet, like her Abuelita Ada was known to say, no man she knew ever asked for pretty; he always asked for pussy. Rita wasn't trying to get into the habit of supplying every man she met with pussy simply because he took her for a pretty, empty-headed good time. Thus, basic training tested her will, while her Drill

Sergeant tested her heart.

Before enlisting, Rita was a man's woman. From catching his eye to snatching his breath away, she could strut the strut to make a man's dick so hard that parts of him went beyond blue to purple. Then there was the raw finesse with which she'd put "that cat" on him that would guarantee he sign his name in blood anywhere she chose: across the bottom of his checks, on credit card purchases, or co-signed big-girl toys. *Cat* brought men down, no matter the breed: cheetah, jaguar, mountain lion, bob cat, or housecat. There was no question about it, Rita Whitlow did with men as she pleased. Never had she encountered a supposed pussycat with an edge, a woman in uniform (so what); a woman that made her feel like she was falling on the inside. Never, that is, until she crossed paths with the woman who made Rita's coochie cat speak her name in Swahili.

It was hot and muggy the August day she and fellow trainees stood panting, fatigued, and sweat stitched in the threads of their uniforms like insignia. On a huge parade field, they were flanked before a captivating Drill Sergeant. Rita couldn't believe the arrogance of the woman. The bitch thought she was God and gave orders to prove it; and today of all days her orders were directed specifically towards Rita. After hours of standing at attention under a baby blue South Carolina sky, Rita had reached her last straw.

"Fuck this shit." She whispered to the short, quiet girl on her left. "Either Uncle Sam ain't the one for me or I'm definitely not the one for this man's army. This woman is going home."

The short, quiet girl's eyes shifted slightly, though her body never dropped its perfectly executed precision.

"I'm tempted to walk right now," Rita continued. "Yet, it might be easier to walk after these stupid maneuvers. Maybe..."

Rita was sure about many things, except that *maybe*. Maybe the wind betrayed her and carried the whispered insubordination to the Drill Sergeant's ears. Maybe it was Cupid's meddling arrows. Maybe the bitch read lips, since the Drill Sergeant wasn't that far away.   Maybe Rita was receiving her wish to have the Drill Sergeant in her face, in a subtle, subconscious sense.   Whatever the maybes, Drill Sergeant Tyme Solomon appeared in her face and suddenly Rita felt a bolt of lightening rivet her to the sandy earth under her boots.

The woman commanded Rita's full attention.   So much so, the shorter woman could neither blink nor rip her eyes from the boiling caramel she saw in the Drill Sergeant's irises that threatened to leave Rita scorched and sticky.   Whatever else the Drill Sergeant wanted, it was clear she wanted to make an example of Rita.

"So Mama's little prissy missy wants to go home, huh? A fucking loser, I thought so."   The Drill Sergeant coughed her words like phlegm.   "Today is a beautiful day to watch your sorry, spineless ass trot across this parade field before these winners, these real-live, recruits-to-be, so they can see the difference between who they are and what they used to be."

The decorated heifer may as well have poked her finger against the tip of Rita's nose and called her out.   Rita opened her mouth to back the hussy up but Drill Sergeant Solomon's eyes held an invitation Rita was leery to open.   Her face took on a commanding tightness and every fiber of her being begged Rita to say whatever was on her mind but somehow...Rita couldn't.   Chalk it up to fear, family ridicule, and personal defeat. Whatever!   All at once, Rita wanted nothing more than to recall her words but once spoken, words could not be recalled.   The Drill Sergeant knew this and smelled Rita's retreat.

"What the fuck you wanna tell me, Miss Priss?"

She stepped close enough for Rita to smell her sweat mixed with a sweet, tangerine scent.   She stepped close enough for Rita to study her brutal fist of a mouth.   She stepped inside Rita's comfort zone and captured Rita with her visual clutch.   Rita knew the difference between a pussycat and a refined ally cat. As she stood there entrapped by the Drill Sergeant, something deep inside of her woke up and made her want to find the nearest wall to sit on so she could yowl for this cat's affection.

"Look at me while I'm talking to you, Trainee Whitlow." The Drill Sergeant's tone snapped, stinging with authority. "I refuse to permit you to waste anymore of my time...of *our* time. Besides, I wouldn't want you in my unit if I were under fire or at peace. A quitter is a quitter is a quitter, consistently."

Rita balled her mouth and stiffened her body. Every ear and eye within ten feet it seemed was focused on her. Tears trickled behind her crumbling anger but she willed them back to wherever they needed to be, until she could comfort herself later in the bathroom of her barracks. The Drill Sergeant's patience thinned lightening fast.

"If you want to quit, Peppermint Patty, walk around me and get the hell off my field right now. If you decide to stay, apologize so we can continue with our formations."

Rita inhaled tangerine, sweat, and power. She shut her eyes and exhaled, involuntarily, desire and resolve. She didn't know much. Not where it would happen nor when it would happen. The only thing she was certain of was two basic truths: one, arrogance had a price tag and two, Drill Sergeant Solomon would pay for hers at Rita's engineering.

She gritted her teeth not to pout. When she could pull herself together, she whispered, "I'm sorry, Drill Sergeant Solomon."

"Say it loud enough for the others to hear, since you interrupted our day, Trainee Whitlow."

Rita struggled to breathe under the Drill Sergeant's chin.

"I'm sorry, fellow trainees!" She bellowed. Her top lip quivered but she spoke loudly, lifted her bosom, returned the Drill Sergeant's level scrutiny, then asked, "Anything else, ma'am?"

"Ma'am?"

"I mean, Drill Sergeant Solomon."

The Drill Sergeant liked this new *back-against-the-wall* trainee. She could have spewed more venom than this little girl could conceive but with a self composure born of control before surrender, Drill Sergeant Solomon's, "Drop. Give me 75 push-ups, and see me later for an added duty," came softer than a caress.

"Yes, Drill Sergeant Solomon."

That year, if the wind taught Rita anything at all, it taught her not to ask why life happened as it happened and no matter what, don't tell whatever comes down from the Top Brass.

She wrote letters almost every week in boot camp. Some to family and a few to boyfriends who hung on right up to when she had to sever their umbilical cords to her heart because they couldn't understand why it wasn't pumping for them. Only one, Larry, read the writing between her words and responded with the line, "So, who's the lucky Drill Sergeant?"

To explain, Rita found the quietest carrel in a secret corner of the post's library and with sun pouring into the lofty windows and joy filling her soul, she began to write a letter of explanation. She wondered just how much she should tell her homeboy turned boy toy turned best friend. She wondered if he could take the truth. She wondered if she could write the truth. Then the more she wondered, the more her fingers itched to tell the truth, and her conclusion emanated from the drift of dust in the sunlight. *He'd asked, doggone it, so be brave enough to tell the truth.* If there were consequences, she'd deal with them later.

***

Without another thought, Rita wrote:

Dear Larry,

Waz up, boy? I miss you so much! This basic training is no joke and that is putting it mildly. Sometimes I wanna pack my bags and never look back. Everything is so official here. Things are done by The Book, under codes of ethics. But, as with any situation, you got your unofficial fun and that, my friend, makes up the good times that are the joint. Like when my crew and I go sneaking into the mess hall's kitchen to buy weed from the cooks, who are cooler than cool, or into the boys' barracks to take care of itches we don't want to scratch ourselves.

I could go on but time to me, has always been, as they say, "of the essence." So, I'm answering your question about my Drill Sergeant. L, I could be dismissed from boot camp for revealing what you'll read in this letter and my baby stands the chance of losing her career over our exposed relationship but human desire is a mothafucker! Don't know how it happened but truth is...I entered the military to come out! There...I wrote it!

Oh Larry, Drill Sergeant Tyme Solomon is dah shit! There is nothing sexier than to see her dressed out, participating in formation, or coming into the barracks to supervise; or to catch her in passing on post; or having her posted up in my face or in somebody else's, giving orders and taking names; or watching her communicating with higher brass.

Damnit, L, she's the epitome of butch sex appeal! I think of her and the seat of my fatigues goes wet. Believe me when I say it, I have never felt this way about anyone, especially a woman, before, ever, so you know it shocks me sometimes. But I love the dyke in her...and in me, for wanting her!

When I see her in that sexy-ass uniform with her flashy silver belt buckles, black boots shiny and clear as a mirror, medals and insignia parade perfect, hat angled to perfection and rolled on one side like she wrote the book on How to be Sexy in the Service, I want a lifetime of orders from her. Forget eight weeks!

Sometimes though, I long to tame the hardness in her but then again, L, the first time she fucked me, I learned her hardness was a part of the military's redesigning, same as I am being redesigned as her trainee. I learned she was gentle under the concrete and I am softer than a baby's smile when she looks at me. That's another story altogether, her stares. They sizzle and are hotter than Armageddon. Boyfriend, they have me battling myself not to break eye contact first. It's like we're locked in a visual embrace. I hope you understand.

Tyme, I mean, Drill Sergeant Solomon...see, the woman addles me and rattles me, even here, in private, on this page.

I'll call her DS. DS is the sort of woman who backs me up. Stops me in my boots, in my heels, and assists me down from my high horse. You know how high I ride them, baby (smile). And you also know I can make most brothas jump, no, run and leap through ringed fire, with a touch, a stare, a peek of skin. Not this woman! She escorts me to the white flag with her infamous, "I will do with you as I please, Miss Priss." And I say again, I love it...and her.

I know this letter is long but I can't write good-bye without writing this. The time she cussed me out for saying I wanted to quit boot camp was the first time she fucked me and assigned me an additional duty. Sounds sick, huh? It was a rush though. How did she do it? I thought you'd never ask. A week after she gave me an extra phone duty, she left a BDU (Battle Dress Uniform) under my pillow along with detailed instructions on how we were going to get by the guard on the post's gate. I thought she was the bitch from boot camp hell, L, but if you'd tried to stop the wheels rolling toward her fucking me, I'd have erased you as much as I love you, homeboy.

Anyway, to land this ship, we drove to her friend's house (it was really a mansion) and we had every square inch of it to ourselves. Boy, she treated me to loving that gave foreplay a whole new meaning. I will never see lips in the same light again. And I dare not mention the rest of her. No offense, but a brotha never took me to the places DS took me. She kissed a fantasy into my punany—her lips were creamy heat, as hard as she is! She kissed climaxes from my nape to my toes. The soles of my feet, the back of my thighs, and the sensitive skin from my armpits to my waist worshiped her.

Every inch of me bowed to her touch. Talk about juice, damn, Homes, my baby had me slick with every flick of her tongue across my clit. Ooooh! That first night was the first time I discovered I could cum...for a woman. I swear she was swimming in my cum. Now if that wasn't the stuff, her ass pulled on a strap, which I'd never imagined a woman would EVER use on this gyrl, and she rode me into a hellava surrender. My pussy did everything she asked and then some! From the front to the back and back again, every part of me ached when she finally let me go...even my ponytail! Hell, I'd volunteer to fight the next war or conflict single-handedly, if DS said she wanted me to.

If I keep writing, L, I'll be here all night. Gotta return to phone duty. Ooops, almost forgot one thing. Even though DS has the up's on a sistah most of the time, I'm still your gyrl, Larry, my darling.

Love U,
Rita

***

Rita parked in a circular drive, paces away from majestic granite steps. The sprawling three-story home with bay windows and a cozy wrap-around porch with garden arrangements that never failed to amaze her held its own in a neighborhood of old bohemia. Affable sunshine draped her shoulders and a playful breeze slipped under her trench coat when she wasn't looking. It tickled her thighs and seemed to caress her legs in good-natured kisses. She wiggled and grinned a giddy, girlish grin. One hand rising to open another button under the trench's lapels offered that mannish draft an easy exit.

She knocked sobering then persistent...then knocked again. As many times as she'd knocked on her former Drill Sergeant's decorative, oak door, excitement still worked her nerves like cymbals. Behind her, Master Sergeant Solomon's street witnessed the familiar drama with a tranquil understanding. Such stately houses had no interest in questions or answers beyond their neighbors' property lines. What they saw, they saw. What they didn't, they omitted. It was a gossip-free street Rita's Tyme had come to appreciate when she wasn't on post; and it was a street Rita appreciated for its ability to record without words. So when Master Sergeant Solomon opened the door, smiled, and raised her chin in greeting, gesturing Rita into a cool, darkened foyer, Rita tipped inside, and the street politely turned its back.

"Hey, baby girl." Tyme crooned pulling Rita into a familiar tangerine fragrant embrace.

Rita didn't bother responding. All she ever wanted to do was hold and be held by this woman, *her woman*. She took her in slowly, one sigh at a time. Dizzy. That's what she wanted to be. Dizzy and so high on Tyme Solomon, they'd have to spend the rest of eternity bringing one another back to reality. It was a good thing the heavy door braced Rita's back. Tyme left a breath's space between them. They remained like that, Tyme standing close, charging her love battery, the current flowing through them tsunami strong. Rita could have easily climaxed but Tyme always knew when Rita's love battery was a hair fracture away from overcharging. Head and shoulders above Rita, Tyme parted her lips and Rita concentrated on what her lover was whispering into her sleek, black curls. Try as she might, Rita couldn't starve the fire that mannish puff of air had sparked under her trench coat.

"Como estas, Private Whitlow?"

Didn't matter to Rita she hadn't been a Private First Class for going on a year. She'd gotten out of the Army to discover her passion organizing and managing four AIDS shelters across the city. Actually, when this woman addressed her as Private Whitlow, Rita did what she always did…she melted, soft, velvety, and buttery. It oozed down her black thongs to her shiny, thigh-high black stiletto boots, leaving her saturated with desire. The rhinestones in the "Bitch" across her ass glittered like a marquee when Tyme removed Rita's trench coat.

Tyme knew her power even after their five years of being together. "You came for private duty?" It was their running joke; their breezeway into active duty. Rita locked her knees to remain upright.

"Private First Class, Rita Florentina Whitlow reporting for any duty you so desire, Master Sergeant Solomon." Rita saluted sharp and sexy.

Tyme leaned over her and gently took her bottom lip between her teeth. "Good. I was beginning to wonder and we both know my thoughts on tardiness."

Rita felt the Master Sergeant's longing in what she didn't say. Tyme was a woman of action and spoke only for emphasis. Undoubtedly, Rita understood her silent craving in the effortlessness with which she unbuttoned her trench coat and in the exact moment Tyme's piped-in music vibrated the red-hot air in the cool living room. Tyme commanded her, ordered her. Simply. Softly. To dance. Rita obliged.

The room was her stage as Rita swayed to music. There was little she loved more than pleasing Tyme with a carte blanche performance of her...back door. Sweat and sugar-baby sweetness drenched her, as she danced, tapping and high-stepping, wiggling and booty-shaking through yet another sensual routine. Squatting, flexing, splitting—she held Tyme in the palm of her manicured hand.

Then, about an hour later, thongs in a corner, she walked her bare bottom over to Tyme, sitting in boxers, legs wide. She smeared herself up and down her woman's strong, wide thighs. Tyme accepted Rita everywhere...on her lap, in her arms, around her waist, across her shoulders. She bent Rita over and kissed her from top to bottom and across every bit of the luscious ass she adored. She made her skin boil and simmer. She stroked Rita's muscled thighs, seasoned and marinated her nipples, fingertips, and clit with her hot tongue machinations. When Rita lay prone on the sofa, Tyme got up and slipped on her piece. Tyme fucked her with deep then rough strokes, then soft and playful forays into Rita's tender places, from different positions that seemed to outnumber *The Kama Sutra*. Rita moaned then screamed loud enough to wake the city not to mention the neighborhood. A Master Chef as well as a Master Sergeant, Tyme had her way, lovingly, commandingly, freakishly, with a woman who would always be the trainee she loved at first sight, a woman for whom she would forever be willing to loose it all for.

"How are you, *mi querida*?" Tyme lay under Rita on the cool hardwood floor after the sofa complained of their sweat in soft, squishing sounds.

"*Bien.*" She loved it when Tyme slipped into Spanglish. Tyme tasted Rita's lips. "*Cansada?*"

"Yeah." *Damn straight she was tired.* Tyme wore her out first, satisfying her. Perhaps, Rita thought, that was the military in her, too, though Tyme swore it was only a butch woman being a butch woman. Rita kissed Tyme's smooth lips and tasted herself on Tyme's tongue.

"*Te quiero,*" Tyme whispered. "*Con todo mi corazon.*"

"With all your heart?"

"Do I have to tell?" Tyme asked with a smile.

"Si! How else would I know?"

"Aaaaah," Tyme murmured. "In the way I hold you. In the way I console you. In the way you get me to consent to things I wouldn't usually entertain. *Si, mami,* in the way you drive me insane."

Rita rolled off Tyme and cuddled into her side and softly praised, "*Como Hermosa, Madam Poetry!*"

"Thank you. Gracias."

Tyme sat up to study Rita. She had to see her, everytime. The curvy hips and thighs in the boots she adored. The sexy touches Rita hooked up did it for her. Like this rhinestone belly chain. She let her fingertips dance over the sparkling adornment and graze Rita's skin before they dipped between her legs. She adored the woman, every inch of her.

They both knew what was coming next when Tyme filled herself with Rita's essence. In spite of Tyme swearing she wouldn't ask again. Contrary to what she didn't tell. Hell, Pablo Neruda verbalized her thoughts poetically: *Those who mattered wouldn't mind, those who did, didn't matter.* Thus, she asked anyway.

"You like this house, don't you?"

"Uh-huh."

"Aren't you tired of running between two residences?"

"Si."

"Then when are we going to make this house a home?"

It had become their chorus line, a trusted refrain, nothing

more until Rita lifted her voice and sang a "Don't wanna lose you" tune.

"If you promise to buy the tickets to Fiji and make sure everybody wears white...even Larry."

Tyme pulled Rita back on top of her. She held her in an octopus hug, her legs and arms controlling shit, cradling Rita close enough to breathe for her.

"I will," Tyme sighed. "I will."

Look At Me When You Come
Tasha C. Miller

HOT ROD – *Young, erotic, African-American, butch lesbian, 6'-0," muscular build, athletic, college graduate, loves the arts, cooking, and working with her hands. She writes poetry and paints. Enjoys going to Broadway shows, candlelight dinners, and walking on the beach. She speaks three languages and is well traveled. Aims to please and always does. You call, she comes, then you cum! Hot Rod is available for discreet encounters, companionship, or social events in and around New York City. Your desire is her specialty.*

ALEXIS

"Alexis, come out for a quick drink," my friend Woo says.

That's all I agreed to but a drink turns into dinner. We end up at *Victor's Café*, a popular Cuban restaurant in Midtown. I leave the table to go to the restroom to wash my hands before our food comes. I put my purse down on the sink and as I check my breath in the palm of my hand, I hear a banging noise and faint moans coming from the corner stall. I turn and look down on the floor to discover a pair of boots and one high-heeled leg. I assume the other is hanging in the air somewhere. The moans get louder and louder. A chuckle involuntarily escapes my lips and I quickly cover my mouth to prevent a repeat of that mishap. *That's hot.* I think to myself, assuming some girl and her boyfriend couldn't wait to get home.

I hear the latch click on the stall. I resist the urge to turn around and instead decide to sneak a peek through the reflection in the mirror while trying to reapply my lipstick without poking myself in the eye. A petite dark skinned woman who looks to be in her early 30's comes out of the stall first. In any other instance, she would be reasonably attractive if not for her disheveled clothes and sweaty, sex funky hairdo. She stumbles before regaining her balance and straightens her dress. She does a quick check of her make-up and tames the wildness of her hair.

"Hi," I say to break up the awkward moment.

"Hello, darling." She says with a thick Jamaican accent. She smiles at me and hurries out of the restroom. I hear the latch on the stall and again I avoid looking in that direction. I rummage through my bag and try to appear uninterested.

"Hi, how are you?"

Shocked to hear a woman's voice, I look up at the reflection in the mirror. I stutter. "Gggood...and you?"

I turn in her direction and automatically begin to explore her entire body, which is covered with hot chocolate skin, a shade darker than mine with eyes like onyx that are shamelessly undressing me too. She is tall and lean with long brown locs that hang nearly to her waist. She is wearing a black leather jacket, baggy jeans, and black boots. My assessment of her is interrupted by my mind's desire to fantasize about her fucking me in that stall.

"I'm well."

She breaks my trance, matching my gaze as she catches me sizing her up. She measures my every curve under my pink cashmere sweater and black slacks. I take the pin from my head and let my hair fall down pass my shoulders. I hear a slight growl from her throat.

"Enjoy the rest of your evening, beautiful." She winks at me and dries her hands.

"You too." I lick my lips and watch her leave visualizing

her naked body under all of those baggy clothes. The light scent of body oil she left in her absence mesmerizes me. I go back to the table where I rejoin my best friend, Woo.

"The food came a few minutes ago. You ok?" She asks taking a mouthful of paella.

"See those two women over at that table?" I tilt my head to the left. "They were in the bathroom fucking."

"For real?" She asks. "Daddy is hot, I'd do her." Woo sighs staring at the woman, probably wondering into the same fantasy I just pulled myself out of.

Woo has been a lesbian since high school. She is a beautiful woman of African and Indian descent, all breasts and ass. Any lesbian would love to get lost in Woo. I, on the other hand, am not comfortable talking about my attraction to females. But lately, all I think about is having sex with women morning, noon, and night.

"Hello! What's up with you? Are you going to eat or watch them all night?" Woo asks raising an eyebrow and pointing toward my plate.

"I'm just curious. She's so sexy."

Woo gives me an evil glare. "You need to come out of the fucking closet that's what you need to do. Aren't you tired of being miserable?"

I roll my eyes at her, take a bite of my empanada, and drink a sip of wine.

"Nothing to say? Thought not," Woo says sarcastically.

I'm married, unhappily to my high school sweetheart. He's an entertainment mogul, record companies, clothing lines, night clubs, car detail shops, you name it. If it makes money, he probably does it. He's a man more concerned with his business and financial status than his relationship with his wife. My role is to play the young, beautiful trophy that agrees with just about anything. He showers me with gifts and money, which he believes keeps my bitching about his extramarital affairs to a minimum. Truth is, I stopped caring a long time ago. He's gone for weeks, sometimes months at a time. I am alone and lonely most nights and it's the same when he's home; but I realize now it doesn't have to be this way.

Woo and I, best friends since high school, had lost touch after I married and moved to Los Angeles. Since I've moved back to the city six months ago it's like we were never apart. Regardless of all my money and possessions, I envy Woo. After high school, I became a wife while she went to college and got her MBA. Now she's a successful investment banker living a lavish existence in her own right. Tonight, she had to practically drag me kicking and screaming just to go out to dinner and a movie. I'm glad she did.

I manage to pull my eyes away from Daddy even though I long to get her attention. What I would do with it if I had it, I haven't figured out yet. The only thing I know is that I want her. I notice from the corner of my eye that she and her date are leaving. I'm trying to conjure up the nerve to run out into the street after her when I notice a flashing light on the table where she sat.

"Where are you going?" Woo asks annoyed.

I dart across the dining room. It's her cell phone. I grab it, scoot back to our table, and drop it into my purse.

"What are you going to do with that phone?" Woo asks, obviously pissed now.

"Tell her to come and get it."

"Are we still talking about the phone?"

I laugh without answering.

"Give it to me." She demands holding out her hand. "Come on. I'll make sure she gets it," Woo says.

"I'm sure you would but I'll make sure *she gets it*." I laugh clutching my purse tightly. "Besides, I thought you had a woman, for whom I've yet to meet."

"I thought you had a husband. You don't know what you're doing." Woo releases a hard breath and surrenders.

When I arrive home I go through the cell phone, it's full of women's names, in every area code imaginable, even overseas. I call my cell phone so I can have her number for myself. Taylor

Dubois pops up on my caller idea.

"Taylor? That's sexy." I smile.

Her phone vibrates in my hand, startling me, and before I realize what I'm doing, I answer it.

"Hello?"

"Hey Taylor, it's Madame. I got a hot one for you tonight."

I interrupt, "Actually this isn't Taylor but I will have her call you as soon as possible." I hang up. My heart is thumping hard in my chest. Still not sure exactly what I'm doing, I decide to call the number from my cell phone.

"Love Unlimited Escorts. How can we service you?"

"I'm calling about Taylor." I say terrified of what I might be getting myself into.

"Taylor? You mean Hot Rod? When and for how long would you desire her services?"

"I'm sorry, let me call you back." I hang up.

I look up Love Unlimited Escorts on the Internet and there she is, *Hot Rod*.

"Damn." I rub the back of my neck as I stare at a picture of her in a pair of boxer briefs sporting a huge bulge and I can't help wondering what it feels like.

Taylor's cell phone vibrates on the desk and snaps me out of my daydream. "Hello?"

"Hi, this is Taylor, you have my phone."

"Yeah, I found it at the restaurant."

"Thank you. Is it too late for me to pick it up tonight?"

"No. My address is 740 Park Avenue, the penthouse." I say feeling bold.

"See you soon."

I take a long, hot shower, but I don't want to appear too obvious so I put on a white tank and a pair of red boy shorts, when what I really want to do is answer the door in the nude.

"Hi." I smile when I open the door. "You remember me?"

"Of course I do. You answer your own door?"

"I gave the staff the weekend off. Come in." I grab

Taylor by her arm, giving it a little squeeze as I lead her into the living room.

"I'm Alexis, by the way."

"Taylor, it's nice to know you, Alexis." She sits on the couch and looks around. "This is, uhm…very palatial," she complements.

"Thank you. Can I offer you something…anything?"

"I'm good actually."

"I bet you are," escapes my lips. Taylor pretends she doesn't hear me.

She and I make small talk. I drop hints that I'm attracted to her but she's not taking the bait. I don't know how to make it any clearer that I want her short of stripping butt ass naked.

Maybe Taylor and Hot Rod are two distinct personalities. I think to myself. *I'll fuck either one of them, it doesn't matter to me!*

"So, if I can get my phone now; I'll be on my way." Taylor says standing up.

Wet and disappointed, I go into the kitchen to retrieve her cell. I walk slow and seductively and make sure she is watching me. *She is.*

"Here you go." I turn around and bump into her chest as I discover she's right behind me. I slip the phone into her jacket pocket then I look down at her hands. "Your hands are huge." I say as I place mine inside of her palms.

"I usually have a response for that comment but I'm not touching that one," she smirks.

"Touch it." I grab Taylor's wrist and place her hands on my chest. She cups my breasts and fondles my nipples immediately harden through the thin cotton tank. She slides her hands under my top and pulls it over my head. I look into her eyes. She has to know how much I want her. She takes my face in her hands. Her breath glides across my lips before she gently takes my mouth into hers. Never have I kissed lips so soft. I hold my breath and my body goes limp against hers. Taylor picks me up and sits me on the kitchen counter and I wrap my legs around her waist. I pull her locs tightly when she grinds hard into me and I realize she's strapped.

"Stay with me."

"I can't." Taylor says breaking our embrace.

"Why?"

"I don't fuck married women." Taylor wipes her mouth. "I have to go, thank you for returning my phone, I really appreciate it." She feels her cell phone vibrate in her pocket and she answers it as she leaves.

My cell phone rings. It's Woo. I don't feel like talking but I answer anyway.

"What's up?" She asks.

"She just left. Nothing happened if that's why you're calling."

"Alexis, she's out of your league. You're not ready…"

I hang up on her and press redial.

"Love Unlimited Escorts. How may…"

"I want Hot Rod, right now. I don't care how much it costs. Right now!"

An hour later, Taylor rings my doorbell.

"I thought you didn't fuck married women." I tease.

"I don't fuck married women for free."

***

"I love your lips." I whisper to Taylor in between kisses.

We are standing at the foot of the massive canopy bed that I usually share with my husband in our plush master suite. Taylor slides her hands underneath my nightgown, up my body, down my back, and rests them on my hips. She digs her hands into my panties as she tongues the side of my neck. Taylor kisses me again, softer and more passionate than before.

"Are you sure this is what you want?" She asks. "I don't want you to have any regrets."

"I want you…but I'm scared."

"I'll be gentle. I promise." Taylor reassures me as she lays me down on the bed.

She licks my breasts and swirls her tongue around each nipple. Taylor slides down to my stomach and teases my navel with her tongue. I grab her shoulders and pull her t-shirt over her head. I squirm as Taylor goes lower, kissing me between my thighs. I moan uncontrollably as my anticipation builds. "Please."

Taylor adheres to my pleas and licks my clit in one long stroke. Then she goes full force and puts her entire face in my pussy. My body yearns to cum and I push Taylor's head deeper into my pussy to drive home the point.

Taylor sucks my clit, gently squeezing it between her lips. Her face is soaking wet from all of my juices. Moans fill the silence of the huge bedroom and my body begins to shake in anticipation of a noise that will break all sound barriers! But before I can climax, Taylor pulls away from my pussy. She kisses me and lets me taste my own sweetness on her tongue.

She works her finger across my slit and into my pussy. One finger, then two, and I begin to rock back and forth, as I spread my legs wider for one more. The slick walls of my pussy start to tighten around Taylor's fingers. She takes my throbbing clit in her mouth and sucks hard while she simultaneously pumps her fingers in and out. I cry out in sheer ecstasy.

"Oooh, please be gentle baby." I beg as she lays me on my back. "Give it to me." I command as I open my legs wide.

But Taylor is in no rush. I impatiently reach down and begin stroking Taylor's dick, lubing it with my own juices. Taylor teases my clit with the head of her cock.

"Close your eyes," Taylor whispers. I shut my eyes and grab hold of Taylor's ass when she lays on top of me. She sucks my bottom lip into her mouth. Taylor slips the tip of her dick inside of my pussy and I can't help but to pull her hips into me begging for more.

I dig my nails into Taylor's back, pushing her deeper inside. She slides in and out with slow expertise. I lock my legs around Taylor's waist as I moan a soft, "Don't stop," in Taylor's ear. I call out her name repeatedly and each time she thrusts deeper inside of me. My body begins to tremble but Taylor continues as she rises up on both hands, pushing into me in long, circular strokes. I could feel her watching me as she continues to thrust within me.

Taylor whispers, "Look at me when you cum."

At the sound of her request, my body tenses up. A wave erupts inside of me, threatening to take over my every thought but I look into Taylor's eyes as the orgasm rips through me. I cry out in sheer ecstasy before finally relaxing and laying quietly in Daddy's arms. This is the night I fell in love.

***

For the last couple of months, I have paid for Taylor's time around the clock. Although our lovemaking is amazing, I know that our relationship transcends that. Taylor has freed me both spiritually as well as sexually! But sooner than I care to think about it, our honeymoon comes to an end when my husband returns from a business trip. The thought of not seeing Taylor drives me crazy. I know that I will be miserable until I can be with her again.

"What have you been up to?" Woo asks.

I look around the deserted East Village diner with little interest for the place or for the conversation. All I can think about is Taylor and when the next time we can see each other. I look at Woo and see the interest in her eyes and decide that at least spending time with her and sharing what I feel about Taylor might help me make it through this long and unpredictable separation. "You have to swear to me that you'll keep this to yourself."

"Of course, I will."

"I met someone." I hesitate for only a second and then release all of the thoughts and feelings that I have been holding inside for weeks. "And I'm in love."

Woo is speechless. Before either one of us can respond,

the slender blonde waitress refills our coffee, breaking my train of thought for a moment.

I pour sugar into my coffee then pick up from where I left off. "We've been together for a couple months. That's why you haven't seen me much."

Woo sits up on the edge of her seat, moving in closer to me. "Who is he?"

For a second I wonder just how much I should be telling Woo but I can't hold it inside any longer. I'm constantly on guard at home, afraid that I might slip up at any moment, yet all the while dying on the inside to scream her name. "Taylor. She's the woman from the restaurant that night," I blurt out.

Woo's mouth drops open. "So you fucked? She fucked you and now you're in love with her?" She raises her voice and leans back from the table.

I quickly put my index finger to Woo's lip. "Keep your voice down," I plead while surveying the restaurant to make sure no one is listening to our conversation. Then I smile at Woo and begin to share just how much we were fucking. "Are we fucking, you ask? Yes and let me count the ways we have *fucked*." I throw my head back in laughter, thrilled to be sharing these feelings, excited about the memory of Taylor's tongue, fingers, and body.

"Spare me the details," Woo responds dryly, not at all sharing my amusement.

"Why are you so upset? Is it because you wanted her for yourself?"

"Does she know how you feel?" Woo asks, ignoring my question.

"Not yet." I admit a little sullen by Woo's lack of enthusiasm.

"Do yourself a favor. Keep that shit to yourself." She advises then unceremoniously get ups from the table and walks out the restaurant.

Jealous. I think to myself. I continue to sip my cup of coffee, reliving my inner thoughts of Taylor alone; and filled with anticipation of our reunion even in light of the departure of my friendship with Woo. *Oh well, who cares?*

While my husband is in town, I portray the dutiful wife in public while trying desperately to maintain my patience. But that soon fades away when I spot another woman sitting in Taylor's lap at a restaurant bar. Desperately trying to prevent the flawless makeup from cracking on my face at the site of the two of them, I rush to the powder room and call Taylor on her cell phone. I'm not surprised when she doesn't answer. Whenever Taylor's on duty, she never leaves a client without the pleasure of her undivided attention. Her voicemail is the only consolation that I have. I wanted to sound reasonable and patient but conscious thought is thrown to the wind just like the words that roll off my tongue.

"You should be with me, you're mine!" I yell into the cell phone.

TAYLOR

I'm Hot Rod. I love what I do. I love fucking. Always have. I get paid a ridiculous amount of money to do shit I would do for free. Making ladies cum is not hard work, it's making them go away afterwards that wears me out. They always fall in love, or want to leave their husbands for me, or want to support me claiming *this cock is theirs*, or my favorite…*let me take you away from all of this*. Get the fuck outta here!

I will admit, I do have my favorites, but I'd never let them know. Some of my clients are so insatiably erotic that it even drives me mad. Like this little Jamaican honey that will do it anywhere at anytime. Luckily I've learned to keep my emotions out of the bedroom but every once in a while, I run across a loose cannon with a bottomless pit of money at their disposal that does not like to hear the word, no.

As I walk towards the Plaza Hotel after receiving the assignment to remain there on duty for the next week, I'm beginning to realize that I've run across yet another fatal attraction with money to burn.   When I enter the suite, Alexis is waiting, sprawled across the bed. I thought with her husband being in town for the next few days that I'd get a pardon from her for awhile.   But as I watch her with the satisfied grin of Cheshire cat on her face, I realize she's found another way to keep me from other women.

"Where's your husband, Alexis?" I asked dryly.

"Don't know. He dropped me off at home and went back out." She says with a careless sigh, then crawls to the end of the bed, and looks up at me. "I told you, I want you all to myself. Stay here, relax, and wait for me. I'll come every chance I get. You can have whatever you want and charge it to the room, baby. Now…" She gets up from the bed wearing only a bath towel. "Are you going to make me beg?"

Watching her move that sexy body towards me, how could I resist. "I like it when you pay but I love it when you beg." I laugh.

***

"I'm leaving him." She confesses as she snuggles in my arms.

"What!"

"I can't live a lie like this anymore. I don't love him." She looks up at me with those bedroom eyes. "I love you. I want to be with you."

"You're joking right?" I get up abruptly, pushing her across the bed.

Alexis gets up from the bed and tries to quickly regain her composure. I can tell from the look in her eyes that I've hurt her feelings. I know she's developed feelings for me that are way beyond sexual. I also know that although I didn't necessarily do anything to encourage it, I didn't do anything to halt or slow things down either. But this couldn't happen and now was the time to bring this fantasy to an end.

"Baby, think about it. Don't give me an answer right now. Just think about it," Alexis pleads.

***

It's been a week since I've ended my arrangement with Alexis but it seems the more I pull away from her, the harder she pushes back. I've booked myself with other clients as far in the future as I could, attempting to break Alexis's thirst for me. But it's not working, instead it's fueling her desire. Now she's sending me expensive gifts to the Love Unlimited offices to get my attention but I just send them right back. The last straw for me was when she sent me a fully customized truck. Now don't get me wrong, it was sweet. But I knew what came with that fringe benefit and I definitely didn't want the job anymore! I thought after returning the truck it would finally be over. But as I hear a familiar voice at my front door, I realize it's far from being over by just my subtle hints.

"What are you doing here?" Alexis yells when Woo answers the door.

"What do you want, Alexis?"

"I'm looking for Taylor. What are you doing here?" Alexis demands.

"T, baby. You have a visitor." Woo announces then closes the door in Alexis's face.

I open the door to find her waiting patiently for me. "How did you find out where I lived?"

"What the fuck is she doing here!" Alexis screams ignoring my question.

"Lower your voice, Alexis." I warn her before closing the door behind me. "Woo, is my woman, not that my personal life is any of your business."

"*You're woman*? I'm your fucking personal life!" Alexis says gritting her teeth. "Bring your ass out here Woo!" She continues her rage, while pushing past me to bang on the door.

"I don't believe we are having this conversation. We are not in a relationship, Alexis. You paid me to fuck you." I say pulling Alexis away from the door.

"Then fuck me!"

Woo opens the door.

"Sweetheart, go back inside." I ask her, motioning for her to close the door.

"No, baby, she called me, so I'm here. What Alexis, what you gon' do? I told you she was out of your league. I told you to leave her alone." Woo says as she takes a protective stance at the archway of our door.

"You just had to take her from me didn't you?" Alexis accuses.

"Taylor and I have been together for nearly a year. I let you borrow Hot Rod but Taylor is mine."

Alexis shakes her head trying to clear all of the words that Woo was revealing to her. She had trusted Woo, confided in her, and had made the ultimate sacrifice to be with this woman, and now it wasn't ending at all like she had dreamed. "I can make her happy. I can give her everything she wants. I left my husband for her!"

"Hey, that has nothing to do with me, Alexis."

"I left him for you. What about all we've shared? The love we've made?"

Woo laughs. "Do you have any idea how much Taylor loves to have her clit licked? Have you ever even seen it? You haven't experienced anything more than any of her other clients have."

Alexis exhales and diverts her eyes away from Woo unable to admit that she hadn't truly experienced very much of Taylor's body at all.

"That's what I thought. You haven't because it's mine. Don't be long, baby." Woo says, ending her conversation with a reassuring kiss on my lips and then a victorious retreat back to the apartment.

"You don't want to lose your job do you, Taylor?" Alexis threatens. "You want to be fired for refusing to give the company's top customer what she wants?"

"Would you like me to tell your husband where nearly a

quarter of a million dollars of his money has gone over the last few months? How about telling him all of the countless ways we fucked in every corner of his penthouse? How you paid me to fuck you and paid me not to fuck someone else when I wasn't *fucking you?*"

Alexis looks into my eyes trying to reclaim the vision of what she saw the first time we made love...the first time we fucked, but nothing's there but what she now realizes is contempt.

"I didn't think so. I have clients lined up. I have nothing to lose. But you, you have everything to lose. I understand you are used to getting what you want but you're getting me confused with my dick. I'm not for sale."

***

I didn't see or hear from Alexis anymore after that afternoon. Sometimes I think about her but not often. It only happens when I see that same look that she had in another client's eyes...that look of lust, even when I know the client thinks it's love.

Bringing Up Daddy
Aimee Pearl

YOUR HAND

"Let me see your hand," I said.

We were naked together in my narrow bed. We'd been having hot, sweaty, vanilla sex for hours. I was ready to get what I had decided you were here to give me. You rolled over towards me, tired but not sleepy, muscular but not menacing… not yet anyway. *Butch!* You moved on me like a dream.

"Let me see it."

You extended your arm. I took your hand in mine and drew your palm to my clavicle. A silent switch flipped on. Your eyes widened. Wordlessly, gently, you pressed in.

"I know what you're thinking," I breathed. "I want you to say it. Say what you're thinking. Tell me what you want me to call you."

No answer.

"Please. Please say it. Please, tell me what to call you."

No answer, just the feeling of your fingers on my throat, your eyes on my neck, and your tortured, ragged breathing.

"Please say it. Tell me. I need to hear you say it. Please. Say Daddy," I gasped.

Your grip tightened.

"Daddy," I sighed.

"Daddy," you instructed.

"Daddy," I pled. "Daddy? What am I, Daddy?"

"My little girl."

"What else?"

"You're a bitch." Your grip became tighter.

"Oh God, Daddy!" My left hand was gripping your hand that was gripping my neck. "What else?"

"You're a dirty little whore."

"I deserve to get punished, Daddy. I've been a bad girl."

"Yes, very bad. You're *filthy*."

"Will you spank me?"

You paused briefly then your hand drifted away from my throat. I turned onto my side to present my ass against you, to tease you. You weren't born with a cock and weren't packing one either but we both knew how hard you were. Desire lay between us like the cock we were simultaneously envisioning on you, thick and heavy, pressing out from you and into me. My ass coaxed it so.

You were ready to spank me now. The first smack landed clumsily, lopsided, and cautiously. When you saw that you hadn't hurt me or caused me to run from the room screaming, you let the full force flow. You attacked my ass like a live thing, each blow more powerful than the last. I think you may have even hurt your hand. Something was unleashed that night and neither of us were the same.

YOUR FEMINISM

We met at a party. The attraction was instant and undeniable. We exchanged numbers, email addresses, and instant messenger screen names. *Ah, the modern age of lesbian courting.* A few nights later, we were instant-messaging each other in that just-getting-acquainted way, and I was starting to learn just how green you were. You'd only been out for a couple of years and had only had a few relationships. You hadn't explored your sexuality that much, other than knowing you were a butch who liked to have sex. *Vanilla sex.* Normally, I wouldn't have wasted my time but something about you called to me. It hadn't just been your light skin and full lips that got my attention; this went beyond the physical. I sensed it *in* you. You wouldn't have caught my eye in the first place if it wasn't already there somewhere. It was buried deep inside of you and I knew it would be worth my while to bring it out.

You sent a message:

What kind of women do you usually go out with?

I gave you a laundry list:

I like butches.

Uh-huh?

I like women who are smart and well-read.

Mmm-hmmm?

Physically, I go for tall and strong. You know, a powerful build.

Yep.

And I'm really attracted to the Daddy type.

The screen was blank for a minute. When you started typing again, it was to change the subject entirely:

So, what kind of books do you like to read?

Bingo. I was on to you. In my mind, the wolves began to circle. I let the conversation drift where it would that night. I let you take the lead. A few nights later, we were talking on-line again, and I knew things would be different. We hadn't even gone on our first date yet, although we had already made plans to do so but I decided to take a risk. I decided to bring up Daddy. The hour was late. We were both sleepy but still in the throes of excitement over getting to know each other and had been instant-messaging for quite a few hours. You were telling me that you and your last girlfriend had not been compatible.

In what way?

Uh...sexually

How do you mean?

Well, uh, she felt that...as a feminist and as a woman of color, she couldn't do what I wanted

to try with her. I tried to let her know that...uh,
doing it that way wouldn't mean that I would expect
her to serve me outside the bedroom...that I'm a
feminist too and a woman of color, of course. But
it was complicated.

I hear that...being both of those things
myself.

You could sense that I wasn't conflicted, the way your
ex had been. I think you knew that this wasn't because I lacked
consciousness of the issues but because I *chose* not to be
conflicted.

These things we desire, they don't belong just
to white people.

You paused.

I bit the bullet and typed:

What do you fantasize about?

Your three-sentence answer came fast and left me wet.

We're in the men's room. My girl's face up
against the wall and I'm fucking her from behind.
The men watch from the urinals.

I moaned and squirmed in my seat. I silently wished you
were in the room with me. I'd be unzipping your pants and
pulling your cock out. Slowly, I began to touch myself

Hello?

Oh, sorry! Still here.

I was embarrassed. Our conversation, up to my question
about fantasies, had been about relationship histories, not about
getting each other off. I wondered. *Should I bring us back to a
casual level? Should I tell you about the stickiness in my panties?*
We had only met once in person and at that time, we had merely
shaken hands. Were we about to have cybersex before even
going on our first date? *That would be a first in itself, for me, the
more experienced of the two of us. And what about my plan to
bring up Daddy?*

And you?

You asked, interrupting my reverie.

Me?

It's an even exchange. The reins are in your hands now. I told you. Now you have to tell me. What do you fantasize about?

Well, hmmm. Let's see. I like bathrooms too...

YOUR COCK

I told you my fantasy:

I'm at a women's club. I've asked my date to pack hard. I meet her at the club and because it's dark, I can't tell right away if she did what I told her. We're standing by the bar and she takes my hand and discretely leads it to her crotch. I can feel the shape of a large, stiff dick stuffed tight in her jeans. My fingers trace its outline and we exchange looks of fire. For an hour we tease each other. We brave the dance floor even as the crowd crushes us against one another and dancing itself becomes an unbearable foreplay. I can feel the moisture gather between my legs. I want that cock inside me.

Finally, I take her hand and lead her to the bathroom. There is a single line but eventually it's our turn. We enter, leaving a line of full-bladdered dykes outside. No one seems to mind that we've gone in together but I know we need to be quick. It's a single stall room, my favorite kind. (I'm somewhat of a toilet connoisseur.) She ushers me in then slams the door behind me and locks it with one hand while shoving me across the sink with the other. Without saying a word, she pulls my mini-skirt up and pulls my g-string to the side, so that my pussy lips are exposed. She tugs her cock out of her jeans and shoves it into me roughly and without ceremony. She fucks three or four fast orgasms out of me, then pulls out just as unexpectedly and sits down on the toilet to piss. I straighten up and turn to watch her, smoothing my skirt down in the process.

"Did I tell you to put your skirt back down?" She asks.

"No. Sorry." I lift it back up.

"Come closer."

I take a step towards her. She reaches out and hooks three fingers into my still wet cunt, fucking me even harder than before, pumping into me, and making me cum again, as the last drops of her urine hit the bowl.

She knows I have a fetish for piss play. She wipes herself and stands up.

"Fix your skirt. Let's go," she commands.

We exit the stall.

The End

HOT!

Thank you. I'm glad you liked it. I have to confess something.

What?

It's a true story.

Even through the computer, I could hear you sigh. Later, much later in our relationship, you told me you were cumming when you read the fantasy. I told you that I knew you were. I was too.

YOUR EVENTUALITY

You call me up and say, "Little girl, I need my cock sucked. Come over here and give me some relief. Service me."

And I say, "Yes, Daddy, I'll be right over."

I come over and immediately I take you in my mouth. I lick and suck until your cum slides down my throat; as I stand and lick my lips you tell me how cute I am and pat my butt. You're tired from cumming, so you take a nap while I wash the dishes in your sink and take your laundry out of the dryer. I fold the clothes up nice and neat then wait.

When you wake, you're hard again. I'm sitting on the floor near your bed, playing with my toys. You sit up in bed. I don't look up. "Come here, little girl," you say. "Come and sit in Daddy's lap."

I put down my toys and start to crawl towards you. On

purpose, I move slowly, a little more slowly than you want me to. I know you'll get impatient with me this way and I'm right. When I get within arm's length, you reach out and grab me by the hair, dragging me head first across the carpet towards you fast and shoving me face down, mouth open, onto your cock.

"Too slow!" You growl.

I choke, gag, sputter, and tears spring to my eyes. I know you think I look pretty when I cry, so I look up into your face to show you. You ignore the tears.

"You like moving so slow, little girl?"

I know you're mad now but when you see the dishes and laundry later, you'll be pleased. I like you happy but I also like you mad…that's when it's my time. You grab me up by the waist and pull me to my feet commanding me to lift my skirt. I obey you and show you that I'm not wearing any panties. I straddle your lap and you hold me up so the tip of your dick grazes my pussy. When my legs are securely behind you, you slam me down onto your hardness (no hand to guide it in.) Luckily, it's at the right angle and slides inside deep.

"Oh, Daddy," I moan.

You look thoughtful and abruptly shove me off your lap.

"I'm letting you get off too easy, little girl," you say. "Go get me a bigger dick, this one isn't big enough for a disobedient slow, little girl like you. Get the one that's on the dresser over there and be quick this time!"

I scramble to do as you say. I bring you the dick, a light brown one that matches your skin. As you put it on, you tell me to pick out my favorite belt. It's time to teach me a lesson, you say. I grab your wide, black, leather strap, hand it to you eyes down, and bend over the bed, ass up like you like. I know what's coming next.

"Now, you've been too slow. I'm gonna have to teach you how to be quicker. Are you ready for your lesson, little girl?"

"Yes, Daddy."

Snap!

You begin to beat my bare ass with the belt. I scream at first but the more you beat me, the quieter I become. The sound of leather snapping through the air becomes musical, a rhythm between us. I breathe you in through the pain and as I quiet down, you become stronger, fierce, until there is nothing in the room but soft delicious torture. When I'm totally silent, you tell me it's time for me to take your bare hand.

"Count down from your age, little girl."

I begin.

"10."

Whap!

"9."

Whap!

"8."

Whap!

And so on, until I get to one. On one, you hit me full force and I know I won't be able to sit tonight. I'm dripping wet.

"You gonna be slow again, little girl?"

"No, Daddy!"

We both know I'm lying. I'll never learn my lesson. You stand me up, turn me around, and kiss and caress me all over.

Let Your Fingers Do The Walking
Stephani Maari Booker

"Why are you being so quiet?"

"Do you want the truth?"

"Yeah, I want the whole truth and nothing but the truth."

"Well, the *truth is*, I'm laying up here with one hand holding the phone and the other hand down my panties. I'm sooo horny right now. I hope you don't mind."

"Naw, that's all right. It's not like I haven't been thinking about you that way while we're supposed to be having a *heavy conversation*. It's been so long for me, you know."

"I understand. It's been a long time since I've even wanted to be with anybody like I want to be with you. I think about you so much and I try to tell myself, *Quit calling her so much. You're running up your phone bill and probably getting on her nerves!* Even though we haven't met, I feel like I miss you. Damn, I wish you were right here!"

"Girl, I feel the same way too. We just have to wait for my vacation time to come up. It's only a couple of weeks away."

"That just seems so far away though. My loneliness and my horniness need to be satisfied now!"

"Well, we've both been doing a good job of satisfying the loneliness since we've been talking on the phone almost every day. As for the horniness…well, you got your hands on your stuff and just before you called I was getting ready to go to bed and play with my toy."

"Your *toy*? Really? What does your toy look like?"

"It's seven inches long and an inch thick. It's black, hard, plastic, and curved at the end. It takes two "C" batteries…"

"Umph, I'm scared of that! I have a toy, too, you know. But it doesn't go inside like yours sounds like it does. It's a plug-in with a big knob on the end that I rub against my special spot."

"Well, I use my toy both outside and inside. Damn, the more we keep talking about it, the more I want to play with it."

"Hmmm…you think you could play with your toy with me on the phone?"

"You want me, too?"

"Yeah, I think I want to hear you get off. Could you do that for me? I hope that doesn't sound too freaky."

"Girl, you talking to the original *Super Freak*! Hold on."

***

"You hear that?"

"Yeah, I can hear it buzzing all over the phone. Tell me what you're doing with it."

"I'm holding the tip of it against my clit. Now I'm rubbing it around and around…and….mmmmm…uh, now I'm pressing it hhhard….against my clit ... mmmmm."

"Oooh, you're making me soooo wet. Keep on making noises like that, baby, do it for me."

"Mmmmm…ooooh …awwwww…oh yeah!"

"You know what I want you to do right now?"

"Oooooh…wwwhat?"

"I want you to take my tongue and lick your nipples…"

"Mmmmph!"

"Then go down from your breasts to your belly and stick my tongue in your belly button and go round and round."

"Aaah, aaah ... oooohh…"

"Then I'm gonna go lower and brush my lips against your pussy hair."

"Oh...oh...yeahhhh!"

"You cumming?"

"Uh...almost...there."

"You sound so good with that moaning. Keep going."

"Mmmmm, kkeep...mmmm...talking to me."

"All right. I'm gonna spread you open and lick your clit. How do you want me to lick it?"

"Awww... suck it...hard…ooh!"

"I'm gonna wrap my lips around it and suck it real hard..."

"THAT'S IT...OH!...OH!...grrrrr...OH!"

"Oh yes, damn you sound so good!"

"Ooh...oh...aaah...mmmm...whewww."

"How about another one?"

"Girl, I'm lying here with my legs wide open, just covered with sweat...oh yeah. I'm about to pass out now. What about you? Can't I hear *you cum*?"

"Honey, listening to you was good enough for me...for now. It's so late and we've been on the phone so long."

"Mmm...yeah...so when you gonna call me to give me mine, woman? You gonna make me wait all the way 'til next weekend?"

"Well, hell, we've talked to each other three times this week..."

"Um-hm?"

"And I'm scared of what my bill this month is gonna look like."

"Yeah, I know...mine too."

"So...well...hmmmm...what time you want me to call you tomorrow night, girl?"

"After eight, after I get home from work and eat. You gonna have your toy ready?"

"Ready and running at super freak speed!"

Once *Bitten*
Submerge

My name is Detective Nicole Miller. I am a prisoner…
a prisoner of my own wants, cravings, and desires. A prisoner
to my body and its carnal appetite for what some may call "the
forbidden." It wasn't always like this and I wasn't either. At one
time, I had been a hard-ass homicide detective with nerves of
steel and an iron-fisted control. I had to be that way with what
I'd seen. After seven years on the job, I had seen enough blood,
guts, and insanity to last me a lifetime until recently that is.

As I sat alone naked, except for the topaz pendant
hanging between my breasts, in front of the raging fire, I had
time to reflect. As I sat alone waiting for my lover to return, I
had time to remember the first time. The first time I encountered
my seductress, my mistress, my taker. It was the time I traded my
control in for abandonment, my dominance for submissiveness,
my life of order and structure for one of chaos and destruction.
If only I had acted differently. If only I had listened to my head
and not my heart.

I had been assigned to a high profile murder. The victim
was Esmeralda Clifton. She was the wife of a Wall Street tycoon.
No one liked her, not even her husband. Her body had been
found in her bedroom, naked and bound to the bed by leather
straps. There was little blood, just a few drops, splattered on her
thighs but no obvious cause of death. The toxicology had come
back clean. The medical examiner had been stumped. I was

assigned primary. We had a witness, the Clifton's landscaper, Danny Martin. He wasn't a witness to the murder but to the victim's last known activities. He saw a woman with Mrs. Clifton. "A *goddess,*" he proclaimed. He had watched them engage in sexual relations. "They had fucked in every possible way," he said. We asked if he had gotten off on it. His response, "Who wouldn't!"

With the description the landscaper gave us, it didn't take us long to find our witness. She was also a well known socialite living in uptown. We wasted no time going to her penthouse apartment to question her. I knocked on the door as my partner, Doug Watson, stood behind me. A giant of a man, in a black three-piece suit, answered. I flashed him my ID. He didn't even glance at it, just stared me straight in the face.

"We're here to see Ms. Grace."

His face was like a chiseled rock, gray even, but it could have been the reflection from the suit.

"I'm afraid that Mistress Grace is not available." He said in a cold deep baritone voice.

"I don't think you get it, Lerch, this is not a social visit. We need..."

"It's okay, Thomas, you can let them in."

The voice had come from around the corner in another room. It had floated through the open door like smoke, seeping into my pores and invading my head. Lerch stepped aside but stayed close enough to remind us of his presence. He was such an awesome and powerfully built man that I don't think we could have forgotten if we wanted to.

The suite was one immense room. It was 1500 square feet of black marble, white granite, and massive Greek pillars. There were little splashes of color here and there. From the blood red throw rug in front of the massive fireplace, emerald green velvet pillows on the black leather sofa, and a few paintings adorning the walls with vibrant splashes of ruby, sapphire, and gold colors. In the center of all the contrasting color, stood a beautiful woman in a long, fluid, black, silk robe.

When the landscaper had called her a goddess, he was not far off. She looked worthy of that title. She could have been a black Aphrodite or Venus. Her hair was the color of coal, falling down her back and around her shoulders. Her eyes, under sharp arched eyebrows, had the color of intensity. They were penetrating hazel that locked me in like a tractor beam. Her skin was pale and flawless. Not a wrinkle, crease, or blemish marred it. She had full, sensuous, crimson lips that pulled into a smile as we entered the room. She was a captivating sista. I was a self assured stud in my own right, yet her beauty and overt sexuality totally stunned me.

"Please sit, Detectives." She gestured toward the sofa.

I had to nudge my partner in the ribs to get him to move. As we sat, she settled onto the loveseat opposite us. She curled her legs up under her like a cat. As she moved, her robe fell open to expose a long elegant leg. I tried not to stare. To compensate for my unusual distraction, I dug out my notebook and looked at it.

"Do you know Esmeralda Clifton?"

"Yes."

"Did you know she was dead?" I asked watching for some sign of guilt. Usually people blinked too fast or their mouths twitched. Grace did nothing but stare at me with her mystifying hazel eyes. I had begun to feel a stirring in my belly.

"Yes. I heard it on the news."

I looked around but could see no sign of a TV or radio.

"Well how do you feel about that?"

"It is a terrible tragedy. I am deeply saddened, of course."

"I would think you would be, especially considering you were fucking her only hours before she was murdered."

A slight smile formed on her lips as she lazily rubbed her hand back and forth across her leg.

"Are you assuming that I'm going to deny that I was with her, Detective Miller? Do you assume that I am ashamed of the acts we performed?"

I said nothing. The things the landscaper had told us

were foreign to me. Leather, latex, whips, piercing. As a cop you see and hear pretty much everything but I was still shocked that these two women would engage in such things.

But you were intrigued, weren't you Nikki?

I glanced around me as the words filled my head. I looked over at Doug to see if he heard them as well. He was staring at me, waiting for me to continue the questions.

"Um… could you tell us what happened that night?"

"Esmeralda and I frequent many of the same charity events. That night it was for AIDS research. We had a few drinks together. She complained about her husband and her dull lifeless existence. Then we went to her home in her limo. This was about ten o'clock."

I checked my notes from the limo driver. No discrepancy.

"We had a few more drinks and Esmeralda told me how she's always found me attractive. One thing led to another and we ended up pleasuring each other for the next two hours. She had an extensive collection of toys."

"Is that what you call them…*toys*?"

Grace smiled overtly and trailed her finger over her lips. I watched her mouth as her tongue peeked out slightly to moisten them. My legs started to throb and a savage hunger gnawed at my gut.

Would you like to kiss me, Nikki?

I tore my gaze from her lips and looked around me again. The voice had seemed to come from behind me. I turned slightly to glance over my shoulder. Doug looked at me curiously. He touched my arm gently and turned his attention to our host.

"What time did you leave?" He asked.

I sat back and let him take over the interview while I regained my composure. Sweat popped out on my forehead and the back of my neck. Little beads had dripped down and drenched the waistband of my khakis.

"Around twelve thirty, I'm sure the driver can confirm that."

Doug continued his line of questions. "In what state did

you leave Ms. Clifton?"

"Are you asking me if I killed her Detective Watson?"

"No. I'm asking you in what state did you leave her?"

"A state of ecstasy, I'm sure."

"Did you tie her up?"

"Yes and I'm sure Mr. Martin already told you that. He secretively liked to watch us or so he thought and we occasionally enjoyed performing for him."

I watched as Grace calmly answered questions. She never took her eyes off me. My throat was dry. My eyes started to water. My nipples tingled as they rubbed against the restraint of my bra. I shifted in my seat to stop the sensation but every time I moved, my briefs would ride up my butt and nuzzle my ass. Grace smiled as she watched me squirm around. I started to feel dizzy. The room quivered around me in heat waves.

Come to me Nikki. Let me pleasure you.

I shook my head but the voice penetrated me regardless. I looked up at Grace. She was standing and smiling at me. She rolled her shoulders and her robe fell to the ground. I nearly swallowed my tongue. Her body was exquisite. Her breasts were high and round with suckable tips. Her waist was slender and her stomach was flat. She had beautiful rounded hips and her legs were long, ending in a perfect V where in between them she had just a sprinkle of curly, black hair. I thought it looked soft, sexy, and hot.

Come to me, Nikki.

I stood and walked to her. She grabbed the back of my neck and brought her mouth down to mine. I opened and let her tongue mate with mine. Her breath was hot and she tasted like licorice. As we kissed, I could feel myself moisten. I could feel myself become open and vulnerable. I felt myself do something that I've not done in years…surrender.

Take off your clothes and lay on the rug.

I did. I was in her power. I would have done anything she asked. I wanted so badly to taste her, to love her, to be one with her. I laid down and Grace laid beside me. I was quivering with anticipation. My breath came in quick short bursts. She gently laid her hand on my breasts and massaged them. My nipples hardened as she circled one after the other with her thumb. She bent over and took one in her mouth. I nearly erupted with pleasure. She bit down and pain exploded in my head. I jolted but she held me down. She bit down again but this time the pain teetered on pleasure and I almost climaxed.

Things started to happen quickly. Legs spread. Sucking on my clit. Fingers inside me. Orgasm. Biting. Anal penetration. My fingers inside her. Orgasm. The images spun around in my head. One blurred into the next. Then I remember lying between her legs. They were spread wide. Her pussy was wide open in front of me. She was pink and red inside. I thought what wonderful colors they were. I inched closer and spread her labia with my fingers. I ceased her clit. I pressed my tongue gently down on it. I could feel her jerk. I pressed harder and began little circles with the tip of my tongue. She moved with my rhythm. I sucked it into my mouth and rolled it around with my teeth. I could feel her climax as her legs quivered. Sweet juices poured out of her pussy. I lapped them up like a kitten laps its sweet cream. She tasted like ambrosia and I wanted more. I wanted all she could give me. I easily slipped three fingers into her and pumped them as fast as I could.

I looked up at her face as her pleasure washed over her. Her eyes were open and they were no longer hazel but ebony. Her mouth was open in a silent scream and I swear that I could see fangs protruding from behind her eyeteeth. They were dripping with saliva and it ran down her lips over her chin. I should have been mortified. I should have been repulsed and disgusted but instead I was in love. She never looked more radiant and stunning as she did at that moment. I rammed my fingers into her and sucked on her clit until she exploded pure pleasure once more.

Nicole, my love, it is you that I have been waiting for.

"Miller? Miller? Are you all right?"

I looked up at Doug's concerned face and wondered why I was on the floor. I felt wet and shaky. I thought at first that I had somehow fell into a puddle of water but realized that I was drenched in my own sweat. I grabbed onto Doug's offered hand. He raised me up to the sofa.

"What happened?" I asked as I wiped the beads of embarrassment off my face.

"Jesus, Miller! One minute you were sitting beside me squirming and muttering under your breath, then the next you slithered to the floor unconscious."

"How long was I out?" I looked up past Doug to Grace. She was standing behind him calm and poised with her hands clasped in front of her. Her eyes glinted and she grinned slightly.

"A couple of seconds."

"You gave us quite a scare Detective Miller. Would you like a glass of water?"

I took a few deep cleansing breaths and looked up at her again. Her eyes sparkled again but this time they turned black. It happened in a split second but I had seen it and I remembered.

"No. Let's go, Doug. I think we got what we needed."

I raised up from the sofa and turned towards the door.

"Are you sure, Detective Miller? Are you sure you got all of what you needed?"

I didn't turn back but stated, "Just keep yourself available."

"I usually do Detective."

I could feel her seductive kiss on my back as I walked out the door. Doug didn't say anything until we were in the car on our way back to the station. I took one of his cigarettes and lit it. I sucked in greedily and nearly choked.

"What the hell happened in there, Nikki?"

"I don't know. Something just overwhelmed me. Must have been the incense she was burning."

I rubbed my forehead. "Maybe the smell did something to my brain."

"Funny, I didn't smell anything," he said as he took the lit cigarette dangling from my trembling fingers. "Must have been a female thing."

I didn't look at him but out the side window into the

night. The street lamps were bright and hurt my eyes. "Yeah must have been."

Later that night, I was in bed with my on again off again lover, Terri. She was a paramedic and we met at a local fundraiser. We dated for the last year but it never turned that corner where it becomes exclusive and committed. Neither one of us had room for a serious relationship. Eventually, we would just phone each other when we felt the need for sex, or in my case, a false sense of comfort. When I got home from the station, I called her. I needed to see her. She showed up half an hour later. When she came through the door, I launched myself at her. She was surprised and pleased at my aggression. I attached my mouth to hers and starting pulling at her clothes.

Minutes later, we were naked and entangled on the bed. I ravished her mouth, her neck, as my hands raced everywhere over her sensual body. Her muscles were pulled taut under her skin and I wondered why I had never noticed how toned she was. How each of her muscles flowed into another. How the veins on her neck and legs stuck out when she was aroused. I licked her tits as I guided my strap into her. I felt enormous as I filled her up. With each thrust, I imagined that she could feel it in her throat. She dug her nails into my back as I passionately pumped in and out. I closed my eyes and let my pleasure take me. I let myself be washed away on waves of ecstasy. I felt her mouth on my tits. She sucked and pinched my nipples hard sending bursts of electricity through my body. I opened my eyes to see her face as I neared my climax. Instead of Terri's face, I was looking into the magnetic hazel eyes of Grace.

I jolted then screamed. She smiled seductively and continued to manipulate my tits. I looked down and it was Grace's mouth on my breasts. Her ample tits were mashed up against my rib cage. I shut my eyes again. I could hear Terri's moans of pleasure as I matched her thrust for thrust. I opened my eyes fearing the truth. Grace was still there, ravishing, sexy, and sucking on my breasts. I wrapped my hands in her hair and held on. I looked down to my crotch and saw that she was filled with my strap and I was fucking her. I let myself go. I surrendered to her and the immense pleasure/pain that she was inflicting on me. I groaned and thrashed about the bed. She spread her legs wider, trying to swallow me up. I found her hot, wet mouth, and fucked it with my tongue. She laughed as I savaged her face. I couldn't get enough. She enfolded me with her legs and squeezed, pushing my pelvis deeper into her with her heels as she now feverishly sucked on my neck. I rammed my strap into her as far as it would go as she gushed hot pleasure onto me. I screamed and cried as my own orgasm racked through my body.

You are mine now, Nicole.

"Oh yes, I am yours. Take me, Grace. Take me!" I moaned as I lifted my head up from her neck so I could see her intoxicating face. Terri stared wide-eyed at me.

"What the hell are you talking about? Who the hell is Grace?"

I turned my head from her glaring eyes and pushed myself off. I rolled over to the side and curled into a ball, hugging my knees.

"What the fuck is going on Nikki? That was the most amazing sex we ever had. Jesus, I thought you were going to kill me! And now you're moaning some other woman's name. Who the fuck is Grace?"

Silent tears streamed down my face and I wiped at them with the back of my hand. "I think you should go home, Terri."

"If I had known you were fucking somebody else, I wouldn't have come."

I turned over and got out of the bed. "Leave, Terri! Just get your shit and leave!"

Grabbing her jeans and shirt, she stormed out the bedroom door. I could hear her cursing all the way through the apartment and out the door. I grabbed my pillow stuffing it into my body and cried. I sobbed so hard my throat ached with strain. I cried because I knew I was lost. I was lost to the deep, intense ache rising in my belly even now. Lost to the woman named Grace. Eventually, I cried myself to sleep.

I arrived at the station the next morning, rumpled, and exhausted. I arrived to a noisy, bustling homicide department. Something had happened; I could tell from the look in the eyes of my colleagues. I searched out Doug and found him at his desk celebrating.

"What happened?"

"Congratulations Miller, we just solved another homicide!"

My throat went dry and I thought I was going to be sick. I reached out for balance and grabbed onto Doug's shoulder. He took it as a gesture of thanks and slapped me on the back.

"What do you mean?"

"The landscaper confessed."

The room started to spin and I found a chair to settle myself in.

"He walked into the station very early this morning like a zombie and wanted to make a confession. He's in holding now. We're just waiting for the paperwork so we can book him."

I couldn't believe what I was hearing. "Do we have any other evidence? Did we check out his place?"

"Oh yeah. We got pictures of the deceased in some compromising positions. Looks like Danny and the socialite liked to play with each other too. He had pictures of her tied up, bound, gagged, and chained, under his mattress. We also found what looks like some kind of weird toxic plant...called moonseed or something like that. I guess it paralyzes the victim then eventually you stop breathing. So we're running the toxicology again."

"What about the blood? Could he explain the blood?"

Doug looked down at me questioningly. "What's the matter Miller, mad that you didn't catch the killer?"

"No. I'm just making sure that we have no holes for the defense lawyer to squirm through."

Doug started to laugh. "Well, you'll love this, speaking of holes. He said he must have accidentally bitten her piercing out of her clit. Could you imagine, Miller, what that would feel like? I bet that hurt a lot."

I rubbed my forehead where an excruciating pain started to develop and sighed. "Well, it looks like you got everything taken care of Doug."

He sneered down at me. "Pissed off that I didn't call you?"

I rose from the chair and offered my hand. "Nope. Good work Doug. I'll let the Lieutenant know all the work you did on this case. Next time you can be the primary asshole."

I turned on my heel and headed for the exit.

"Hey Miller, are you all right? It's not that *female thing* again, is it?"

"Yeah Doug, it is. Don't worry, I'm going to get it taken care of."

Thomas, the giant, opened the door when I knocked. He stepped aside as I walked into the suite.

"Is she here?"

"No, but she left instructions that if you should show up that you could wait for her here."

"Great." I said as I collapsed onto the sofa. My head was pounding and my eyes were stinging. "Do you have any Tylenol or something?"

The giant went into the kitchen and poured something into a glass. He came over to me. He moved silently for such a large man. He handed me the glass.

"Try this. It is an old family recipe. It will also help you relax."

I looked suspiciously at the dark thick liquid in the glass. It smelled like pennies. I took a sip. It was tangy but surprisingly pleasant. I downed the rest of it in two gulps. Soon my head felt light. I laid back on the sofa. My eyes felt heavy so I closed them. A total sense of euphoria washed over me and I grinned.

Wake up, my darling. Wake up, my Nicole.

I opened my eyes. Grace was standing over me wearing only a g-string in red velvet. I reached up to her. She bent down and kissed me softly on my mouth. She gently stroked her hand over my skin. I looked down and noticed I was naked with only a topaz pendant hanging between my breasts. I wrapped my hand around it, feeling its warmth, its gift of life.

"Is this a dream?"

"No, my love, from now on everything will be more real than you could imagine."

"Will you bite me too?"

Grace covered me with her pale body and gazed into my eyes. I wrapped my arms around her and submerged myself into her hair, drinking in her engaging scent.

"I already have, my love."

Love
Phase 3

Is This Love?

Is this love that I feel
taking over inside of me?
Is this love that is running
wild like flood waters through me?
It has captured me;
captured every inch of me,
and won't let me...
won't let go.
It won't set me free not even for sleep.
See, she keeps coming back to me,
reminding me
that she is the one;
the one who was created to love me.
To fill me...
fill me up with a love most of the world will never know
because they were too scared to answer the door.
Too scared to believe in so much more...
so much more than
hours, minutes...
hell, seconds
of the best thing.
Too afraid to like it enough
to beg the feeling to stay.
They were too scared to believe it existed today.
So I ask the gods to send an answer to me.
Is this love filled up inside of me,
so exposed inside of me?
I can't hide or deny, it is a relevant part of me.
So the question still stands,
bugging the hell out of me,
is this real love?

From Friends to Lovers
Shonia L. Brown

"Tell me what you're thinking?" The voice came across my telephone like a bedroom whisper that seemed so close, I swear I could feel the warm breath rustle the little baby hairs across my forehead.

"About you," I replied softly.

Small, girlish giggles came from the other end of the phone and then a deep sigh. "What about me?"

"Your smile and the way it warms my heart. Your big, brown eyes and the way they make me feel giddy and at the same time aroused. Your skin and how soft it is when you gently brush your hand against my face."

"Erin, why do you always know just what to say? It's like you're reading from the pages of a novel but that voice of yours is more like my very own private movie made for two."

I could hear the faint sound of papers being shuffled around and a tiny grunt from Serita's lips as she got comfortable on the other end of the phone. I silently envisioned what she was wearing and instantly images of white lace or a silky satin bra and panty set caressing her soft, milk chocolate skin came to mind. My hands clenched together as they fought off the desire to feel the warm body that lay beneath the lingerie. As I listened to Serita continue to describe how my voice made her feel, I couldn't help wondering how we had gotten to this place of intimacy.

For two years, we had been distant friends. Although we

lived in the same city, only 20 minutes away from each other, it felt like we lived on the opposite ends of the earth. Serita is an airline stewardess for Delta and I am an art teacher at Kennedy Middle School. Our first encounter was at a party a mutual friend had given two summers ago. My girlfriend at the time had stood me up and I decided to go solo. Serita came with two friends that spent most of the night making everyone feel like we had invaded their private bedroom. Serita wasn't a shy woman and had no problem leaving the couple in blissful harmony to circulate throughout the room. I, on the other hand, had "shy" as my middle name. I spent most of the evening out on our friend's deck stargazing and occasionally looking at my watch hoping that the *polite two hour time frame to spend at a party you don't really want to be at*, was growing closer. Just as the last 60 minutes approached, so did Serita. It was a little breezy that night but the outfit she wore, made me feel as if it were 100 degrees instead of the 65 degrees that the weatherman had forecasted.

"*Now* what are you thinking about?"
Serita's voice invaded my private daydream and I was suddenly brought back into the reality of our late night conversation.

"What else...you."

She giggled again and then let her laughter drifted into a seductive sigh. "What now?"

"I was thinking of when we first met."

"At Shey's party?"

"But of course. Remember what you were wearing?"

She paused for a few seconds then fain ignorance in her response, "No, I don't think I do."

I knew she remembered which outfit it was as I remembered oh so well two years later. It was one that neither one of us would forget because I made sure of that. Every time I was bold enough within our friendship to remind her of that outfit, I would.

"You wore a black halter top that embraced your upper body and accented your broad shoulders like a possessive lover.

Your scrumptious bottom and curvy hips paraded around me in a tight black leather skirt with the split up the side, which complemented your delicious strut in a pair of thigh high boots. Remember now?"

She sighed again. "Yes...I remember now."

"I almost dropped my cocktail when I saw you walk onto the deck. You just smiled at my clumsiness and quickly caught my falling glass."

She giggled. "You looked like you needed a little help. I was happy to oblige."

"And so was I. The touch of your soft hand against mine did my body good, gurl! It was like suddenly a dark cave that had been absent of fire was illuminated with the warm rays of a never ending sun. I glowed."

There was silence on the other end of the phone for a few minutes and I wondered if I had said something wrong. But Serita quickly assured me with yet a deeper sigh that I was saying all of the right things.

"So what took you so long anyway? I've been waiting two whole years for you to give up that girlfriend of yours," she said teasingly.

"I thought I was in love with her and I wanted to remain faithful, even though from the first day I saw you, I couldn't get you out of my head."

"Is that why I hardly ever heard from you, because you couldn't get me out of your head?"

"Exactly."

"Bullshit!"

"Serita, watch your language gurl!" I teased hoping to lighten up what was heading towards a darker mood.

"I'm serious, Erin. Why did you avoid me for two years?"

"Because I wanted you...but I felt I had to be faithful to the woman that I was already with. I wouldn't be able to stand being around you so much and not being able to touch you."

"Yes, you would have."

"No, I wouldn't have."

"Yes, you would have. I'd made sure of it."

"You speak as if you would have had complete control over the situation," I retorted. I felt my ego getting a little bruised as Serita challenged me with her own aggressiveness. For a femme gurl, she was unstereotypically mannish.

"Trust me, Erin. I would have been in complete control. I've always been in control of when and where I would allow myself to be taken by any lover. My last lover waited for months before I allowed her to touch me. We slept in the same bed together many of nights, dressed in only our underwear, and I allowed nothing to happen."

"Now that's bullshit! No way would you sleep in my bed and not be consumed by my eyes, my hands, my lips..."

"Really?"

"Yes, really."

"And what would you do if I came over there right now and undressed to my bra and panties, and climbed in bed with you, and spooned my body to yours, but refused to allow you to *really* touch me?"

"Just imagine us lying in bed together, me in my Joe Boxers and t-shirt, and you in a pair of white thongs and matching bra. Our bodies are so close that I feel your heart beating against the palm of my hand. You exhale on a soft sigh and the smell of vanilla escapes into the air. Can you feel me?"

"Yes, I feel you."

I began telling Serita the fantasy that I had envisioned night after night for months now; and as I told the story, I began to feel as if she really were in bed next to me, cuddled up in my arms. I could feel her chocolate body scantily clad in a thin pair of silk thongs and matching bra. I felt her meticulously styled, short permed hair against my face. I saw her manicured nails wrap around my wrists and hold me tightly as she forced her body to quiet itself. I could feel my pulse quicken as my hands removed themselves from her grip. My left hand climbed slowly up her arm, leaving chill bumps along the way. She moved slightly against my lower half as if preparing herself for a good night's sleep but sleep was not on my agenda. I stroked her shoulder softly then allowed my fingers to travel down her neck to rest on her chest. The tips of my fingers danced playfully along the edge of her bra and waited for signs of resistance but found none. My fingers dipped quickly inside her bra as if they were testing bath water to see if it was too hot but the heat that I discovered in between the satin and her soft skin was comfort to my hands.

"Tell me stop," I challenged softly, whispering my command in her ear.

She moved her body slightly, just enough to allow my hand full entry into her bra and access to her steadily rising nipple. The dark little berry bloomed under my fingers' guidance and I stroked it until I heard Serita utter a moan that definitely sounded like an approval not a reprimand; but I persisted with my challenge.

"Tell me stop, Serita."

She stifled another moan as I increased the pressure against her nipple. I could feel the warm flesh of her body press against my pelvis and I longed to feel her skin against my hairy, moist pussy lips, but I wanted her to beg me for it. I removed my hand from her bra and I heard her utter a noise that sounded like a mixture of a cry and a moan. I wet my lips as the anticipation of claiming this woman for mine heightened my desire and made my heart beat in time with her rhythmic movements against my body. My hand trailed from her breasts to her stomach and smoothed the small little rolls of flesh back and forth like a tidal wave in a deep, blue ocean. She moved shyly against me, as she motioned for me to stop caressing her stomach.

"I know, I know, you can pitch more than an inch."

"What are you talking about? I'm not sizing you up, baby, I'm feeling you up," I teased.

She responded to my jest with girlish laughter then replaced my hand on her stomach. I continued my exploration of her soft, warm, round belly and wondered briefly how it would feel when she had a life growing inside of it, a life that would be raised by the both of us. As her desire increased with every movement she made, my exploration of her body grew bolder. The fingers traveled from her stomach to the top of her thongs.

"Tell me stop, Serita."

Her body froze in time and I could feel the exact moment when she stopped breathing. For just a few moments, she was deathly still as she patiently waited for my next move. As my hand slowly crept inside her panties, the aroma of wild flowers and a warm spring rain seeped into the air, and suddenly my fingers were drenched in her wet, sticky honey. The breathing returned to a rapid pattern and her body jerked at my mere touch.

"Tell me stop, Serita. Tell me now, damn it!"

As the heat that rushed between my legs ignited my desire, I felt the blood pulsating through my veins. My heart beat rapidly as I stroked her throbbing clit and dipped into that honey pot of sweet juices.

"Oooooh, oooohhh! Yes, Erin, yes!"

I smiled with confidence, as my hands nimbly unwrapped this beautiful gift and devoured her body like the best dessert I'd ever had. My tongue dipped and sucked on the thick clit that swelled more and more with each caress from my mouth. She opened her legs to me and allowed my head to rest snugly inside her warm embrace. The forest of curly black hair tickled my nose and lips, as my tongue delved deeper into its darkened pleasures. Soft, slender hands greeted my larger, thicker hands, as she guided me to all of the places within her that longed to be touched by only me. I felt the honey drip down to her bottom and I couldn't help but follow its trail with my thumb right into the depths of her ass. She opened her bottom to me like a woman dying of thirst and starvation, needing to be filled with completeness. As my mouth fed her clit, my thumb fed her hungry ass, and we sucked and grinded to a place of no return... a place where our bodies and souls would join. Her sighs and screams of "Yes! Oh damn it, yes!" sent me over the edge and

I climaxed against the cotton sheets of my bed as she climaxed within the warmth of my mouth.

As I finished my description of our bedroom encounter, I could hear heavy breathing on the other end of the phone. I opened my eyes and I was quickly brought back into the reality of my darkened bedroom and the empty space next to me. It was just a fantasy but for the first time, I had taken Serita with me into my dream world.

"Serita, are you there?"

"Yes...I'm here," she said softly.

"Are you okay?"

She paused for a few moments before responding. "Yes... it's just that no one has ever gotten me this wet before...not just by their words...I think I need to change my boxers...you've got me soaking wet!"

I smiled at the acknowledgement that my story had that effect on her. I had spent too many nights of sheer frustration and pent up desire wanting to be near her, wanting to touch her and not be able to, without having her now share some of the same frustration. "I'm glad I could please you," I half teased.

"You know it'll be different."

"What? What will be different?"

"Reality may not be as good as your fantasy," she explained.

"I doubt that seriously," I said matter of fact.

"Do you really want to know for sure?"

Now it was my turn to pause. I didn't know why I was hesitant, after all I had been waiting for this moment. I guess I was just a little surprised that it was coming sooner than I had anticipated.

"Yes, I want to know."

"Then come over."

The dial tone rang in my ears like the sound of a church bell. *Then come over!* Had she really meant that she wanted me to come to her apartment tonight? Was she really ready to have me in her bed for more than sleeping? I hadn't even had a chance to drop a few pounds before I pranced around her in my boxers. *Damn, I knew I should have called Jenny Craig!* I paced around my bedroom trying to figure out what to wear, what to say, what to bring, what to do. But as the minutes ticked away, I knew I couldn't keep procrastinating. I had to go over there and get exactly what I had been longing for the past two years. So I showered in peppermint bath oil, dressed in some loose fitting jeans, and a black button down, and sandals. I quickly packed an overnight bag, presuming that I would be staying over night and headed down I-20 in my green Montero Sport.

Twenty minutes later I was buzzing her at the access gate of her apartment. At the press of a button, the gates into her world opened for me, and I slowly drove my truck towards her door. The lights of her apartment were dimly lit and I could hear soft music playing as I grew closer. When she opened the door to the apartment, I was not prepared for the beautiful vision that I saw, and my big grin completely gave me away as the lust in my eyes matched the heat in my boxers. Her smile was a mirror image of mine. Sculpted in a red, oriental corset with matching thongs, thigh high stockings, and a pair of black and red stiletto heels, she was my Aphrodite in the flesh! Her matching red, *O·P·I's I Don't Do Dishes* manicured nails beckoned me into the fragrant and warm confines of her world. I hesitated for a moment as I contemplated this turn of events but my delay was short lived as we moved together from friends to lovers.

Titilayo
W.L. Tracy

"Morning Grand. I picked up the mail for you."

"Oh, thank you baby. Just put it on the kitchen table."

I smiled as I watched my oldest grandchild switch her way to the table. She was just like me, from that button nose, to her milk-chocolate skin, ample breasts, and birthing hips. It was as if I spit her out but she was my grandchild.

"Grand?"

"Yes, dear." I answered while standing at the kitchen counter mixing up a batch of my famous biscuits. Well, they were famous among the people at my church.

"You got a letter from someone."

"Really?" I smiled. Teane was like her mother, Spirit in that she could be very nosy but would beat around the bush even if she were paid a million dollars to get to the point of her snooping ways.

"Yes, ma'am. But it is addressed to Mae West Johnson. I didn't think anyone called you that anymore?"

Stunned by the name my grandchild used, I dropped the spoon in the bowl that I was stirring and went over to her. I wiped my hands on my apron and took the letter from Teane's delicate hand. As I read the envelope, I noticed that the return address was here in Georgia, near Atlanta, but there wasn't a name on it to let me know from whom.

"Are you going to open it?" Teane looked curious with her right eyebrow raised at attention.

I hesitated a few seconds longer, contemplating whether I wanted to open it in front of Teane. She was very adult like but she was still my grandchild and a teenager nonetheless. I had no idea what was in the letter or who it was from. I inhaled deeply and let out a long exhale as I opened the envelope slowly. I pulled out a piece of yellow legal pad paper and unfolded it to reveal handwriting I had not seen in years but would never forget.

Dear Mae West,

I hope that this letter finds you healthy and happy. I know that it has been a number of years since we have talked to one another but I want you to know that I have never forgotten you. In fact, you may be shocked to know that I have kept up with you, even with your name change. I still like the name Mae West and that is why I used that name on this letter.

Believe it or not, I was both happy and sad to know that you were able to find true love. After everything that happened between us, especially the way things ended before they had a chance to begin, I think that it is wonderful you were able to do what I was not capable of doing...to love another woman. I am truly sorry to hear that your love has passed on. I pray that you and your family find the strength that you need from God.

I am sure that you are wondering why I am writing this letter. The fact is, I am not in the best of health and there is something I needed to tell you. Even though the years have passed, my love for you never did. I have always loved you. I know that you are aware that I did remain with my husband until his death over eleven years ago. We were always good friends and we had made a promise to each other to take care of one another. There were many other reasons why I chose to stay with him but none of that is important. What is important is that I should have spoken to you before now. I should have told you why things had to be the way they were. I did not want you to hate me. That is why I need to let you know what was happening then and why I chose to remain in a relationship that was not passionate.

To begin, the era that we were in, your mother finding us, and my commitment to my husband played very big parts in my decision. But to be honest, because that is what this letter is about, the biggest part of my decision was based on my fear. I was young, you were younger, and I was afraid of my feelings. I was afraid of a love that I have wanted my whole life. There were the beatings of Blacks and other racism that I worked hard to fight against but I could not deal with anything else like that. Could you imagine how it would have been for two women who loved each other the way we did? I suppose you do. You were stronger than obviously I was. This is why you were able to find true love with a woman despite the world around you. I applaud that but I was not as strong. Plus, we had not known each other for very long and at that point in my life, I felt that a relationship with you would not be the best thing for either of us, which is why I left. I just could not bring myself to see the hurt in your eyes anymore than I saw that day in the park.

I have regretted my choice but regardless, I stand behind my decisions. As I stated earlier, my health is failing me. The reason that I am writing this letter is two-fold. One, I wanted you to know how I really felt and still feel about you after all these years. The other is a bit more complicated. I would like for you to come see me before my final day. I know that this request might be a bit strange but I would really like to see you. If this is possible, my address is on the front of the envelope. I hope that I can see you soon.
Yours,
Margaret H.

I was shocked to have a letter in my hands from Margaret Hayes after all these years. Before I knew what happened, before I could control them, I had tears in my eyes. This was a woman that I thought I would never hear from after the park, yet here I stand, with a letter from her saying that she has always loved me. I didn't know what emotions to have.

"Grand, who is Margaret H.?"

I smiled. I had never shared the story of Margaret with anyone because I did not think it was a story worthy of sharing, until now.

"Margaret Hayes. She is the first woman that I ever loved." I said in that all too romantic tone to be talking to my eldest grandchild.

I shook myself out of the trance that I was in and continued with my thoughts to Teane. "Margaret was a woman that I knew many years ago, before your Grandmother Adwoa. In fact, I think she somewhat prepared me for your grandmother and the difficulty in being in a same-sex relationship."

"How long did you know her?"

"That's the funny thing, we only met one day and spent an afternoon together. That's it. We never had a real relationship, per say, but the short time we were together meant a lot to me."

"Are you going to go see her?" She said with all the maturity of a much older person. Often, I forgot how young Teane was because of her disposition. She was so much like me when I was 17.

I smiled. I didn't have an answer for her. A part of me wanted to but I loved Adwoa and thought that it would be rude to meet with a past love that was never a relationship because I had spent my life with Adwoa. I didn't know if that would be honoring her memory or tarnishing it. I was so confused.

"Grand? Why don't you tell me about her, maybe that will help you make up your mind?"

"How did you know?"

"It is written all over your face." She said with a big grin on her face.

"I'm not sure you need to hear about someone other than your Grandmother Adwoa."

"Grand, you mean the world to me. I can tell that this decision is a hard one. I loved Grandmother Adwoa. I know that nothing will replace her but you have to do what makes you whole. I am sure that Grandmother Adwoa would say the same thing."

I hugged her tightly. Her maturity was what I needed right then. Maybe talking about the past would finally put it to rest and I could go see Margaret without feeling guilty.

"Well baby, it all started…"

***

In 1965, I was 17 and about to graduate from Barker High School. I was engaged to Darryl Morrison, a neighborhood guy that all the girls had a thing for. He was the center for the high school basketball team, fine in all those ways that girls wanted to lose their virginity to. That was all I used to hear, *Girl, your man is fine* or *How did he end up with you?* The fact was, I didn't know why I was with him. I mean, he was very sweet and never pressured me into having sex but I didn't want to be with him in any way. I tried but he was not for me. Honestly, none of the boys were for me. I had plans that didn't include marrying Darryl or any other guy for that matter.

But in my home, my mother ruled and I was not strong enough to stand up for what I wanted, for fear of the consequences. That along with the fact that Darryl has always been smitten towards me since we were little kids and his mother and my mother have been planning for this day since before I could remember, I said yes when Darryl proposed to me. Unfortunately, I was not that happy bride-to-be. But when Darryl told my mother of our engagement, you would have thought that he asked my mother the way she was jumping up and down when I showed her the ring. At least one of us was excited. She told me, "Gal, get happy 'cause men like Darryl don't just fall from trees. He's a good man. Get yo head out them clouds and start actin' like a wife-to-be!"

That was easier said than done. I didn't love Darryl, not in the way that a woman is supposed to love her husband. On top of that, my mother wanted me to go to teaching school and I had no desire to be a teacher. I had bigger dreams but apparently what my mother wanted was more important than what I wanted.

On the day that mother set up an appointment with some lady from a local teaching school, I had plans to go to the park with my note pad and pencil. Once again, mother changed all of that. To make myself feel more at home in a situation I didn't want to be in, I scheduled to meet the lady, Margaret Hayes, at the library at noon. As I walked to the library, passing by all of the storefronts and office buildings, I dreamed of going off to college far from my small hometown in Georgia. I had dreams of grandeur to do something in advertising and I was going to make those dreams come true one way or another someday.

As I walked into the library, the smell of the books and the excitement of the knowledge that I knew they possessed, filled my spirits with an immediate joy. That's why I picked the library. It was my favorite place because I had constant distractions with books all around me. Plus, whoever this lady was, she would have to whisper, so I could daydream, which was one of my absolute favorite pastimes. Gwendolyn, the head librarian greeted me as I walked through the doors. I stopped and chatted with her about the on-goings of the library. Gwendolyn was an older lady, maybe in her fifties, but she had the spirit and energy of a teen. I loved talking to her. She was like the mother I wish I had.

I looked down at my watch and noticed that it was 12:10 p.m. I knew that it was past time to meet the lady from the school but I really had no interest in doing so. But then I could hear mother's voice in my mind and I figured that I had better do this or my home was not going to be fit to enter later today.

I told Gwendolyn that I had to meet someone and moved towards the table where I spent most of my time. As I glided my stacked heels towards the table, I noticed it was already occupied with a woman sitting, legs casually crossed at the place I called my second home. She was so breathtaking that I stopped dead in my tracks. My thoughts turned into wild desires as I looked at her. I was stunned, to say the least. Once I regained my composure, she looked me dead in the eyes, making my heart skip and parts of my body I didn't know existed, take attention. The only time I had feelings like this were from the women I saw on "Petticoat Junction" and "Soul Train."

"Hello." She said in the sultriest voice as she stood to greet me. *I thought I was going to fall into her arms right then and there!*

"Hello." I managed to whisper.

"I presume you are Mae West Johnson? I am Margaret Hayes, the recruiter from Clark College."

"Oh, hi." I said stupidly and reached to greet her outreached hand for a quick handshake.

"Um, would you like to sit down?" I managed to say as I slumped into the nearest chair.

"Yes, let's." She said as she sat those beautiful curvy hips into the wooden chair.

She was utterly gorgeous. She was as chocolate as the sweet chocolate bar I had eaten on the way to the library with a big fro like my drama teacher and the most beautiful hips that could sit in a pair of jeans I had ever dreamed about. But she was better than any dream, she was real.

"So, let's talk about this teaching thing." I said loud enough to get an equally loud "Shhhhhh!" from Gwendolyn.

"Sorry." I lipped to her with an embarrassed blush on my face and quickly turned my attention back to the beauty sitting next to me, hoping she did not think that I was immature.

"Do you want to go somewhere else so we can talk?" I asked suddenly wanting to escape my usually safe haven.

"Sure." She said with the biggest, white-toothed smile I had ever seen.

As we got up, I noticed a ring on her left hand ring finger. *Dang, she was married! Well hell, I was engaged myself and she was probably not interested in women anyway. But a girl could dream, couldn't she?*

We walked out of the library, turning right towards Joe's Snacks n' Things. That was the perfect place to talk to the lovely that made me second guess my already second guessed engagement to Darryl. Walking into Joe's, the smell of French fries and burgers wondered up to my salivary glands. I was hungry but for far more than food, I wanted to get to know Margaret. We sat down at a booth towards the back of the restaurant. Although we as Blacks (or coloreds as the Whites called us) were struggling to be served in the front of the restaurants, I wanted as much privacy as possible.

"So," Margaret started as we looked over the menu, "you are interested in becoming a teacher. Why?"

Why? Why did she have to ask me that? Why not start with personal things or anything except why I wanted to be a teacher. I didn't. My mother wanted me to be one but I couldn't say that. Could I?

Noticing that I didn't know where to start, Margaret went on. "I have written an outline of a schedule that you might have in your first year of teaching school. Mae West? Are you okay?"

"Huh? Oh, I'm sorry. Please, just call me Mae. I hate the fact my mother loves Westerns enough to have named me that. Uhmm, what were you saying?" I tried to procrastinate.

Smiling, she put down the paper. "Mae, why do you want to be a teacher?"

I returned her tender smile and simply asked, "Do you mind if we order first?"

"Of course not."

We signed for the waitress to come take our orders. I always had a very healthy appetite so I ordered the largest burger on the menu with fries and a shake, while Margaret ordered a salad. She stated that she was a vegetarian after the waitress walked off, which made me like her even more. She was cool in a very nonchalant way. Her essence was speaking volumes to me and I had to have more.

"So Mae, why do you want to be a teacher?"

There's that question again. I wanted to talk to Margaret about so much but why I didn't want to be a teacher was not one of them.

"Why did you want to become a teacher?" I asked to try to give me a good answer rather than the truth.

"Well, I liked the idea of shaping young minds. You know, help them see the world in a different light. It was rewarding and fun."

"Was?"

"Is."

"Are you sure about that? I mean, you did say *was*."

"Listen," Margaret began in a more stern voice, "I am here to interview you, not the other way around." She ended with that gorgeous smile.

"I'm sorry it's just that you said was, like it is not the same for you or something. I just thought that you might want to talk about it. If not to me, then maybe to your husband?"

Now why did I say that? Now she knew that I noticed that she was married and why should I care? Fact was, I did care and I keep getting this weird feeling from her that told me to keep pressing. So I did.

"How did you...? Oh." Margaret looked down at her wedding ring and twirled it around her finger. "I see you're quite observant. Why is that?"

"Just the way I am I suppose. Just like I have noticed that you have not told me what is really going on."

"My, you are a feisty young thing! I don't know why but I feel like I can talk to you, but this is completely inappropriate behavior for a recruiter. I could get fired."

"Listen, I have always been told that I behaved as if I'm older than my years and I take that as a compliment. You are not that much older than me but I feel that life has weighed a heavy burden on you. It is obvious in your demeanor. I am not trying to dove into your personal business but I have a feeling about you as well, and I can sense that you need to talk. That is what I am good for, an ear to hear your woes and a shoulder to cry on."

"Well, there is something, but please don't let anyone

know that we had this conversation. I need my job but I really need someone to talk to and although we just met, I feel like I can confide in you."

"I promise that our conversation will not go any further than this table." I said as I did my scout's honor pledge.

"I love to teach, I love being a teacher, but I know there are other things in my life that I would love to do equally as much. Lately, my passion for painting has made its way to the dominant forefront. That, plus the fact that my husband and I don't love each other, is causing me to rethink my life choices."

"Well, I would say that is a lot to burden you down. What do you want to do?"

She smiled that ginger-sweet smile and shrugged her shoulders.

"Well, why don't we start with your husband?" *Of course I would want to start with him. I was getting a very strong vibe from Ms. Lady and after she made a point to tell me that she did not love her husband, all bets were off.*

The waitress returned with our food, so Margaret waited until she was gone to give me a response to my statement. It felt as though it was taking this lady forever to put the food on the table. By the time she asked, *"Will there be anything else?"* all I could do was snap, "No!" With that, she retreated quickly but not before throwing me a look that cool kill. I felt bad for a second but when I realized that Margaret did not notice because she was staring down at her wedding ring, I knew that I had done her a favor by hurrying the waitress away so she could release her burden without the pressure of on lookers.

"Mae, I just don't know how all of this happened to me. I mean, I love him, but I am not *in* love with him. I never have been and now that I want to pursue another career and he doesn't support me, it is making me feel like I don't even like him, you know what I mean?"

I shook my head yes. I felt her pain for more than my attraction for her. I realized that I could be her in about a year. I didn't love Darryl either.

"You see, my marriage was not my idea, it was my family's idea. They wanted me to *marry up in life* and when my husband showed an interest in me, they took full advantage of it. And here I am...a woman with dreams that will never be realized as long as I am married to him. To be honest, I would much rather not be married at all. That would suit me just fine. Then I could concentrate on my art and maybe even teach part-time. Then I would be happy."

"My grandmother always says that things happen for a reason and that people are in our lives, no matter how brief, for a reason as well. I truly believe that we were meant to meet each other. You seem like you need a friend and I do too. A lot of what you have said about your life is how I feel. You have shared so much of your life with me but I have not been completely honest with you."

"Honest with me?"

"Yes. You see...I don't have the desire to be a teacher... that is what my mother wants for me. In fact, the reason that I am engaged is because of her."

"Really? Why don't you tell her?"

"Why didn't you tell your mother?" I looked at the solemn, shaken-up look in her face and regretted the way that came out. I was not trying to be rude but I often get defensive when it comes to my relationship with my mother.

"I'm sorry. I didn't mean to pry."

"No, I'm sorry. I can get defensive. I like talking to you. I don't know why but I feel close to you."

"Yes, I know what you mean." There it was again, that beautiful smile that melted me every time I saw it.

We continued to talk about our lives and our dreams for another couple of hours. It was the first time I had opened up to anyone about some of the things that I wanted in my life, not what my mother wanted. It felt great.

. "Are you finished?" Margaret looked at my half-eaten burger and then at me. *What was I supposed to say? Yes because although I find you incredibly attractive, there is no way that I can tell you how I feel?*

"I'm not as hungry as I thought." I lied with a half smile on my face. She was not buying it.

"Listen Mae West..." She started and then smiled that perfect way she does. "Mae, I didn't mean to upset you earlier. I was way out of line and for that, I apologize."

"You don't get it. I really am interested in you and what is going on with you. Our lives are so paralleled and I have never connected with anyone the way I have with you. You have helped me understand *me*. I know we just met but I feel like I can trust you, open up to you. Besides, I...I..."

She let out a deep exhale, parted her lips as if to say something, apparently changed her mind and smiled. I had gone too far but I couldn't help it. I had never had feelings like this before and I could not keep them in.

"What are you saying Mae?" She finally asked with the strangest smirk on her face.

"I am saying...I am...just saying...that I am, uhh... concerned about you. I mean...my mother wants me to go to teaching school, which is not where my heart is. Until I met you, I thought that I had to do what she wanted. Don't you want to do what you want to do for a change?"

The look she was giving me was making me wet again in a region that had never experienced wetness before and I couldn't think straight, but I tried to pull myself together. It was no use falling apart in front of a married woman.

"What I am trying to say is what I said earlier, you seem as though you need a friend. I thought that I could be a friend to you. We have so much in common."

"Is that all?"

Where was this lady going with these questions? I mean, first she was uptight about telling me too much about her life and now, now it seemed as though she was flirting with me. Wasn't she?

"What do you mean? *Is that all?*"

"Listen, Mae West," Margaret said as she put her hand on

top of mine, "there has been some tension between us since we first met. I mean, I figured you were not interested in teaching since you kept changing the subject and we have this very strange chemistry. So I wanted to know what you are really thinking. Is there something that I need to know?"

"Not that I know of. Is there something you feel you need to tell me?"

"Isn't there another question you would rather ask?"

"Like?"

I was not going to give in that easy. I now knew that she was flirting with me but I would not be the one to cross that line. Besides, she was married, whether she wanted to be or not. She removed her hand from mine and looked around the restaurant to see if anyone noticed. *I don't know if anyone else did but I did and it felt great!* Very warm and tender was her touch. I had never felt a touch like hers before. I wanted so badly for her to do it again.

"How about we pay our bill and walk off some of this food?"

Gosh! This lady changes the script every five seconds. But she still had my interest, so I grabbed the paper that she had written the schedule on to have something of hers and stuffed it into my purse before replying, "Okay."

We left out of Joe's and headed towards the park. It was a great day for the park with the sun high in the sky and a gentle breeze cascading over our skin. Not to mention, most people were at work since it was only 2:45 in the afternoon and it would be pretty empty. I would finally have some alone time with my walking dream. As we walked, we continued to discuss our lives and how we felt about different changes going on within the world today, especially about the happenings going on one state over in Alabama earlier in the year. In Selma alone, a lot of change and violence had occurred against Blacks as well as the Whites that helped them. We talked about that awful Sunday that hundreds of civil rights marchers gathered in Selma to protest voting rights and were Billy clubbed and tear-gassed by local and state police. We discussed, in detail our thoughts about Malcolm X's assassination at his mosque in New York as well as the white priest, James J. Reeb that was attacked by a white mob and later died due to massive head injuries. We talked about the impact of President Johnson's decision to introduce the Voting Rights Act. Some say a little too late but at least he did it. In the midst of all of the civil rights protest, America was in the middle of fighting the Vietnam War. A war that many Americans, regardless of racial or economic differences, bonded together to protest against. Things were changing in America and the world and we just hoped the changes would be for the best.

By the time we reached the *Negro's Side* sign, we had covered the globe and back. Margaret grimaced at the sign and walked on towards a nearby bench then sat down. I sat down next to her, feeling even closer to her than I had earlier, or to anyone else for that matter. She certainly was a unique person that I was glad to know.

"Mae, we have talked about everything concerning your feelings about the world, the government, even your mother, but what I want to know about is you. There is something about you that is making me drop my guard. I feel close to you the way that I should feel about others in my life. Why is that?"

I pondered how to really answer that question. *Could I, should I, tell her how I really felt. What was really going on with me? What could I lose? Nothing!*

"Margaret, I really like you. There is something about you that I am highly attracted to. Your smile, your voice, your, well…pardon me if I offend you, but I am sexually attracted to you. Since the moment I saw you, I have been and I don't know how else to tell you."

There! I had finally told her how I felt. She was beautiful and I had a feeling that she had not heard that enough in her life, especially from her husband. There was a long pause that felt like forever for me. She put her hand to her mouth. I could tell that she was thinking about how to respond to the downpour of affection she was just given.

"Well, I never thought that you would say that! Mae, I must admit that I have an attraction for you as well. I have tried to hide those feelings especially since I am trying to recruit you for school but your demeanor, your openness, the way you are, I can't fight those feelings. They are the same feelings that I have tried to hide for many women. Mae, I have to tell you the truth about my life."

She took a deep inhale and I knew that what she was going to tell me was going to be very hard but I wanted her to know that I was there for her. I put my hand on top of hers and squeezed it to reinforce what I had told her earlier. I cared for her very deeply. I wanted to make her life easy and to make her happy. She looked at my hand on top of hers and smiled...that contagious smile that could melt the South Pole with a single glimmer.

"I married my husband because I needed to marry him. I never loved him. I have never been in love with any man. I am a lover of women. He knows that but he hopes that one day I will change and love him but I won't." She said shaking her head.

"I understand. I am engaged to a man I don't love. I secretly lust over the women that I see on television. I think my mother knows but she doesn't say anything, she is just glad I said yes to Darryl."

I hesitated to say the next thing but I knew that it was right. I had to tell her again, to let her know how I felt; that I did understand. "I really like you. The way they teach us to like boys. I really do!" And with that, I leaned over and kissed her. Right there in the park. Right there for the entire world to see. I kissed her the way Darryl always wanted me to kiss him. I kissed her to get rid of all the times she had not felt loved. I kissed her to show her that I was the one for her. I kissed her with all the passion I had ever felt.

"MAE WEST JOHNSON!"

I stopped kissing the woman that made me feel whole and looked into the steaming eyes of Leslie-Kay Johnson, my mother. We stood up quickly to face her wrath. She looked as though she could boil over at any moment. But no matter what, I was not ashamed of what I had just done. I tried to grab Margaret's hand to reinforce my feelings but she snatched it away. She moved closer to my mother and further away from me telling my mother that it was all a misunderstanding.

Mother didn't give Margaret eye contact the entire time she attempted to *explain the situation*. She only looked at me with as much contempt as I had ever seen. That was the major turning point in my life…the moment that I knew who I was… when I knew that I had to stand up for myself. Especially since the woman I just shared my feelings with was now turning her back on me.

After that day, I moved out of my mother's home…well, she kicked me out. I moved to Atlanta with a cousin who lived there. Found a job and got on my feet. I never talked to my mother again. The next time I saw her was at her funeral. I often wished we had been able to put the past behind us. I loved my mother but she couldn't love a lesbian.

As for Margaret, I heard that she and her husband had moved closer to Atlanta from Rome, Georgia because he got a better job. I never ran into her but I did keep up with her whereabouts for a while. That is until I met Adwoa (ah-doo-wa). When I learned that Adwoa's name was a Ghana name meaning Peace, I knew that I had finally found *my place* in this world. We shared a life together full of spirit, strength, and struggles of growth until her death last year. I am now 57 years old and still growing, but on that day many years ago, I became the woman that I am today. After meeting Adwoa, I changed my name to Titilayo (tee-tee-lye-oh). I chose that name with Adwoa's help. I wanted a name that symbolized what I was about, what I believed in, and as a way to continue in my beliefs. My name is from the Yoruba tribe of Nigeria and it means *Happiness Is Eternal*.

"Well, my dearest that is the story of your Grand's long lost love. I loved your grandmother but there was always a place in my heart for Margaret."

"I think that you should go see her Grand. I think that it would be good for you and her."

I hugged my eldest granddaughter. She was so bright and caring, I couldn't ask for a better grandchild and the Lord blessed me with three. Of course Teane was the one that I was the closest to and right now, I needed that. It made me miss her grandmother even more.

"Yes, I think that I would like that. Would you take me?"

"Of course, Grand. You did not even have to ask."

Nora's Lover
Sue Harmon

Whap! Whap! Whoosh! Whap! Whap! Whoosh! The rhythmic sound gave an assurance to her heart as she walked into the kitchen of the café. Her heart was assured of two things, Nora's rolls would be ready for the customers and Nora was the only person in the café. Admittedly it was the second part that made her giddy as a girl of sixteen. She shook her head as she tried to reconcile the giddy teenage feelings with the reality that she was a grandmother four times over.

"Hmmmm, Hmmmmm, Hmmmmm," Nora hummed to herself as she worked the dough for her rolls. Her thoughts slipped to her children. From her children her thoughts slipped to her now ex-husband, who had done nothing to discourage the older boys from enlisting. "Damn fool!" She shouted into what she thought was an empty room. In her mind, he was the reason she would lose her sons to this war. They so much desired to be like their father. She prayed daily they would be better than their alcoholic, womanizer daddy.

"Nora, Nora, you ok?" Mrs. Bell asked after she heard the phrase *damn fool*. She must be thinking about her ex-husband, Abraham. Mrs. Bell rushed over to Nora to provide the *comfort* she had been thinking about when she had walked into the café. Standing beside the statuesque woman, Mrs. Bell placed her arm around Nora's shoulder.

"Is everything ok?" She whispered into Nora's ear.

"Miz Bell, stop that, now. I'm a making bread." Nora

said in her non-pulsed manner that after all of these years still left Mrs. Bell wondering about Nora's emotions. "Besides, nothing is wrong. I just got to thinking about my boys and from there I started thinking about Abraham." Nora said as she continued to knead the dough.

Mrs. Bell moved to stand behind Nora dropping her arm to Nora's waist. "If it is money…"

Nora cut Mrs. Bell off quickly "No, it is not money. It is the war and my boys being overseas." She disliked when Mrs. Bell would try to give her more than what she earned at the café. There was a great deal Nora disliked in the world. Mrs. Bell's arm on her waist was not part of that great deal. Still kneading the dough, Nora leaned back a little into Mrs. Bell.

"Miz Bell, it is about time for the others to come in." Nora said as her thoughts began to turn from ex-husband, children, and war to the feel of the woman behind her. The woman she had loved since before she could spell love. However, 1968 was no better time than 1928 to be a *bull dagger*.

"I locked the door. You know they won't come in here one minute before they gotta. I know they hate me. Hell, even the White men hate me for not marrying one of them after Paul died." Mrs. Bell said a little breathless as she pulled Nora against her body. She placed a kiss on Nora's neck. Her hands brushed Nora's bodice. Shivering with need, she said, "I need you, now. We have time."

"Miz…Bell…I   have   bread…d'oven.   Hmmmnn. Ummm…Ahhh…" Nora found speech hard as she became lost in Mrs. Bell's hands on her bodice. Her body on its own accord began to move against Mrs. Bell with the urgency of a new bride's pent up passion.

This batch of rolls would have to be thrown out. Mrs. Bell also knew she was tanking her profit by not being able to control herself with Nora at work. However, since the arrival of Nora's grandchildren, work had been the only place they had to be alone. Her hands moved from Nora's bodice to her hips. Despite six children and over fifty years of living, Nora's body was still the same as when she first became a woman. The day that she first became Mrs. Bell's woman.

Mrs. Bell began to thrust harder against Nora's luscious bottom. Each thrust an attempt to wipe out the feelings of betrayal she still felt at the birth of each of Nora's children. "Mine, damn it, mine," Mrs. Bell said in a harsh whisper. The same frustrated phrase she had been yelling since the eve of her own wedding. The same phrase she whispered into Nora's ear on the eve of Nora's wedding.

The faint sound of voices brought them back to the reality of 1968 Mississippi. Mrs. Bell still quivering forced herself from Nora. Nora looking at her own bodice, asked for an apron to cover the holes where the buttons should have been, buttons that had become victims of their brief passionate interlude. Mrs. Bell eyeing Nora's bodice asked the question that had been the source of many arguments since Nora's divorce.

"Will you leave with me? I can just sell everything and we can go. I am too old not to be with you every hour of the day. We have done our duty to our families."

"The apron please...Honey," was Nora's only reply. As always the word *Honey* deflected any argument that could arise.

It amazed Nora that despite being five years older than she, Mrs. Bell still did not understand what their relationship meant even in 1968. Where could a couple of lesbians, one white and one black go? They were too old to try to move now. They should have done it before either one got married or got kids.

"I am sorry about the buttons," Mrs. Bell murmured against Nora's lips, as she placed the apron over Nora's head. "I guess I should let them in before they get curious. No need to add fuel to the fire that has been going on about us for all of these years."

Mona Mae was the first to enter into the café. Her night at the juke joint still clung to her. Nora hated the smell because it reminded her of Abraham. The question of why she married him came to mind. Why did she not just run away? She could have gone to live with her great-aunt in New York. Her aunt had escaped to the North years before Nora was born. She had ran from an overseer who was determined that any child she bore would belong to him. No sense in woulda, coulda, shoulda now. She and Martha, who she called Mrs. Bell when they were alone, had had their moment.

As Nora cleaned her station of the excess dough and flour, she allowed her mind to drift to her first time. Her husband may have thought he was the first, however, in her mind, Martha was the first, and since her divorce, the last. She thought about how she had always loved going with Papa to deliver the eggs and milk from their farm. Martha was a town girl a few years her senior and White. Nora knew she loved Martha the moment the thin girl touched her hand when she paid for the milk. White folks never touched coloreds. Amongst the coloreds, Nora's family was thought to be high and mighty, however, Nora's constant interactions with Whites kept her aware of her place. Only when she would meet Martha on the milk run did she feel out of her place. Papa told her not to make much of Martha's behavior. He told her that Martha would change when she got older.

Papa was wrong. Martha, having something of a wild streak, would seek out Nora. Nora remembered the '28 Studebaker and the lies Martha told Nora's Papa so they could enjoy time alone in her new car. The only thing that changed about Martha was her decision to marry Paul Bell. Although Nora understood why Martha did it, her heart could not accept it. Her heart never accepted Martha being enjoyed by another. Her heart's mind caused her to visualize the first time they kissed.

Martha had asked her to come inside one winter day to get the money for the milk and the eggs. In one of those rare times, Martha was home alone. This time when she gave the money to Nora, she asked, "Nora, do you like me?" Remembering her place in society, Nora gave a non-committal answer. Martha sensing Nora was not being open in her reply, she asked again.

Nora, ever cautious, replied once more in the non-pulsed manner she had been taught to treat White folks. At that point Martha cursed and then pulled Nora into a kiss. Looking into Nora's eyes, Martha asked Nora once more if she liked her. Nora, a little shaken by the realization of her fantasy, could only shake her head in an affirmative motion.

Martha then told Nora, "I have liked you, like this for so very long. I need to see you again. Can you meet me at my grandfather's house?" Nora, still dazed, replied she could. It was not until she had gotten back to Papa and the wagon that she realized she did not know where Martha's grandfather lived. White people were White people to her except for Martha.

Her Papa had asked what took so long. Only when he asked about the money did she realize she had dropped the money. Jumping from the wagon she raced back to Martha's house to get the money.

"I don't know your granddaddy. And I left the money in here," she said somewhat winded by being near Martha again.

Smiling, Martha kissed Nora again before handing the money to her. Martha then said, "Don't you worry about meeting me at my grandfather's house. I have another idea. Just you be home tomorrow."

Nora, still an untried girl, did not understand why Martha could make her tingle with a smile. However, that is just what Martha's smile did to Nora. She skipped to the wagon. Her Papa did not question why she left the money. Nora was known to be a bit of a dreamer. She told Papa that she just loved the houses in town. Her Papa told her to be thankful for her home in the country.

Martha arrived at Nora's house the next day to ask her parents if Nora could work at Martha's granddaddy's house. Nora's parents agreed that Nora could do the work, as long as Nora was still able to do the milk run. Nora's Papa was not big on working for White folks. Nora was excited by Martha's take charge manner and mostly by Martha's desire to see her again. During the night Nora had replayed their kiss over and over again.

"Well gal, com'on, I don't have all day." Martha's words shocked Nora into rejoining the conversation about Nora's new job as a nurse maid to Martha's granddaddy.

Quickly Nora packed a few things before joining Martha in that shiny, new Studebaker. Martha pulled the Studebaker to the side of the road once they were out of Nora's parents' sight.

"I hope you don't mind. My granddaddy does need a nurse and I need you." Martha held Nora's eyes with her own as she spoke. Nora could only think of the kiss they had shared. Martha seeing Nora's desire responded to it with a kiss. The first of many lingering and youthful passionate filled kisses they would share down the lane from Martha's granddaddy's house and in his house.

"Nora! Nora! I need your help out front." Mrs. Bell called to the kitchen.

Nora, brought back to the present by the sound of Martha's voice, replied, "I'm coming," as she quickly finished the cleaning of her station.

Mrs. Bell did not like having to call Nora out to the front but Nora worked better than the young White girls less than half her age. She did not like the way the men would approach Nora. She especially did not like that Clyde Monfort, who had been chasing Nora ever since they shared the same foot tub as babies. It galled her to hear him tell of his childhood with Nora. She could not understand how he could have a successful farm and still have time to chase *her* Nora. Today she would stop him before he offered to give Nora a ride.

"Nora, after the rush, I'll take you home." Mrs. Bell spoke to Nora but kept her eyes on Clyde. Owning almost half the real estate in town, Nora's father owned the other half, gave Mrs. Bell a little room to be so bold.

Nora would have been angry had the situation not been so funny. There was Martha telling Clyde to back off in a room full of people. Nora thought to herself that all of them were too old to be acting like this. She caught Martha's eye and then shook her head. She liked Clyde. He had been a good friend for years and not just to her. He never told anyone about finding Martha and Nora together in that Studebaker down the lane from Martha's granddaddy's house. *Yes, Clyde was a real good friend.* She and Martha owed him to this very day for keeping quiet.

She walked over to the counter where he sat to fill his coffee cup. "Would you like something sweet to go with the coffee?" She asked Clyde before she thought about her words. "We have pie and a hot peach cobbler that I made this morning." She added quickly to cover her slip.

A slow smile crept across Clyde's handsome, married face; his day had just been made. "I'll just have the cobbler." The look on Martha's face was enough for him.

Nora went to the back to get the cobbler. Martha was close on her heels. "Nora, before you take that cobbler to Clyde, will you come to my office? I just checked the register and it is not right."

Nora knew the register was fine. "Yes, Miz Bell, I'll be right there," Nora responded.

"Mona Mae, take that cobbler out to Clyde. I need to talk with Nora about the register." Mrs. Bell shouted to Mona Mae who was bent over the counter holding her head.

"Yes'um." Mona Mae replied as she moved slowly to cut the cobbler.

Mrs. Bell closed the door behind Nora. Behind the closed door all pretenses were dropped. "Don't play me with Clyde," Martha breathed into Nora's neck.

"Stop acting jealous, Martha," Nora responded. "I love you. I have loved you since that moment you first held my hand to pay for the milk my Papa sold." Nora wrapped her arms around Martha's neck, running her hands into Martha's hair. "We are too old for jealousy, Honey," Nora continued.

Martha moaned in desire. "We are also too old for the floor. Let's go to my place." Martha said as she moved her hands along Nora's waistline.

"We have a business to run." Nora said in hopes of

reminding Martha where they were. Looking into Martha's glazed eyes Nora realized the point of reminding had passed.

A knock on the door followed by Mona Mae's still groggy voice kept Martha from raising Nora's dress any higher. "Yeah, Mona, tell Lucy she can use the register. Nora has shown me what she did." Martha said without any attempt to cover the desire in her voice.

Righting her clothes, Nora moved to the door. Martha grabbing Nora's arm, pulled Nora back into her arms for another kiss. Nora knew she would have to leave early for Martha was in a mood not to be denied. Those moods had almost caused them to be caught many times over the years. A shaken Martha, slowly allowed Nora to leave her embrace. Martha leaned against the office door after Nora had left, shaking her head. "I am too damn old for this," she said to herself. Holding herself, she moved slowly to the office chair. A slow smile crept to her face as she considered the various reasons Nora could give for leaving early today. They had to leave before the young'uns got out of school. Whatever reason Nora gave it would need to allow enough time for some rest. As she left the office a huge smile came to her face.

"Nora, why don't you come over to my place to see if your young'uns can use some of those things Katie Mae left?" Martha asked. She prayed Nora would not turn her down again.

Without missing a beat in the communication, Nora replied, "Miz Bell, I don't have a way to get over to your place before I haft to be home to get the children."

Martha, excited by the *Yes!* she heard in Nora's reply said, "I can take you there now. The girls got everything in hand here. Right, Mona?"

"Yes'um," was Mona Mae's slow reply.

Once they were inside Mrs. Bell's house, they held each other with the desperation of years of lies, games, and longing. Behind closed doors there was no need for any of those things. The only need that was acknowledged by their embrace was the need for each other.

Pulling back for a moment, Martha said to Nora, "Let's get into our bed." She guided Nora toward the bedroom. It felt great to say *our bed.*

Sitting on the edge of the bed they kissed gently, as they had when they were younger at Martha's granddaddy's house. Nora pushed Martha onto the mattress using her body's fullness. Slowly she began the motions that had brought them to climax for forty years. A slow cry escaped from Martha as she allowed the pent up desire to escape from her still clothed body.

"Let's undress," she suggested. "Remember how we would spend the night together at Granddaddy's?"

Nora smiled as she remembered the freedom or foolishness they shared. Slowly they undressed then climbed into the bed.

"I wish I could hold you like this forever. Really, what is keeping us from each other now?" Martha asked.

Nora looked at Martha as if she were crazy. *Did she really not see the turmoil in the country?*

"Nora, I have given all I planned to my kids and this town. We can go out West. Things are different in the West."

Pulling Martha closer to her, Nora spoke, "Martha... North, East, West, and South, our love is the same no matter what direction. We have lasted forty-years; I do not need to move to love you more." So saying, Nora began again to express the forty years of loving she had shared with Martha.

Steps Are Made for Climbing
Renair Amin

"Toya!"

I ignored my "little lady" as she tried to get my attention. Then she ran in front of me, jumping up and down, trying to get my attention. However, I prevailed at our game. I always do. It is hard but my secret is: if I look straight ahead, she never jumps into my view since she is only 4 feet tall.

"Toya, I know you hear me."

I continued to ignore her as her ponytails bounced into my peripheral vision. I had dressed her in her favorite yellow sundress, which I bought for her last year.

"Blue sock, black sock." She sang as she danced around my waist. I looked down and realized that I had on mismatched socks. That is what happens when a screaming six-year old startles you out of your sleep insisting you take them to the park.

I bent down and kissed little lady's forehead and looked at her pretty face. People always say how she looks just like her mother and they were telling the truth. She took my hand to begin our walk around the park. As usual, she breaks away and runs towards the swings. Normally, I would chase her but I hadn't had my coffee yet. I watched her in awe as she determined which swing she wanted to ride on. Tears began to run down my face; I had been so emotional lately.

Robin, also known as the "little lady," was the daughter

of my wife, Sharice. Sharice and I had been together for a total of four years, give or take a few months. We met at a local bookstore. She had just purchased a book that I also had come to buy. When she heard me ask the cashier for a newly released lesbian novel, not only did she tell me where to find it, she gave me her analysis on the book. I was impressed. Before I knew it, I was in that bookstore more than usual. I ran into her at least two more times that week which eventually led up to her asking me out to dinner.

We dated occasionally over the next few months but my heart was on full speed. I had fallen in love with her hazel eyes. Not to mention, she had the hottest dark chocolate body that I had ever seen. I called her my "chocolate kiss" because she was so small and sweet. Her height was only 5'5" which was average but in comparison to me, she was tiny. However, she would joke that just because I was 5'11" didn't mean she could not climb to the top. Dating her was hard because we were taking it slow. I tried not to notice how my body would react to her touch even if we were just holding hands. The key word is *tried*. It didn't help that she always wore the sexiest suits and my favorite cologne.

I noticed that she never would invite me back to her place. I started wondering if she was seeing someone else. Plus, she always had something else, besides work, to do. When we were out on a date, she was always excusing herself to answer the phone.

After about several months of dating, she called me one day and said that she had someone she wanted me to meet. I was excited hoping this was a signal that we were getting serious but I was nervous. When she pulled up in front of my door, I went out to the car not knowing what to expect. At first, I didn't see anyone in the car so I thought we were driving to the person she wanted me to meet. Upon approaching the car, I saw the top of a head. When I reached the car, I saw in the front passenger seat, a mini version of Sharice. She was the carbon copy of Sharice all the way down to her hazel eyes. There was no doubt in my mind that she was Sharice's daughter. I just laughed at my mind's previous assumptions and was so glad I didn't act on them.

Sharice rolled down the window and said, "Robin, this is Ms. Latoya. Remember, I told you about her. She will be going with us today, okay?"

Robin just nodded and we drove off into a world of our own. I mean, in truth, at the time, Robin was only three years old. *What did I expect her to say?* After that, Sharice would pick me up every Saturday and we would relax and play with Robin at the park. It took awhile for Robin to loosen up. I expected the awkwardness, though. I, too, was adjusting. Dating someone with a child was something I hadn't done before.

Over time I got to know Robin. She was just as hyper then as she is now. I loved that about her. She was always happy and could always make me smile. Even before I moved in, if I needed a laugh, I would call to hear Robin's voice.

"Toya, why are you crying? You miss mommy, too? I know I do."

I squatted to meet her eye to eye. I grinned and wiped my tears. She smiled. It was clear that she would be short like Sharice. There was going to be no way to avoid that gene since it appeared that it ran through every woman in Sharice's family. Unless she would eventually take after her father, Sharice always said he was a tall gentleman.

"Yes, lady, I do. As a matter of fact, I will call her for you."

I picked up my cell phone to call Sharice. She had gone away on a business trip and was scheduled to return tomorrow morning. I hadn't seen her face in almost five days and it was murder. This was one of the longest trips that she has taken since starting her new job. I missed her immensely but it gave me more time alone with my little lady. I let it ring but I got the machine. The caller ID would let her know I called so I just hung up.

"Can you tell me a story?" Robin asked.

"Sure, Robin, which one would you like to hear?"

"Tell me the story about the princess who lived happily

ever after."

"Robin, are you sure you want to hear that story again? I have told you that story so many times."

I actually enjoyed telling that story. I had been telling it to Robin since she was four and she loved it more each time. It had taken Robin and me a long time to get to this point. In the beginning, we had our rocky times but in the end, we worked through it. I learned to let her come to me. I never forced my friendship on her.

Once I moved in, I realized that trying to get us to form a bond was going easier than trying to get her to understand her new family. She was only a child but there was still a level of understanding of our relationship that she would need. We managed a way to explain everything and that was the start of the "Princess" story. There were many chapters to this story that we would add as she grew older and new situations arose but she always liked the first chapter the most.

"Toya, come on." Robin whined as she pulled on my arm.

"Alright, Robin."

I walked over to the picnic table and sat down. Robin sat next to me, kicking her feet; she was too short to reach the ground. At that moment, my cell phone started ringing. I looked at the name and it said "Mommy." I nudged Robin and answered the phone.

"Hey, Mommy."

"Let me speak to her." Robin shouted excitedly as she snatched the phone out of my hand and began telling her all her events of the day. She hadn't been able to speak to her since yesterday so she had so much she had to tell her.

After about ten minutes, she passed me the phone. I guess she was done but I could still hear Sharice talking.

"Baby, she is done."

We both started laughing. Robin would hold your attention as long as she wanted you to have it. Then she was onto the next topic. I listened as Sharice told me about her day. It was so nice to hear her voice. Although I got a little sad because I missed her so much, I knew that she was taking care of business for her "women," as she would always say.

She asked me what I was doing. I told her that I was just getting ready to tell Robin, the Princess story. I figured that would be the cue for Sharice to call me back but instead she asked me to put her on speakerphone.

"So Robin, you want to hear the Princess story. Well, let me see if I can help."

I smiled. Sharice knew the story as well as I did. She was definitely my queen on the throne. The love that I had for her was beyond words. Sometimes I would just sit in my house and stare at my surroundings. I was overjoyed at what has happened in my life over the past few years.

"Okay. Once upon a time, there lived a princess in a castle far away. She lived there in a castle with her mother, the queen. She was a beautiful princess with long flowing black hair, a pretty smile, and beautiful hazel eyes like her mother. One day, another queen came to visit the castle. The princess, who was very shy, would always hide away when other queens would visit causing the queen to always have to summon the princess to her side. However, the visiting queen had been there several times and the princess was used to seeing her."

I was so caught up in the story that I jumped right into the story. Robin just rested her head on her hand and looked at me.

"Yes," I interjected. "The princess had become familiar with the visiting queen and would always come down to watch her whenever she would visit. After a long period of time, the queen herself had become smitten with the visiting queen and had taken her as her wife. The princess was not fond of the idea because it was all new to her. However, the queen tried to explain that although her family was going to be different, it was still *her* family. She told her how the love would now be two-fold and they would each love and treat her as the glorious princess that she was. In the beginning, the princess had to get used to the fact that there was someone else in her and her mother's life. Out of confusion of what to call this new woman in her life, she decided that she would just ask the new queen. One day after dinner, the princess asked the new queen, 'Are you my stepmother?' 'Steps are for climbing my dear,' the queen responded. 'I am your friend and whenever you need me, I am here,' she promised."

Sharice's voice came through the speakerphone to continue the story.

"The princess accepted that answer and smiled with delight. Even though the princess would grow to be a queen of her own land one day, she would always remember the words that had been spoken to her that evening. And the new queen was true to her word and was always there whenever she was needed."

Robin smiled. "I love that story."

"I love it too, baby. And Toya?"

I could only imagine what was next. Sharice was a silly character so I knew it was going to be something to make me laugh.

"Yes, dear?"

"Why are you wearing one blue sock and one black sock?"

"I don't know. I told you not to put that dull light in the bedroom."

It took a second for my brain to compute her question as I explained my response. I paused and looked around. How could she have known what color my socks were?

"How could you know the color of my socks, unless…"

"I was right behind you." She said as she finished my sentence.

I turned around, smiled, and pointed at Sharice. Robin let out a squeal as she turned around and saw her mother.

"Mommy!" She cried as she ran down the hill into her mother's arms.

Sharice looked at me and smiled as she held Robin. Like a child, I ran down the hill too. I missed her so much and it showed. I leaned in and kissed her on the cheek. I would save the real kiss for later.

Time was a blur on our ride home. Sharice told me how her trip was cut short and she wanted to surprise me. But when she called the house and I wasn't home, she figured we were at the park. She took a chance but when she called me back and I confirmed the location, she knew she had told her cab to drop her in the right place. I asked what she would have done if we were not there. She said she didn't know but that it worked out in her favor.

We were home in no time and Robin was doing her famous "what you bring me" song and Sharice was singing along with her. I just laughed because they both were so comical. Sharice fed her, gave her the gift, and tucked her away in bed, which took longer than usual, but it was expected. She was excited about having her mother home.

I sat down in my living room and looked at the home Sharice and I had built together. I walked over to our family photo and ran my fingers over the edge of the frame. From behind me, I could hear Sharice enter. She walked over to me and placed her arms around my waist and put her head in my back.

"Are you being sentimental again?"

"No," I answered through the tears.

As I said before, I never knew we would come to this point but we had connected on other levels and before I knew it, two years had gone by and she was proposing. Robin was an adjustment but I just had to learn to be patient. She would come to me when she was ready and she did.

Now look at us, two years later, Sharice is the manager of her investment department while I stay home to take care of Robin who was only in school for half the day. I had worked for 7 years as one of the lead accountants at a CPA firm and had taken an extended non-pay leave of absence from work. Hopefully, I can go back to work once Robin starts school full time unless something else comes up.

Sharice rubbed my stomach. We had been trying to have

a baby for the past year with a close friend of ours who offered to be our donor. We had everything checked out and had taken all the necessary steps to complete the process. The first two times nothing had happened. I felt so bad for Sharice. She would be so anxious only to be told that it did not take. I swore I would never tell her about any pregnancy signs until I was absolutely sure and if she asked I would tell her that I hadn't heard from the doctor. However, lately, I had been noticing some changes with my body and had gone in for a pregnancy test. I didn't want to tell Sharice; she would be too excited and I didn't want her to be let down again.

I went to the phone to pick up the messages off the machine. I listened to each one hoping that one would be the message that I wanted to hear. Either way, I would have to go back to the doctor either for prenatal care or to attempt the procedure again. I listened as the doctor's prognosis came over the receiver then hung up the phone. I sighed and instantly could feel my eyes watering. I turned around expecting to see Sharice but she was gone. I assumed she went up to bed; she *had* to be exhausted.

I began my journey up the flight of stairs, the same steps that she had carried me up when we returned from our honeymoon. As I walked towards our bedroom, memories flashed through my mind like a movie. Each step took me closer and closer to the woman I loved. My hands touched the photographs along the staircase. I smiled at the pictures that showed us in our earlier years. Although they were not taken that long ago, I knew I had grown so much over the years.

I stared down the hall at the bedroom door that led to the room that had brought us so much pleasure. Our bedroom was our make-out spot, break area, and conference room. This is where we would take time every night to go over important matters of the house. I would lay in her arms and talk about my day with Robin. She would tell me the stress of her meetings, who she had to fire, and who she wanted to hire. We would kiss goodnight and as our little joke promise to take over the world again tomorrow. I opened the door to a dark room.

"Come here, baby."

"You know better than to turn out these lights. I can't see as it is," I fussed.

Out of nowhere, she playfully tackled me. I started laughing. As she sat on me, while pinning my arms under me, I came face to face with the eyes of my true love. There was no use in me struggling; she was definitely in better shape than me. She would always win and I would always be winded. I just smiled to myself. In no other place or time, would I feel what I felt right now. In the darkness, she couldn't see the tears fall down my face but I knew I was on the verge of breaking down. She began to kiss my face. She paused as her lips encountered the wetness of my tears. I could see her face as a light appeared through the blinds that had shifted from the night's wind.

She placed her mouth on mine and slid her hands underneath my waist. The intensity of the kiss grew with the ferocious movements of her hips. Our bodies spoke in tongues as I began to claw at her back. In one movement, she ripped every button on my shirt. I whimpered at the feeling growing below my waist. She moved from my lips and took my nipple in her mouth. She slowly tugged at the hard knot until it was red. *My body was shaking and she was just beginning!*

Sharice began to kiss me slowly down to my navel. She stopped, put her head on my stomach, and told me she loved me. Her hands had began to move towards the heat that was rising between my legs. I could hear her moan at the wetness that had formed. She parted my legs and took me in her mouth. The warmth of her mouth caused my body to erupt sooner than I expected. I began to convulse until I had released all that was stored.

Sharice got up and walked into the master bathroom to get a wash cloth. She always enjoyed cleaning up her "messes" (as she calls them). I enjoyed the warmth of the wash cloth against my swollen mound. She was gentle as she cleaned me. I wanted to feel her again but I could tell that although she was still turned on, she was tired. After she was done cleaning me, she went back to the bathroom to freshen up. I got up and walked to the hallway bathroom to complete the process that Sharice began. She does a good job but I needed to do some extra feminine things. Plus, I also wanted to go check on Robin who was peacefully sleeping through the night. I just leaned there against her doorpost and watched her for what seemed like an eternity. Again, I sighed and journeyed back to our room.

In the bedroom, Sharice had lit a candle and the room was full of lavender which she knew was my favorite scent. I removed my robe to reveal a black nightgown that I had brought while Sharice was on her business trip. I had it in the bathroom under the towels awaiting her arrival. I wanted to wear it when we first got into the bed but when she tackled me, I lost all train of thought. The candlelight danced around her head revealing that her eyes were closed in a restful manner. I slid into bed next to her and put my head on her chest. I listened to her heartbeat as it slowed to a rhythmic pattern. I assumed she was sleeping until she spoke.

"Latoya, I love you so much. You have made my family complete. I will always thank God for allowing me to experience that feeling."

"That was beautiful." I said as I fumbled with the button on her pajamas.

She positioned her arm around me so that her hand rested on her stomach. "Baby, you are such a wonderful mother to Robin. She loves you so much. One day, we will have another little one to add to our family. "

"Would next year be a problem?" I said slyly.

"Why would next year be a problem?"

"Well, Sharice, I am not sure of the exact date until after the ultrasound. But you said that one day you would have another little one added to your family so I was just giving you an approximate time. At least that is when Dr. Williams said in her message to me."

"No, baby, next year is fine for me."

I waited because I knew that her brain had not computed what I said. I could hear her heartbeat steadily increase. It was only a matter of time before I would be able to feel it attempt to jump through her chest.

"Latoya, what are you saying?"

"For you to be book smart, I swear." I chuckled.

Sharice pulled me up off her chest and repositioned my face. I watched as water began to gather in her eyes. In the years that we had been together, I had never really seen Sharice cry. She was always the rock. I mean I am sure she cried but where no one could see her. Tears began to roll down her face as I watched her body quiver with emotion.

"Imagine you a step-mother." I said sarcastically as I slowly turned her on her back.

"Who's a stepmother? Nope, that is not now or ever. Robin and the new baby are our children. They are *our* children *together*. Anyway, steps are made for climbing."

"Oh, Sharice, you are right and I am definitely about to start climbing…right now." I giggled as I began to mount her.

Bye, Bye, Beautiful
Tanaine Jenkins

It is 1997, my senior year at Ribault Senior High School, and this year is destined to be the best year of my life. It is six months from my 18th birthday and 8 months away from graduation. The middle of October brought 67 degree weather, overcast skies, and breezes the desert would kill for. Football season was just starting and you could tell it by the chanting in the hallways. Every football player had on button up dress shirts and ties; some over did it and put on their Sunday best but dress up was a requirement on game days.

I was dialing the combination on my locker when I heard my name over the commotion in the hallway. I looked up and saw Nick coming toward me. Nick and I were joined at the hip ever since the sixth grade. Nick was just a half an inch shorter than me at 5'7" but her shoulders were wider and she was about 20 pounds heavier. She played tail and running back for the varsity football team and was damn good. Me, I wasn't with all that hitting and grunting. Basketball was my forte, give me a ball and a hoop to put it in, and I am in heaven.

"Nikaya!" I said as she got closer.

"What's up?"

"Another way, another day." I said taking my literature book out of my overly stuffed locker. "You on your way to Phys Ed?"

"Yeah, Coach said he wants me to bulk up a little."

"Hell, you already are!"

We laughed. Nick pulled her shoulder length hair from her face and back into a ponytail using the neutral color rubber band on her wrist.

"Hey, Jordan."

"Hey, Nickaya!"

She sighed at my smart mouth. "What are you doing after practice?"

"Hopefully one of your cheerleader friends!" I laughed

She shook her head. "I didn't ask you who you were doing; I asked you what you were doing."

"Oh, my bad. I don't know, why?"

"I need to talk to you."

"About?"

"I'll meet you at your house about 7:30," she said brushing off my last question.

"What do you need to talk to me about?"

She looked around to see if anyone was in earshot. "I got…" The third period one minute bell rang before she could explain. "I got to go. I'll see you tonight."

I shrugged my shoulders and took off in the opposite direction. The late bell rang before I could turn the knob on my third period classroom door. When I opened the door, Ms. Palmer's eyes darted my way.

"Ladies and Gentlemen, it looks like we have our first volunteer." Everyone looked my way. "Miss Taylor, do you have your poem ready?"

"Damn!"

"Excuse me?"

"I said, damn." Ms. Palmer and I never saw eye to eye. I don't think she liked jocks much.

She narrowed her eyes. "Did you just curse at me?"

"No Ma'am, I cursed at the situation. You know…that whole first amendment right thing. The reason we had to write this poem in the first place," I said giving her just as much eye contact as she was giving me.

"Freedom of speech at the right time," she warned. She

stood up from her dark chocolate leather swivel chair and rounded her desk. She perched her 5'8" frame, with her bird nose, and matching bird chest on the front of her mahogany desk.

"Well?" She said giving the floor to me.

Oh how she made my blood boil! I exhaled, then began...

"I want to grow into love and I want my love's roots to travel deep beneath the earth's surface and resurface at the pearly gates of Heaven and tickle the nape of St. John Paul's neck. I want my heart to grow fond of her and bond with her soul. I want to be out of control yet in control all at the same time. I want my mind to wonder to the ends of the earth only to find her there smiling back at me. You see I want to grow into love. I want to be able to look back 50 years from now and have only one regret, and that's not falling in love with her sooner, like in my Mother's wound or in the twinkle of my Father's eye. I want to scream at the top of my lungs that in love I have one and I am deeply rooted with no signs of buckling and every sign of making love ours, with no interruptions and no misinterpretations of what love really is. I don't want to fall into love, because if you fall in you can fall out. I want to grow roots. I want to grow limbs and leaves. I want to grow. I want to grow old and young. I want to grow. I want to grow into love and I want my love's roots to travel deep beneath the earth's surface and resurface in Heaven."

There was complete and utter silence.

"And what book did you steal that from?" Ms. Palmer asked.

"Sorry to disappoint you but this is my own computation."

Ms. Palmer stood up from her desk. "Is it finished?"

"Yes."

"I don't think it is."

"Well I do."

"I want you to finish it by the end of the week and at that time I want it on my desk typed and double-spaced."

"How am I going to finish something that's already

finished?" I asked clearly aggravated.

"I just want you to finish what you start," she said. "You may be seated."

I opened my mouth to object.

"You MAY be seated Miss Taylor," she said with a little more authority.

Oh, she made my ass hurt!

I walked to the back right corner of the room and slid into my assigned seat. I saw others continue to go up to the front of the class and present their poems or raps in the format of poems. I didn't hear any words that came from their mouths because my ears were still steaming from my encounter with Palmer. But when Damita graced the podium she snapped me into the present.

"My crush," she began. "I fall asleep late and wake up early with them on my mind. Their face is haunting me and taunting my mental state, sometimes I don't want to awake from the dreams that they visit me in and when I do it's like the beginning to the very end. I wish I could tell them how I feel. I wish I knew how to tell if my crush is real. But until I get the nerve to speak up and let it be known, my crush will always just be...my crush."

She gathered her papers and hurried back to her seat. I watched her every move. Our eyes met and she looked away.

"Ladies and Gentleman, words are a form of expression, when you pick up a pen and begin to write, you can write yourself into another world. You can open doors to your mind and ideas and thoughts flow through your pen and onto paper."

The bell rang. I grabbed my literature book and hurried towards the door.

"Jordan!" I heard Ms. Palmer call my name from behind me but I didn't turn around. She waited until the rest of the class left. The door closed and she came around to stand in front of me.

"I'm only hard on you because I see so much potential in you." She put her hand on my face.

I pushed it away. "I'm still not interested," I said walking past her and out of the door.

I exhaled. Since the beginning of the school year she's been trying to…I don't know…get me. The more I turned her down the harder she made it for me. As I quickly moved towards the smell of food, my Palmer troubles were soon forgotten. It was lunchtime and a Tuesday, which meant *Traveling Taco* day. The cafeteria staff took a bag of Ranch Fritos and threw them together with some cheese and taco meat and Voila, a dollar and twenty-cent lunch.

"Jordan!" I smelled her before she came to my side.

"Hey, Beautiful!" I put my arm around her shoulders. "You buying me lunch?"

She sucked her teeth. "If you buy my lunch, I'll buy yours."

"It's a deal."

Beautiful was her real name, not a nickname. She said the first time her mother held her all she said was, "Beautiful!" That was an understatement. She could be an *Ebony* magazine model. She had long jet-black hair and was thick all in the right places. She was that *pretty black* or at least that's how my grandmother would explain it. Her dark complexion made her light brown eyes seem lighter and her smile…well her smile could make the devil weep. She was a 9 ½ on a scale from 1 to 10. Beautiful's mental state mirrored mine and that was a turn on. She was smart so I had to be smarter, she challenged me to be perfect, and I loved that.

Beautiful and I had been together since the beginning of the summer. I took notice of her when summer league basketball started and she would come into the gym to watch her brother practice. It turned out she was watching me more than she was watching him. One night after a game, she stayed around and we played around on the court…talking mostly. At the end of the night, we exchanged numbers and we have been together ever since…going on four months now.

When we got to the cafeteria Nick was already at our table.

"Jordan, I'll go get our lunch," Beautiful said holding her hand out.

"What's that for?" She shifted her weight from one foot to the other. "You got funds!" I said teasingly.

She sighed. "Jordan..."

"Gimmie a kiss first." She smiled and leaned towards me. Her lips were soft and tasted like cinnamon sticks. I reached in my back pocket and pulled out my wallet and handed her the whole thing. "Here, just take it," I said acting as though she had taken my breath away. She laughed and walked off.

Nick sucked her teeth. "Man, you are whipped."

"Ya daddy!" I laughed. "So what's up? What's so important that you need to talk to me about it?"

"Later, it's not something I want to discuss right now, not here." She said fixing her ponytail.

I got comfortable at the table and surveyed the room. "Hey, you know ya girl broke up with her boy."

"Which girl, what boy?" Nick asked looking in the direction my eyes were focused.

"The cheerleader girl and the wrestler guy!"

Nick shook her head. "You mean Kennedy and Sean?"

"Who?" I asked with a frown on my face.

"When did that happen?" She asked ignoring my comment.

"When did what happen?"

"You know what Jordan? Sometimes I think that you have ADD," Nick said shaking her head.

I shrugged my shoulders and began to look for Beautiful.

"The break up Jae, when did they break up?" Nick said getting more aggravated by the minute.

"Oh, over the weekend."

Beautiful came back and handed me my wallet. "What do you want to drink?"

I took the two Styrofoam plates from her hand. "Sweet tea, please."

She walked off to get the drinks and I prepared the tacos.

"You got that girl waiting on you hand and toe," Nick said in disgust.

I stopped putting the sauce on the taco. "Am I not

preparing the tacos so that when she comes back all she has to do is sit down and eat?" I said in my best English accent. "Besides, I paid!" I added.

"Anyway," Nick said rolling her eyes. "They'll be back together by the end of the week."

"I don't know. I heard muscle head really fucked up this time."

"How bad?"

"David Justice, Halle Berry bad," I said as I opened another pack of taco sauce.

She let out a long whistle. "That bad huh?"

I popped a Frito in my mouth. "Now is your chance."

She laughed. "Whatever. I'm a commoner, she only talks to kings, lords, and maybe a prince every now and then."

"What are you two talking about?" Beautiful said as she sat down and put the two cups in between us.

"Camille and Muscle Boy…"

"Kennedy and Sean," Nick said interrupting me. "Broke up and Jae thinks I should try my luck."

"Why not? I heard she's a little freaky," Beautiful laughed.

Nick frowned. "One she's not gay and two, I am not a king, prince, or lord."

"What?" Beautiful said looking puzzled.

I shook my head. "Don't pay her any mind," I turned to Nick. "What does not being gay have to do with anything?" I stuck my fork into the Frito bag. "Beautiful is not gay," I said sticking the fork in my mouth.

"What do you call it?"

"She just wanted to see what it was like and she got hooked." I looked at Beautiful; she was reading an *Ebony* magazine with Halle Berry on the front not paying any attention to the conversation at hand.

"Beautiful?" Her eyes didn't move but her lips did.

"Yes baby?"

I didn't say anything so she looked up and saw that I was staring at her. She smiled.

"Captivated by my beauty?" She joked.

I smiled. "Always."

"Oh gimmie a break," I heard Nick say.

We laughed.

"Don't hate cause, I got one!"

We laughed again.

"Beautiful, you think Nick has a chance?"

"With Kennedy?"

I shook my head yes.

"Nick, all she can say is no," Beautiful advised.

Nick shook her head. "Not gonna take my chances."

"I took my chances with Jordan and look where that got us."

I smiled.

Nick sucked her teeth. "It got Jordan giving up her wallet and you smiling funny. Thanks but no thanks."

"Okay, suit yourself," I said with a shrug of my shoulders.

"That's just what I will do."

We finished our lunch and went our separate ways to finish out the school day. I told Beautiful I'd meet her at my car after school so I could give her a ride home. Not before long, the bell rang letting us know the end of the day was here. I went to my locker, put my science book up, closed it, and began walking towards the parking lot. I was weaving in and out of student traffic when I felt a small hand on my elbow.

"Jordan?" I glanced back and had to do a double take.

"Can I talk to you?"

I nodded and made my way to the side of the hallway.

"What's up?"

Kennedy looked around nervously and bit her bottom lip; she played with the end of one of her braids. I looked at my watch. She shifted her weight and looked around again to see who was watching her.

"Never mind," she said and walked away.

I watched her.

"Like what you see?"

I turned to see Beautiful by my side.

"Now I do," I told her as I put my arm around her shoulder.

"What was that all about?"

"I don't know," I said confused. "She said she wanted to talk to me then she said never mind."

"Humph!"

"What?"

"Don't let her get you in trouble!"

I pulled her close to me. "Whatever."

We waited for a car to pass before we crossed over into the student parking lot.

"Beautiful! Beautiful!" We heard her name being called from behind us and turned around.

"Oh shit." I took my hand from around her shoulders.

Beautiful's mother was running towards us in a slow trot. When she got a few feet away she slowed to a walk…this was not a good thing. Mrs. Anderson didn't know about our relationship, she had her suspicions but this here…was not good.

"What are you doing?" She asked Beautiful through clenched teeth.

"Mom, what are you doing here?" Beautiful said with surprise in her voice and on her face.

"Hey, Mrs. Anderson." I said, trying to take the attention off of Beautiful. Mrs. Anderson shot me a nasty look.

"Okay," I said rocking back on my heels. "Beautiful, I'll go wait by the car," I said pointing in that direction.

"Jordan, I'm taking Beautiful home so you might as well go home yourself."

"Jordan, no, you wait." Beautiful looked at me, then at Mrs. Anderson. "I'll be there in second."

I looked between Beautiful and Mrs. Anderson and walked away. There was no way I was going to get in the middle of that. Once I was out of earshot all hell broke loose. There was screaming and shouting that stopped passing cars. It was Beautiful over talking Mrs. Anderson and then Mrs. Anderson over talking Beautiful. From what I could hear, Beautiful was never permitted to look at me again and that she was an embarrassment to their family. Five minutes later when Beautiful came my way she had an aggravated look on her face and tears in her eyes.

"You ready?" I shook my head yes and opened the door for her.

"I guess home is not the destination?"

"Let's go to the lake," she suggested.

"Baby, that's two hours away."

She looked out the window.

I sighed. "Let me get some gas."

The lake she was talking about was in Tallahassee, Florida, two hours from Jacksonville, Florida. If you took Interstate-95 to Interstate-10, you would run right into it. When I was little, my dad would take my brother, sister, and me to the lake on weekends to go fishing and camping. Years later, Beautiful and I would come up here to think or when we just wanted to get away from the real world for a moment. We were quiet the whole ride there. We pulled up to the lake about 6 o'clock and the view was gorgeous. The sun was trying to set and made pink, purple, and orange patterns in the sky. There was a light constant breeze that made the grass dance a slow waltz and the trees wave at the passing cars. We got out of the car and climbed into the back seat. I layed the long way and Beautiful rested against my chest.

"You love me, Jordan?"

"I do." I said as I smoothed her hair down.

"How much?"

Sigh. "So much it hurts."

"Make love to me, make me feel your love for me."

***

We left the lake at about 9 o'clock and I pulled up in front of Beautiful's townhouse after eleven. She looked up at the house as if she was going to her death.

"You okay?"

"No," she sighed. "Love you!"

"Love you, too."

I reached home about midnight. When I walked in the front door of our three bedroom, two-story house, my father was in the den watching T.V.

"Jordan?"

"Yes, sir?" I asked coming from the dark hallway into the light of the den.

"Where you been?" He asked.

"The lake."

"Something wrong?"

I shook my head no.

"You wanna talk?"

"No, sir."

"Nickaya came by looking for you."

"Aw man, I forgot she was coming over. Was she mad?"

"I don't know," he said rocking in his chair.

Silence.

"Mrs. Anderson called looking for you."

"Oh, she did?"

"Was Beautiful with you?"

"Yes, sir."

"What time did you get her home?"

"About thirty minutes ago."

Silence.

"Goodnight, Jordan."

"Goodnight, Pop." I walked over and gave my father a kiss on the forehead, he patted my shoulder, and I went to bed.

That night, in my dreams, all I could see was me running to Beautiful. Everytime I would get within her reach, she would disappear and reappear somewhere else. I could hear Mrs. Anderson calling her name over and over again.

"Beep, beep, beep!"

I opened my eyes only to see a pair of size five feet resting comfortably next to my head. I jumped back.

Sigh. "Justice!" I pushed the feet and the body they belonged to off of the bed.

Thump!

"Man, Jordan!" Justice cried, still laying on the floor.

"You know there are two beds in this room right?" I swung my feet over the edge of the bed and stepped over her on my way to the bathroom. I used the bathroom, brushed my teeth, washed my face. I looked in the mirror, my hair needed braiding and my eyebrows were in need of a good razor.

Bam, bam, bam!

"Jordan, man, c'mon, I gotta pee."

"Go downstairs!"

Julian sucked his teeth and continued to beat on the door.

"Pee in a cup."

"Jordan!" That was my mom that time.

"Ma'am?"

"Stop hogging the bathroom and let your brother in there!" I opened the door and walked out. Julian licked his tongue at me and I shoved him into the bathroom straight into the tub.

"Ma!" He screamed.

"Jordan!" She yelled back.

"Ma'am? He tripped!"

"I'm a trip you!" She sighed. "Go get ready for school."

I walked back into my room and Justice was still on the floor. I kicked her with my foot and stood half way on her back.

"Ouch! Jordan...stop...get up!"

"I'm not going to be waiting on you all morning. So get up, wash your face, brush your teeth, and get dressed. I'm going to start making you take the bus."

I took my foot off her back and she pushed herself up to her knees then to her feet and walked in the direction of the bathroom.

I opened my closet and looked at all the dry cleaner bags with clothes in them. It was October and fall was sneaking up. Moms took all our clothes to the cleaners so it would save time in the mornings, plus, I think she hated ironing just as much as I did. I pulled out a pair of heavily starched jeans along with my brown sweater vest and beige long sleeve shirt.

Justice came out of the bathroom and stood by my side in front of the closet.

"Jordan, what should I wear?"

I sucked my teeth. We went through this every morning.

"Justice just pick sumtin," I commanded as I grabbed my Timbs. "And none of my clothes either."

I went to the bathroom, took a shower, and got dressed. When I walked back into the room, Justice was putting her braids in a ponytail. I looked her up and down. "That's what you wearin?"

She looked down at her orange shoes, purple jeans, and brown shirt then looked at me. "Yeah!"

"Okay." I went to my dresser and took the Joop cologne from the top drawer.

"Jordan, why you wanna smell like a boy?"

I ignored her.

"You dress like a boy too, the girls in my class thought you were my big brother when you dropped me off."

She paused…I listened.

"I told them that you were my sister. Then they started picking at me and saying that my sister was a boy."

I put the Joop back into the drawer. I walked over behind her and put my hands on her shoulders.

"Who it is?"

She smiled. "Who it ain't."

"You my sister?"

"You my sister."

"Forever?"

"Forever."

"Together?"

"No matter what the weather."

"No matter what I smell like, dress like, or look like, I will always be your sister. Okay?"

She shook her head yes.

"Finish your hair and I'll meet you downstairs."

"Okay."

"Love you."

"Love you, too."

I walked downstairs shaking my head from side to side. I leaned up against the wall and took a deep breath. My mom was the only family member that I confided in about my life style. She said she wouldn't be the one to tell my father, she said that was on me…whenever I was ready. I just don't want to disappoint him. He is my father and I know he loves me but I don't think I could deal with him looking at me differently.

"Jordan, Justice, Julian! Time to go." Julian and Justice ran downstairs past me.

"Stop running in your father's house!" My mother yelled from the kitchen. The fast footsteps quickly slowed. I walked into the kitchen.

"Morning," Mom said smiling. "I heard you had a late night, get enough sleep?"

"Yes, ma'am."

She smiled that knowing smile. "Mrs. Anderson called here yesterday."

"Pop told me."

She busied herself with brushing Julian's hair. Grace Jonnie Mae Taylor was beautiful; some people wished they looked like her at her age. She had that short Halle Berry cut that let everyone know that she could keep up with the changing times. She had a little waist and child-bearing hips. Ex-military, she could still run a seven-minute mile. Her 5'9" frame held her 175 pounds very well. Even after three children, she was still pulling phone numbers in grocery stores and stopping cars in parking lots.

"Alright, Justice, Junior, let's go." I said walking out of the kitchen.

There were three schools within walking distance of each other. Sally B. Mathis is where Justice and Junior attended. Justice was in the second grade and Junior was in the fifth grade. Ribault Middle School was 6th grade through 8th grade and Ribault Senior High School was 9th through 12th grade. I was a proud graduate of two out of three of those schools and soon to be three for three.

When I got to school I usually sit in the car and listen to the Doug Banks Morning Show but I wanted to see Beautiful before classes started. I waited at her homeroom but she didn't show. I was sitting in my homeroom staring out the window when there was a knock at the door. I saw Nick's head peeping through the 4x4 window. She opened the door.

"Ms. Watson?"

My homeroom teacher glanced toward the door. "Yes, Nickaya?"

"May I have a word with Jordan?"

"Jordan, don't be long." She said looking at me over her glasses.

I got up from my seat and headed towards the door. I closed the door behind me.

"What's up?"

"Jason said they're sending Beautiful to North Carolina."

"What!" Jason was Beautiful's older brother. He knew about our relationship and he was cool with it, to a certain extent.

"Where is he?"

"Gym."

Before Nick could get the word out good I was running in the direction of the gym. Nick was by my side.

"Jae be cool."

"I'm always cool." I ran through the doors of the gym. Jason was playing basketball. "Jason!" He turned and immediately began to walk my way. "What happened?"

"Last night before she got in my dad had packed her bags. When she came in he said no daughter of his would be a dyke," he said apprehensively. "She's at the bus station as we speak."

My heart sank. "What time does she leave?"

"They wouldn't tell me because they knew I'd tell you."

"Nick?"

"My car's closer," Nick said reading my mind.

We pulled up in front of the bus station and I saw Mrs. Anderson in the parking lot smoking a cigarette. I jumped out of the car and went inside. Beautiful was standing in front of the window facing the bus dock.

"Beautiful?"

She lowered her head. "I knew you would come if you knew." She turned around, her eyes bloodshot red and swollen.

"Baby," I put my hand on her face.

"Jordan, he's sending me to live with my aunt. He said he will not have me embarrass him and my mother by being a dyke." Tears started to fall from her eyes and then mine. "My mother said that it was probably just a phase that I would grow out of with a little counseling," she sniffled. "I told them I knew who I was and who I loved. I told them that we are in love. I told them it didn't matter that you were a girl. I told them I didn't see you as that." Her tears began to flow more freely.

"Shhhhh," I said trying to calm her. "Baby, I'm sorry."

"He said that I was forbidden to see you and if I continued seeing you I would be sorry. He said that you wouldn't see another birthday, Jordan. He said that you tricked me or had me on some kind of drug and they were going to get me help.

"Baby, don't cry. I am so sorry." I said holding her tighter.

"Not your fault," she said shaking her head from side to side. "It wasn't meant to be, at least not now."

I pulled her to me.

"I love you, Jordan."

"And I, you."

"Beautiful! It's time to go." Mrs. Anderson picked up Beautiful's bags and walked towards the loading area towards the bus that was taking her out of my world. She kissed me like it was the last time she ever would and in my heart I knew that would be the case. I watched her get on the bus and I watched the bus until I couldn't see through the tears that clouded my eyes.

"Jae?" I felt Nick's hand on my shoulder. I blinked and

the reality that she was gone.
        "C'mon man, let's go."

Space and Time:
Theory of Relativity

C. Renee Stephens

She lays on the floor beside me, her feet in my lap, and the length of her body giving the seated "L" of me a third dimension. *She makes me bigger.* She has just hung up from a conversation with her daughter who is happily away at camp, allowing us this space and time together. As she relates the conversation, I gaze at her bright, round face and lush body wearing the proclamation **WHATEVER** in bold blue letters across her broad white T-shirt. Her red cotton shorts are surprisingly loose on her hearty thighs-of-steel. I reach to pick a tan speck off the red. I pause to confirm that it is a bit of chocolate chip peanut butter cookie then pop it in my mouth.

I chuckle, "My Lord, girl, did you get any of that cookie in your mouth?"

She laughs, "Well, I obviously needed to share some with you. Do you want another cookie?"

Our laughter is soft and deep. I lengthen it by acknowledging the second crumb I have eaten off her lap. I questioned what others would think if they caught me doing that. Softer still and deeper the laughter as I recognize the intimacy of the act and its primal simplicity. I was an ape picking grubs from my mate's fur, a cat licking my kitten's coat, a woman eating crumbs from her lover's lap.

It is the beginning of the fifth night, the end of the fourth and final day, and I long to reach the sun and hold it still in the sky for just a moment longer. Failing that, I try to put her on pause as she asks me when I will return. To think of return, I have to first think of leaving and I can't. Instead of answering, I relate all the activities that have filled these four days, beats in this strangely arrhythmic composition of long, lazy adagios, followed by blinding prestos, Chinese food dinners and love-making, car rides and conversation, shopping and sleeping, working and playing, looks and touches. I ask her, without forming the words even in my own mind, to linger here in the pleasure of these days a little longer…tomorrow is too far for me to go now. *How could she hear me?*

We had danced in the living room to Marvin Gaye and Tammy Terrell's *It Takes Two*…in the car to James Brown's *I Got the Feelin'*…in the bedroom to The Staple Singers' *I'll Take You There*. The depth and tempo of our sensual joy is rhythm and blues. We had conversed listening to Miriam Makeba, Bob Marley, and Kathleen Battle, exotic melodies distant enough not to distract while intriguing enough to fill the silences. She explains that African Americans truncate English because African languages require less distortion of the mouth and lips…her PhD dissertation was in linguistics…just listen to Miriam. I explain that I was first introduced to South African vocalists when I saw the film *A Warm December* as a teenager and the music made me cry though I didn't understand the words. I remark that my daughter really likes Bob Marley and that I never understood *I Shot the Sheriff*. She tells the story of how her best friend told her to listen closely to hear the poignant political statement beneath the boppin' melody. She jokes that Kathleen Battle's coloratura is orgasmic and I counter that the incredible soprano has a beautiful, melodic bird trapped in her throat.

Yet, this interlude was not all harmonious. There were jarring shrieks of a tired parrot on the third day. We traveled over four hundred miles so that my lover might meet my very dear friend of twenty years. This friend, an insomniac, has two parrots that also had not slept that night and raucously voiced their imbalance. Like Poe's *Raven*, these birds were prophetic as my friend's need for comfort and twenty years of acquaintance between us weighed heavily against my new love. We three formed an acute triangle with my lover too often the angle farthest away. Having been without a romantic relationship for over eleven years, I am unpracticed in equalizing the distances between us. I suffered with my friend's anxiety about her fragile new love affair, my lover's isolation, my social ineptitude, and the parrots' cries.

And though I cringe at the pain in that day, my heart swells when I think of that evening, of the drive home when my lover offered me silence ("do you need time to yourself?") to assuage the hurt. I had not even recognized the extent of my distress until she touched it with her understanding and concern. Like a homeopathic remedy, her love forced the deepest levels of dis-ease to the surface and my stomach cramped so that I had to stop at two consecutive service areas on the NJ Turnpike…the unconscious made conscious and flushed away.

Also, in that long third day, there were vivid moments of truth. My friend remarked that she liked my lover and liked us together because of the ebb and flow of our supportive energy. I believe that we each have a vision of the other and those visions are closely aligned with the ones that we would like to have of ourselves. So, because she sees me as I want to be, she helps me to become that teacher, that priestess, that warrior. And I pray that I help her to become that teacher, that healer, that princess that she is in the eyes of my heart.

My friend, the seeker, also asked about the relativity of time and of its subjectivity. She explained that time always seemed to pass so slowly when she was in unfamiliar situations, yet time moved more quickly as she became more and more comfortable in them. I remarked that I had read a book that said that Africans had a keener sense of the relativity of time and space than Europeans. As I have written this reflection, I have felt that relativity powerfully. I have felt the length, height, and width of time. I have seen years stretching far behind me as I try to think of my life before meeting my lover. I have tried to grasp the brief moments of ecstasy I have shared with her and hold them longer and deeper within me. I have felt time as music, with changing tempo, rhythms, harmonies, and melodies. And I dance.

But what is dancing but making love set to music playing? Like Shirley Horn's breathy contralto croons co-mingled with the dance that is lovemaking set to the Jazz of a different kind entirely; the moans and croons and shrieks and gasps of improvising bodies trying to express experiences beyond words. I have tried to reduce the climax of this dance to metaphor, mostly to enjoy my lover's blush and her "Early Morning Premature Ejaculation Weeping Orgasm." Awakening in gratitude and disbelief in the arms of my beloved, I am embraced by the scent of dawn and smooth, warm, soft flesh. I gaze at the changing morning light on the hard and soft curves of her toasted pecan profile. Her eyes open and her spirit whispers "Good Morning," like a spark to the fuse that burns quickly. My fiery body begs. Her body still wrapped in sleep, heavy, and dozing, acquiesces.

I mount, search her eyes (her spirit whispers, "Take me"), explode, and overflow with tears of gratitude and disbelief in the magnitude of the gift of the "Long, Slow, Oceanic Swells Orgasm." Standing hip-deep in the ocean, watching the swells building toward breakers, hoping to catch a Big One and body surf onto the beach, I lay beneath her. Her weight pressing into me as if she could sink inside me, melts within me beginning with hips and thighs then stomachs, breasts, shoulders, faces. Our hips begin to undulate, making swells that I watch, hoping to catch a Big One. But these are not breakers and are too long and slow. Their power is deceptive, pulsing through me rhythmically, sapping my strength while filling me, stretching me, expanding me wide and deep as the ocean like a "Rapid-fire Orgasm." Her mouth is hot, deep, and sweet. Soft lips open... grasping. A nimble tongue is darting...searching. I taste her sweet heat, sipping first then gulping in great draughts, my greed frustrated by the impossibility of my need to drink her in.

I lift my head and gaze upon her beauty, feel the steam rising from her blush. Her hips rise in slow circles, the power of her steely thighs lifting me. I moan. Sink my head to taste her mouth, the line of her chin, the flush of her neck that is salt-tinged. The gate in the deep of me opens. Her hips rise with determination. I bury my head in her neck as her thigh strokes my clit. Her hand rises to my breast. My clit explodes in spasms that are bullets to my brain fired in short spurts. I can hardly catch my breath. The pleasure borders on pain in its intensity but fades quickly to small tremors that radiate in rings...echoing pleasure. The feeling is like after a terrifying roller-coaster ride that makes you beg to do it again even though while you were riding, you wanted it to stop and silently vowed that you would never do it again.

The Big One. How do you describe an experience that blows me out of my body and makes me feel for a moment, a second, less, more, completely alone in the universe, yet impossibly united with it? How do you describe the subtle difference between the two Big Ones? There is the implosion that contracts all the muscles of my body starting with and towards my sexual center, fiery, and exhausting, leaving me breathless and thirsting...a star dying into a black hole. The other one is an explosion that sends shards of icy energy outward through every limb, blowing off the top of my head, leaving me reeling and dull-witted and shivering...a star is born.

How vibrant and elemental and universal this loving. Objectively, all of this experience and more have transpired in four days. Subjectively, it is impossible to imagine the length, width, and depth of it fitting into 96 hours. Relatively...well, two women of our mass exploding at the speed of light squared would indeed represent the birth and death of stars. Yet, and still, beneath the rhythm and blues, the world music, opera, and jazz, the metaphysics and quantum physics and geometry, there are quiet conversations, walks in the park, and candlelit meals. There are small moments of simple mathematics in which one plus one equals one.

She lays on the floor beside me, her feet in my lap, the length of her body giving the seated "L" of me a third dimension, stretching me as large as the universe...and growing.

Love Has Never Felt Like This
Jewells

I'm nervous.

Somewhere in the airport a special someone is waiting for me. Someone whose words I fell in love with, the woman, whose melodious voice made every word sound like a song, sending chills down my spine. In a few minutes, for the first time, I'll stand face to face with a woman I fell in love with online.

At the top of the escalator there are families holding stars and stripes signs welcoming their soldiers home and children waiting in anticipation for a parent coming home from a business trip. People are all over, flowers in hands, smiles on faces. There are so many people but no one resembling the face that I've only seen on a computer screen. There is no one possessing those deep brown eyes that hold so much hunger for me. I search and search to no avail. I reach for my cell phone and hold down her number on speed dial. Automatically my phone flips shut, disconnecting the call, when I feel a tap on my shoulder. I turn around expecting to see the radiant smile of the woman whose teeth are so white, Clorox bleach would be jealous. Instead a man in a black suit stands in front of me.

"Can I help you?" I ask in a voice dripping with irritation.

He uses a dingy handkerchief to wipe sweat from his bald head. He doesn't say anything, just holds a sign in front of my face with my name written on it in black marker.

I nod my head. "I'm Camille Thomas. Who are you?"

He looks me over, flashes a sincere smile. "You look just like she described."

"What did you say?" I'm unsure whether I should be flattered or offended.

"I...I didn't mean anything by it. Your friend, Ms. Jada Woods, she said when I saw you, I'd know. She said your eyes held the key to life and that your smile would melt a blind man's heart."

My cheeks grow warm at the memory of when Jada told me those very words over the phone when I emailed her a picture of me for the first time. She had been in a meeting with a client when the chime of a new message popped up on her computer screen. She checked it immediately because the client she was with had her husband email a listing of a house that they wanted to check out. When Jada saw that the email was from me, she told me she contemplated whether she should open it or not. She opened it. As soon as she saw my picture, she excused herself from her client, went into the hallway and called me. Her Phyllis Hymanesque voice sang out like a Jill Scott poem when she gave me the warmest compliment ever.

"When did you see me smile?" I want to know of the man in front of me.

"When I tapped you on the shoulder. I guess you thought it was your lady friend."

I had thought it was her, wished it was her and not some man in a suit. I feel so vulnerable, so foolish for letting a stranger see my anticipation.

"Your picture doesn't do you any justice," he continues.

"She showed you a picture of me?"

"How else was I supposed to know how you looked?"

I shrug, look around, feeling silly for asking such a rhetorical question. My chauffeur picks up on my nervousness. He reaches out his big hand to introduce himself. "I'm Benny. Benny Robinson."

His palm is moist. I refrain from rubbing my hand on my

jeans not wanting to be rude. He is my transportation after all. Benny grabs my carry-on bag and walks me to baggage claim to pick up the rest of my things. He tells me that Jada had a last minute business meeting. "She wanted to be here for you but business is business."

Business is business. Wonder whose words those were. His or Jada's? Maybe this wasn't such a good idea. I mean, really, how much can you learn about someone over the Internet? Here I am, traveling over a thousand miles to meet a woman I fell in love with over the Internet. If that didn't make sense, her not being here to pick me up definitely does. Benny tries to make small talk as we wait for my luggage. I've watched my bags go by twice on the luggage carousel not once making any attempt to grab it or point it out to him. For ten minutes I've been contemplating with myself; trying to decide if I should grab the little bit of cash I have and give it to Benny for his wasted trip and send him on his way. Each time something inside me begs me to wait things out. Maybe business *is* business. What would I do if my job demanded my attention while the woman I loved waited for me at the airport? How would I respond if the tables were turned?

Benny's hard breathing lets me know I need to make a decision. "You haven't seen your bags *yet*?"

I look up at the big, dark man standing next to me with impatience in his eyes. The carousel is no longer turning. There are only two bags on it and both are mine. Without me saying anything, Benny moves to get my bags. He grabs my suitcase and garment bag off the AirTran belt. "Ready?"

I nod an unsure nod.

"We're right out front." Benny uses his head to point us in the direction of his vehicle. He walks us to a black Lincoln Town Car then sits the bags on the curb as he reaches in his pocket for the keys.

I place my hand on top of his before he unlocks the trunk.

"Hey, I'm sorry about that." I gesture back toward the

sliding glass doors we just walked out of. "Back there, I had a lot on my mind. This isn't what I expected. I didn't mean to make it uncomfortable for you."

Benny puts his left hand on top of mine, smiles without showing his teeth. "I understand. I've been around a lot worse."

He pops the trunk open. There's a purple bag, my favorite color, lying in the center of the trunk's floor. A single white rose sticks out. He picks up the bag and hands it to me. Inside the bag is an envelope. Two hearts intertwined are drawn on the front. One has my name on it and the other holds Jada's name. There's also a homemade CD entitled *HeartBeats,* a bottle of my favorite Neutrogena body oil with the light sesame scent, and two small bottles of essential oils: Blue Nile and Pussy. I smile at the innuendo.

I read the card while Benny puts my luggage in the trunk.

Dear Camille,
I never thought I'd feel this way for a woman I've never met. You came along just when I had given up hope. From day one you've shown me nothing but sweetness in a world full of sour. You've shown me that good things do come to those who wait. I'm very grateful to have you as a part of my life. I can't wait to hold you in my arms.
Yours truly,
Jada
P.S. Can't wait to smell you. Smooches!

I'm smiling so hard my cheeks hurt.

"I take it your lady friend has a way with words," Benny says. All I can do is smile even harder. He opens my door but I don't get in. The smell of lavender stops me in my tracks. The scent that Jada adores dances around my nose.

I look back at Benny. "Can't be."

"What?"

I ignore him. Bend my head down to look inside the

car for myself. I feel like the Geto Boys. I feel like my mind is playing tricks on me. I blink my eyes twice.

"Your vision is fine," she speaks.

"Oh, my goodness...you're here!" I don't make any attempt to contain my joy. I almost trip into the car as I move to hug her, feel her body in my arms for the first time.

"Jada, I can't believe you're really here."

"Don't know any place I'd rather be," my Internet lover says.

I truly melt under the sound of her voice and the embrace of her warmth. Benny is still holding the door open. Jada turns to him then winks.

"Thank you," she whispers.

He closes the door. I playfully slap her across her thigh.

"You had me worried for a minute."

"Camille, nothing could've kept me from being here with you...nothing."

"I didn't think so." I cover my face with both hands to hide my shame. "But when I saw some strange man holding a sign with my name on it, I didn't know what to think."

Jada pulls my hands down from my face and brushes her thumbs over my closed eyes. "Sweetie, look at me."

It's hard for me to open my eyes. I feel guilty for thinking so negatively of a woman who has brought me nothing but sunshine. She's the reason I'm here. I shouldn't have let a moment of uncertainty take that away. Slowly I open my eyes.

"I just didn't know what to think." I repeat, tears forming in my eyes.

Jada holds my hand in her lap. "Camille, listen to me. Even if I did have a business meeting or a demanding client, there's no way I'd pay some stranger to pick you up."

"But..."

She shakes her head, points her finger toward the driver's seat. "Benny is my cousin."

My mouth hangs open in disbelief.

"I can't believe this. I got punked by my own girlfriend

and her cousin."

We both laugh.

"If you ever had any doubt about how I feel for you, you can throw that demon out the window right now," Jada says.

She moves her head towards mine and rubs her nose back and forth across mine. Her lavender scent relaxes me, calms my anxiety. She reaches behind my head to move my lips closer to hers. Her soft lips touch mine and I swear my heart stops beating. I lose myself in her kiss.

"I love you," she whispers without separating her lips from mine.

"I love you, too."

The Lincoln comes to a stop behind a silver Mercedes-Benz CLS500. SHETHNG is on the Florida license's plate. Benny gets out and puts my luggage in the trunk of the Benz.

"We're going to take my car from here," Jada tells me. She gets out of the car and says a few things to Benny. He looks back at me through tinted windows. He can't see me but smiles anyway.

My golden complexion lover sways back over to the car she surprised me in. Her skin is the color of honey, kissed by the sun. I'm captivated by her. Her jet black wavy hair is pulled back in a bun. She looks regal, yet sexy at the same time. The only makeup on her face is a pink tinted gloss that makes her lips beg for my attention…and that she'll never have to do. I want to remove the white sundress from her body and make sweet love to her. I want to hear her sing my name and harmonize with her. I feel myself getting warm just watching her. The disappointment I felt minutes ago no longer matters. I feel as if that insecurity never transpired.

Jada opens my door, reaches out her hand to help me out. "There's been a change in plans," she says. "I know you've got to be hungry."

"Yeah, after a seven hour flight, I can eat."

"Good." She smiles.

Over Pad Thai we talk about our first emails, those first

words of attraction. "When you first emailed me, I was expecting the same old foolishness," she tells me. "I was tired of women sending me messages saying one thing but when it all came down to it, they weren't ready for anything serious."

I nod in agreement. "I read your ad and knew immediately that I could fall hard for you."

Jada's eyebrows raised in amazement. "Really?"

"Really. You just had a way with words," I tell her.

"You've got to in my line of business. If you don't say the right thing, you can kiss your client and a fat commission goodbye."

"Oh, so you're admitting that you said what sounded good and what you thought women wanted to hear?"

"I think you know the answer to that."

She's right. I look in her eyes and see nothing but honesty. I hear her voice and only truth resonates from her lips. I inhale another forkful of those sweet noodles and shrimp and wash it down with a sip of water.

"Good, huh?" Jada asks.

"This is some of the best Thai food I think I've ever had."

"Sometimes I come here two, three times a week. And it's not close to my house either but it's my favorite restaurant."

My interest peaks. "So, what made you punk me like that at the airport?" I smile.

Jada doesn't smile back. "I regret that."

"Huh?" I'm confused.

She puts down her fork and puts her hands in her lap.

"When I first thought about it and talked it over with Benny, it sounded like a good idea. It sounded like something I wouldn't mind having done to me. It's all about the element of surprise, you know. But when I saw the look on your face when you walked up to the car, the look of someone who had been let down, I wanted to hit erase and start all over again."

"Really? I looked that disappointed?"

She nods. "If I had to do it all over again, I would've

done what everyone else does. Stood at the arrival gate with my arms open wide to welcome you to my world, welcome you home." Her eyes twinkle with sincerity.

"I'm going to be honest. I was hurt at first. I felt let down. I wondered if it was a sign of things to come. I thought about turning around until Benny opened that door and I smelled you. At that moment everything changed." I throw my hands in the air. "Let's just forget about all of that. What happened doesn't even matter anymore. You're here and I'm here. That's all that matters."

Jada reaches across the table. My hand meets hers halfway. Our fingers intertwine. Silently we comfort each other. We finish our food with idle chatter. Not really talking about much, just enjoying each others company.

"That was good," I say as we walk back out to the car.

"I'm glad you liked it."

"You definitely have to bring me here again before I fly out."

"Don't remind me." Her voice drips with sadness. "I'm missing you already and you just got here."

I rub Jada's hand as it rests on my thigh. "Me too, baby. Me too."

She winks her eye at me then blows me a soft kiss before putting the car in reverse. "Take a little nap. We have a thirty minute drive ahead of us."

Between the long flight and the anxiety from the day's events, closing my eyes is the best thing I can do right now. Plus, *itis* is kicking my butt something serious. I lean my head back on the head rest, close my eyes, and enjoy the ride.

"Wake up, my sweet. We're here."

Somewhere between Fort Lauderdale and Miami, I lost consciousness. Jada lives in Coral Bay, a town about twenty miles north of Miami. Being a real estate broker she has the upper hand when it comes to property. She told me that her home was about fifty grand cheaper here than anywhere within an eighty mile radius. "I definitely got more land and square footage moving out here," she admits.

"This is great." I compliment when we pull into her three car garage.

"It was a steal." She comes around and opens the car door for me. "Come on, let me show you around."

From the outside you could tell that the house was big but the inside looks like a mansion.

"Every room represents a different mood," Jada says.

My eyes wander in awe.

"I can count the times I come in here." She says, referring to the first living room. "It's basically just for show."

The room looks like something you'd see in a magazine. Hardwood floors, contemporary tan leather furniture with a chaise lounge representing different shades of brown. On one wall is a German shrunk in dark oak that one of her clients from Germany bought her as a gift. On the other wall, opposite the window, are two pictures in sepia color: one of a woman, the other of a man.

"Those are my grandparents," Jada explains.

We bypass the kitchen, sun room and the other living room. "This is the imagination room," she stops in front of a closed door. "Anything goes on in here as long as you leave your inhibitions at the door." A sly grin crosses her face. "We'll go in there in a few."

She grabs my hand and leads me to the master bedroom.

"This is huge. It's almost the size of my whole apartment back in D.C."

Jada points to a room inside her room. "Check out the bathroom."

In the corner of the bathroom, under a window, is a Whirlpool bathtub; one that I could sit in forever. A walk-in-shower is to the left of the tub in its own little corner. The bathroom is nice and spacious. It's decorated in the color of ivory, pure and innocent. She comes up behind me, wraps her arms around my waist, and kisses me on the side of my neck.

"How about a nice bath to get you relaxed?"

The touch of her lips on my skin causes me to shiver. My answer comes in the form of a moan. Jada turns the water on. Mostly hot with just enough cool not to scald me. She pours in some lavender bubble bath and a little of her own bottle of Neutrogena.

"When you told me about the oil, I went out and bought some. I wanted to know what you smelled like," she reveals.

My cheeks spread from ear to ear. She looks at me. "You know what makes your smile so beautiful? Your eyes smile too. I can have a bad day and all I have to do is look at a picture of your smile and my day gets brighter."

"Awww, that's so sweet, Jada."

"It's the truth."

She comes over to me, puts her hands on my face and reintroduces her lips to mine. She kisses me so delicately. I could stand here and kiss her forever but she stops our kiss. "There's more where that came from," she assures me. "But first, go ahead and finish looking through the rest of the house. I'm going to get your bags." She blows me a kiss on her way out.

I decide that I have the rest of the week to tour the house. The calming aroma coming from the bath calls out to me in a whisper. I test the water with my hand; it's just right. I undress where I stand. "This feels so good," I say aloud once I've emerged in the water. I lay my head back on the bath pillow and let the water take me to another place.

"I see you started the festivities without me."

"How long have you been watching me?"

"Long enough." She says, dropping an article of clothing with every step she makes toward me. Hunger is painted in her hypnotizing brown eyes.

I stand up and let the suds slide down my tanned skin. My nipples grow hard from the shock of the cool air and my burning desire for the woman standing in front of me. She steps into the tub. "You're beautiful," she tells me.

I tell her the same thing. "I've waited a long time for this moment."

"Eight months but who's counting."

We giggle like two schoolgirls. Our lips touch again. Desire takes over. Her tongue touches mine. My knees buckle. I almost slip but Jada holds me up.

"I got you," she says.

And that she does in more ways than one. We wash each other, slow and delicate like newborn babies.

"I've been dreaming of this moment ever since I first heard your voice," I tell her.

"What is it about my voice that took you there?"

"It's so alluring, so enchanting. It's like when you talk all I hear are possibilities that I want to turn into reality."

"That's deep." She moves a loc from my face. "I love your locs."

"I do too. My mama's genes didn't make it easy though."

"That just makes your journey more meaningful. You've spent time with them, talked to them, nurtured them, watched them grow to be what they are now. If they loc'd overnight, you wouldn't appreciate them as much because there was no process."

"I never looked at it like that." I run my fingers through my freshly twisted locs. "I guess I always find some kind of reason to resent that Mexican side of me."

"You shouldn't, baby. That's a part of who you are."

"See that's why I love you. You bring so much positivity into my life."

She kisses me on the forehead. "And I love you for the happiness you bring into mine." She puts her hand in the water and reaches for my legs. She rests them on top of her left knee. She lathers a purple sponge and washes my feet. I'm so self conscious about my toes; I've never thought they were cute. But she kisses them, each one as if they're the best set of feet she's ever laid her eyes on. That gesture alone makes me toss my insecurities out the window. We finish washing each other, leaving no body part unclean. She pulls the plug to the bath.

"We'll rinse off in the shower."

We help one another out of the tub and hold hands as we walk to the shower. We rinse and dry each other off. Jada hands me a white robe. "This is for you."

The robe has my name sewn on it with purple thread.

"Awww, thanks."

She puts on hers with pink letters. We stand in front of the door where we have to leave all inhibitions behind. "You ready?"

I nod in agreement. She opens the door to a room that has a Moroccan theme. It's filled with deep burgundies, lilacs, golds, turquoises, purples, and greens.

"This is my favorite room in the house," she tells me.

The walls are painted in a deep lilac color. In the middle of the floor is a huge, elevated floor cushion with burgundy satin fabric sewn on it. Under the cushion is a large North African designed rug that covers most of the floor. Around the edges of the room are a variety of pillows that coordinate with the room's theme. Sheer lace hangs from the ceiling surrounding the floor cushion. Candles and incense are everywhere.

Jada pulls the lace back. "Lay down," she instructs.

She goes over to an accent table by the window to light a few Sandlewood scented incense. I watch as the dancing smoke permeates from those slender brown sticks and intoxicates my senses with a dose of faraway. It makes me feel high and carries me to another place.

"You okay?" She asks.

"I'm just caught up in the moment."

She removes her robe, then mine. "Lay on your stomach. I'll be right back."

Seconds later I feel her straddle me. Her warmth rests on my backside. She pours a warm liquid owning a familiar sesame scent on my back. I moan in contentment as she rubs my upper torso. Her pleasure in pleasing me brings a smile to my face. She leans down and I feel her nipples making an impression on my back. She kisses my neck. I turn my head towards her. I want my lips to make a connection with hers again. She raises her body up just enough so I can turn my body over. This kiss holds more passion, more hunger than the previous one. It lasts for what feels like two eternities!

Jada kisses me on my neck, making her way to my breasts. She traces her tongue around each nipple, back and forth, back and forth, teasing them. She takes both of my double Ds in her mouth at the same time. "Damn, Jada," I moan.

I feel myself getting wetter and wetter by the second. This feeling is too good to be true but I'm loving it all the same. She releases my breasts and makes a trail of light kisses down to that soft spot in between my thighs. "I've been waiting forever for this moment," she tells me. Her eyes connect with mine and she smiles. I smile back. My hips rock in anticipation of her first breath on my love below. I spread my legs wider from Coral Bay to Africa. She inhales me and intoxicates her senses in my scent. "You smell divine."

Softly she kisses my womanly lips. She parts my folds open with her tongue. Her mouth is so warm and it feels so good. I feel myself losing control and it is exactly how I want to be. I want to lose myself in Jada and I want her to lose herself in me.

"Dame mas," I tell her in my native tongue.

She loves it when I speak Spanish. She wraps her arms around my thighs, pulls me closer and goes deeper. She gives me more just like I requested. My moans grow louder and become words. I feel myself shaking underneath her.

"Not yet," Jada pleads.

She unhooks her arms, comes up for air, and lays on top of me. She puts her thigh in my wet spot and straddles her moistness across my thigh. Her breasts make love to mine. She rides me and I ride her back. Together we're in sync, making sweet music in Morocco.

"You feel so good," she whispers in my ear.

I smell myself on her breath and it turns me on even more. She hums in my ear words from a song I've never heard before. Her heartbeat against my chest beats faster and her breathing is harder. She's somewhere else and I'm at the same place she is. The euphoria has taken over me and it lets us moan in harmony.

"Camille," she sings. Her voice sounds ever so sweet as she reaches her peak. I feel her throb against my thigh. Within seconds my walls contract. My body jerks underneath her flesh. Jada rests her head in the groove of my neck. I rest my head on top of hers and we lay there letting the aroma of our love making engulf our senses. The scent of lavender and sesame, a smell I never want to stop smelling, permeates the room. We lay still as we try to get our heartbeats back to a normal pace. She rubs her fingers through my locs. I play with a few of her curls that have fallen from her bun in the heat of passion.

"I don't want this moment to end," I tell her.

"Then stay. Don't leave."

Somewhere between calming down from my high and the love of my life asking me to stay, I cry. Love has never felt like this.

The Place for Pride
Dillon Watson

Dee Hall sat back in her chair and rubbed her dry eyes. She had spent the entire morning reading through the minutia of a financial report. Blinking, she reached for the ringing phone.

"Dee Hall, PBS Financial Group."

"Hey Dee, it's Keisha. I'm calling to remind you about dinner Thursday."

"Uh, what did I promise again?"

"Damn, Dee, you need to get away from work sometime. You agreed to go to dinner with me and T. I'm just letting you know her friend Shay will be there and we're *not* trying to hook you up."

Dee gripped the phone. "Shay? I don't remember you guys talking about a Shay." She said despite the lump lodged in her throat. *There was no way this Shay was her Shay.*

"Shay Foster. She's one of Dee's girls from…"

"Sorry, Keisha, I…I've got to go. I'll get with you later this week." Dee hung up the phone and put a trembling hand to her forehead.

"Shay." She whispered as she felt the sting of tears against the back of her eyes.

For two years she had wanted so badly to believe she was going on with her life without the woman who had once been everything to her but now…no! Now, nothing, she wasn't going to relive those old feelings of pain and betrayal. She'd learned to live with the fact that Shay didn't want to be with her anymore.

Pushing back her chair, she paced around her plush office, trying to get her emotions back under control. But despite her best effort, she couldn't block out the memory of the day Shay told her it was over. Dee came home from work exhilarated with the news she had received the big promotion she'd been angling for. It meant a move to Atlanta but both she and Shay had agreed that was what they wanted. *But then things changed.*

Dee covered her mouth against the pain and took a deep breath. Shay was the past and Dee would make sure she stayed there. She returned to her desk to call Keisha and cancel. There was no way in hell she was going to allow her ex back into her life or her soul.

As she reached for the phone, her hand stopped in mid air. "Shit, maybe I should go and show her I'm completely over her."

Grabbing her stomach, she rested her head on her desk. *Did she have the strength to face the woman who made her ache with a mere glance?* She closed her eyes and forced herself to remember how good they'd been together and how bad she felt when it ended. *Did she really want to chance her heart again?*

"No, I paid my dues. I have nothing to prove." Pushing Shay to the back of her mind, she returned to her notes without making the call.

***

Damn, am I doing the right thing?

Despite her early resolve, Dee couldn't pass up the chance to see Shay again. Round and round she'd gone until going seemed the only thing to do. In the end, she decided facing Shay would give her the upper hand and prove she was okay. Frowning, Dee stood in front of the full length mirror checking her reflection carefully. She wanted to make sure she looked good but not like she was trying to impress someone. Her white, button-down shirt was crisp and the sleeves were rolled up just enough to show off the dark skin of her forearms. The seams in her loose fitting jeans were tight. At the last minute, Dee decided to pull back her shoulder length dreads into a ponytail and forgo the usual baseball cap. Before she could talk herself out of going, she grabbed her keys and headed out the door.

Twenty minutes later, with her heart beating like wild drums, she pulled into the parking lot of *Reggie's Place*. Accepting a ticket from the valet parking attendant, she opened the heavy wood front door and stepped inside. The dim light in the restaurant caused her to remove her sunglasses.

"Dee, over here."

Steeling her mind, she turned and started walking in the direction of Keisha's voice. She tried hard not to look too closely at the familiar figure sitting next to Keisha and her girlfriend T. It didn't matter. Even a cursory glance at Shay made her breath lodge in her throat. For a moment her world tilted and she was surprised when her body didn't. Exhaling quietly, she tried to get her mind back together as pain battled lust for dominance.

"Shay," she said acknowledging the other woman.

"You know each other?" T asked, looking curiously from one friend to the other.

"Yeah." Dee replied, trying to seem nonchalant as she dragged her eyes away from her ex lover.

"Old story." She added and put her sunglasses back on. But even the darkness couldn't dim how good Shay looked or ease the throbbing between her thighs.

"Not that old." Shay protested with an easy smile as she stood up.

"You still look the same." She dipped her head in greeting.

"So do you." Dee was proud her voice didn't reflect the pounding of blood in her veins.

How had she forgotten how much that rich, deep voice affected her? Against her will, her eyes returned to Shay. Her ex was about her height at five feet eight inches with a short cut fade. Her light skinned, muscular body was the same as it had been two long years ago and she still had that boyish look and crooked smile that made Dee so damned hot.

"You visiting or what?"

"Interviewing. I have some prospects lined up." Shay watched Dee intently as if looking for a reaction.

Be cool, she's watching. Dee nodded, ignoring the knot that had formed in her stomach. *Shit, she can't move here!* Before she could comment, the hostess announced their table was ready.

Throughout dinner, Dee was quiet, replying in monosyllables when addressed. She played with the food on her plate, her appetite for food gone, replaced with another.

"I'll be right back." She finally said and headed for the bathroom. Once there and safely away from Shay's overwhelming presence, she took out a paper towel, silently cursing the shakiness of her hands. Wetting it, Dee pressed it against her hot cheeks. As much as she tried, she couldn't block the memory of how good the heat from Shay's lips had once felt against her face and body. She fought the memories of the amount of time they had spent satiating each other's desires. She was feverishly staring at her reflection, wondering how the hell she was going to get through the rest of the evening when the door opened. In the mirror she saw Shay walking toward her.

"You a'ight?" Shay asked. Her eyes were trained on Dee's reflection as she stood beside her, shoulder to shoulder.

"I ate too much." Dee lied and looked down.

Shay turned to look at Dee. "I'm sorry if you were nervous on account of me but I'm not sorry I came. I had to see you again."

Dee balled up the paper towel and turned to face Shay, her eyes glittering with anger. "What the hell for? You're the one who told me you didn't want a damn thing to do with me, remember?" She said bitterly.

"I was wrong, Dee." Shay said, her tone pleading. "I tried for two years to get you the fuck out my heart." Her eyes zeroed in on Dee's lips. "But here I stand wanting to kiss you so goddamn bad I can taste it."

"That's not going to happen." Dee backed away until she was up against a wall. "I don't want to kiss you anymore." She said with more bravado than she truly felt.

"Bullshit!" Shay advanced on Dee with the smile of a predator. "Why back away then? You scared?"

Dee lifted her chin. "Hell, no! Don't give yourself so much credit. I got on with my life."

"Prove it. Kiss me, it ain't gonna hurt nothing."

Dee licked her dry lips and swallowed the lump in her throat. She was trapped. If she ran, Shay would know, but if they kissed, Shay would know. She stood still knowing how easy it would be to lean forward and press her lips to Shay's and how satisfying it would feel to welcome Shay's warm tongue into her mouth. Her stomach muscles tightened and she shivered.

That was the sign Shay needed. She put her hands on the wall, leaned forward and kissed Dee passionately, not holding anything back. Dee's senses swam when Shay's tongue entered her mouth. She put her hands behind Shay's head, holding her closer. The tightening in her abdomen moved down between her legs and she got wet. Shaken, she pulled back, panting as her limbs trembled. Dee dropped her hands as if they were on fire. She wanted to run away from the pleasure humming through her body but the heat pouring off Shay's body was too enticing.

She looked into those golden eyes bright with desire and she was lost. With desperation, she reached for Shay, bringing their lips and bodies together. This was what she had been missing for the past two years. This was why she worked so hard, leaving no time for thought. Her heart and body wanted *this woman* in her arms and *no one* else.

Shay pushed her thigh forward, parting Dee's legs. She grabbed her hips and groaned when she felt Dee's heat on her thigh.

"Baby." She whispered passionately and moved her mouth to Dee's neck. Although it had been two years, she found that extra sensitive spot with no trouble and bit it gently.

"Shay!" Dee pressed her center against Shay's hard thigh. Her only thought was relief from the throbbing in her clit.

Shay slipped her hand between their bodies and unfastened Dee's jeans. She shivered when her fingers dipped into Dee's silky wetness. Parting Dee's sex, she painted her clit with the juices and began stroking…slowly at first, then she picked up the pace as Dee's breathing became more ragged.

"Cum for me, baby." She whispered, her breath hot against Dee's ear.

Dee stiffened her legs as the pressure inside built until it had nowhere to go, but up. She bit her lip to keep from screaming as wave after wave of ecstasy exploded through her body. Spent and trembling, she rested her forehead on Shay's shoulder and began to come down from the euphoria.

"This…this doesn't prove anything, Shay." She said, disgusted that she had succumbed so easily. But she was even more disgusted by the hunger still left in her body and her heart.

"Tell me you don't want me again." Shay's husky voice raised goose bumps on Dee's arms. Shay raised Dee's chin and looked into her eyes. "I want you…but more than that I want so bad for you to be my girl again," she said softly. "I'm sorry I threw away two years 'cause of my stupid pride."

When the door to the bathroom opened, Shay used her body to shield Dee. The older woman who entered eyed them suspiciously before entering a stall.

"You broke my heart." Dee whispered fervently, her eyes on the occupied stall.

"I know," Shay whispered in return. "I wanna make it up to you, please?"

"Maybe we should talk about this later."

"Tonight," Shay pressed. She reached for Dee's hand and brought it to her lips. "Please?" She begged unashamedly as moisture gathered in her eyes.

Dee nodded, suppressing a moan. "I want to hate you." She said and let out a sound that was a cross between a laugh and a sob. "You can come to my place but only to talk."

"Just talk." Shay agreed before sneaking a quick kiss.

***

Dee let herself into her apartment an hour later and wondered what the hell she was doing. She'd be crazy to give Shay another chance with her heart but deep inside she already knew. Walking through her place, she quickly straightened up the already clean rooms. By the time her doorbell rang, her heart was hammering in her chest. Taking some deep breaths, she went to answer the door.

Her heart jerked and her body began to tingle when she saw Shay standing in the doorway displaying a sexy smile.

"Come on in," she said breathlessly. "You want something to drink?"

"I'm cool for now." Shay entered the loft and looked around. "Nice place." She complimented, checking out the stylishly furnished room. "I like it. Looks like you."

Dee smiled. "Thanks." She said with her eyes drawn to Shay's smile.

She touched her own lips and it was as though she could feel Shay's imprint from earlier. Dropping her hand, she exhaled.

"You wanted to talk." She reminded Shay as she led her to the soft, white sofa.

"Uh...yeah." Shay cleared her throat, studying her blunt cut nails. "Dee, you know I ain't much for words. Shit, I was scared you'd move here to the big city and see I was a *nobody*," she admitted looking up. "You know that I'd lose my pride... but without you, I am nobody. I wanna be back in your life; and whatever I have to do, I'll do it."

"You realize I make even more than I did before?" Dee asked feeling compelled to bring up the source of past arguments.

"Baby, I don't care," Shay said, meaning every word. "I

love you. My pride has no place between us. Please, please give me a chance to prove I've changed."

Dee's eyes glistened with tears. She had dreamt of this moment so many times while laying in her cold, lonely bed. *Did she dare trust Shay again?* Dee looked at the proud woman who for the first time was willing to beg and she knew she had to take a chance to get back the love she'd lost.

"Shay, will you kiss me?"

Shay was on Dee almost before she could finish her request. She took Dee's face between her hands, looking into her big brown eyes.

"I love you." She said and placed a gentle kiss on the brown lips she thought she'd never feel against hers again. She continued to place light kisses on Dee's mouth until Dee grabbed her head and held their lips together. Licking Dee's lips, Shay moaned when Dee's lips parted. Stroking her lover's mouth with her tongue, Shay's hand slid down to squeeze a small, supple breast. With one last lingering kiss, she sat back and smiled sexily.

"You still hate me?" She asked, unbuttoning Dee's shirt.

Dee laughed throatily, running her hands along Shay's strong arms. "What are you going to do to change my mind?"

Shay spread Dee's shirt and let her eyes travel down dark chocolate skin. She licked her lips at the sight of the glittering belly ring. "Oh, Dee, this is *so damn sexy*." Running a finger from Dee's lips down to the top of her jeans, she asked, "You got a bedroom, baby? I don't think this white couch can take all I plan to do."

Dee led the way up the winding staircase to her bedroom which overlooked the downstairs. She walked over to stand near the bed.

"Man, this is nice." Shay came to a halt and looked around at the expensively furnished room.

Dee, noticing what had Shay's attention, quickly got undressed. "Come here lover," she beckoned.

Shay turned and took a few steps as her clit hardened.

"Dee…uh…" She stopped trying to talk and just looked at the perfection before her. Dee had always been in good shape but now her body seemed leaner and more toned.

"See something you like?" Dee teased. She loved the feel of those bright eyes on her skin. When Shay moaned, she stepped to her and pulled her close so that they were breasts to breasts, hip to hip.

Shay moistened her dry lips. "You." She said and slid her arms around Dee's back. "Only you." Leaning forward, she kissed her with something close to reverence.

Dee wrapped her arms around Shay's wide shoulders and deepened the kiss. She moaned at the tightening in her groin.

"You have on too many clothes." She murmured and nipped Shay's ear.

Shay's hips jerked at the feel of Dee's teeth against her ear. Hard and throbbing, she let Dee go and grabbed the bottom of her shirt, pulling it up over her head. Dee hummed appreciatively at the expanse of taut skin exposed. She ran her hands along the strong shoulders she'd missed so much. After kissing each shoulder, she lowered her hands to Shay's belt. Undoing the buckle, she unsnapped her jeans and pulled down the fly.

"Pull off your pants." She ordered, her eyes bright with need.

Shay smiled knowingly. She pulled her jeans off slowly and kicked them aside. Dee's breathing quickened as she took in the sight of her lover in her sports bra and knit boxers. She helped Shay pull off her bra and attached her mouth to a hardened brown nipple. Switching to the other nipple, she sucked until she heard Shay hiss.

Dropping down to her knees, Dee kissed her way to the top of the boxers. The push against the back of her head from strong hands made her clit swell and moisture painted her thighs. She ran her tongue along the ridges of stomach muscles, thrilled when Shay shivered. Reaching for the boxers, she slid them down and helped Shay take them off.

Dee leaned back and looked up at the magnificent body in front of her. The thatch of brown curls stood out from the golden yellow of Shay's body. She breathed in the musky scent of arousal and her pulse quickened. Leaning forward, she parted Shay and caught the drops of passion with her tongue.

"Shit!" Shay groaned, cupping Dee's head and pulling her tongue closer to her throbbing need. "That's it, baby." She bit her lip and concentrated on keeping upright.

Dee licked Shay's clit slowly. It had been two long years and she didn't want to rush anything. Reducing the pressure, she twirled her tongue around, never lingering too long in one spot. Hearing the increase in Shay's breathing, she slowed down even more and used her face to rub against Shay's wetness.

"Harder, baby!" Shay ordered, grinding against Dee's face. "I need it so...bad." She said and caught her breath as the pressure in her groin started to build. She spread her legs further, allowing more access.

Hearing her frustration, Dee pressed harder and held the flatness of her tongue against Shay's clit as her lover rode her mouth. She felt the tightening in her lover's thighs and knew she was close to release. Increasing the movement of her tongue, Dee almost came herself when she heard Shay cry out. She didn't let up until Shay reached down and eased her head back.

Shay collapsed into a heap on the thick carpet next to Dee. Her breathing was ragged as the spasms continued to surge through her sex. Taking deep breaths, she waited for her heartbeat to return to normal.

"Damn baby, that was good. Me and my body missed your sweet touch."

Dee smiled and stroked Shay's stomach. "My touch has missed your body." She sniffed her upper lip. "And I missed the smell and taste of you."

"I was so blind." Shay blinked against the threat of tears and stood up. This was not the time for tears. She held out her hand to help Dee up and they moved to the bed where they laid on their sides looking at each other in wonder.

"This is where I belong. Thank you for giving me another chance." Leaning forward she gave Dee a kiss. "I'm sorry I was so stupid. And girl, it might take me all night, but I'll show you just how much." She ran her fingers over the curve of Dee's hip.

Dee rolled over and arched her back, saying, "I have plenty of time."

Straddling Dee's hips, Shay spread Dee's arms above her head. "I got you now." She rocked her hips against Dee's damp center. Letting go of Dee's hands, she propped herself on her elbows and dropped fleeting kisses on Dee's lips, enjoying the taste of her own passion.

Growling, Dee laced her fingers behind Shay's hand to maintain contact. She arched her hips when Shay's tongue entered her mouth. Dee moved her hands down Shay's back until she cupped her behind and brought their centers closer together. Shay let go of Dee's mouth and rotated her hips to stoke the fire between her thighs. Bending down, she sucked a large, dark nipple into her mouth.

"Yes!" Dee shouted, bucking against Shay in abandonment. "Oh Shay, I'm going to cum!" Concentrating only on the pressure building against her throbbing clit, she stiffened her legs and panted. With a flash of light behind her eyes, she raised her torso as the pressure exploded. Tears stung her eyes and she could only gasp for breath while Shay continued to grind against her.

"So close." Shay hissed then came with a loud grunt. Sweating, she rested her forehead against Dee's shoulder as her body trembled. "Oooh, that was good." She whispered, blowing out air. "But I want more. Maybe after a couple more times, I can go slower with you."

Dee licked her dry lips. "Hmm, maybe after a couple of more times I can let you." She said and reached for the woman who owned her heart.

The Birthday Present
C.R. Hill

Today is my birthday and I get to celebrate with 500 of my closest friends. I always have my party at the club cuz I work there as the manager. I love it. I'm surrounded by lots of half naked, somewhat intoxicated women, hot music, and a clean up crew in case we trash the place. There's always a huge cake and two or three of my beautiful ex's (dressed in next to nothing) who volunteer to serve the patrons and me. For one night, the club turns into the lesbian "playboy" mansion, and of course, you can call me, Hef.

I'm sitting at the door taking money, giving Ugly Grace a break. It's cool cuz as I take the money I'm also collecting birthday kisses and presents. Working the door gives you first crack at all the cuties. Sexy Sistahs, Lovely Latinos, Beautiful Asians, and even some fine ass white girls, all have to file past me. This job is a dream, especially for a good looking stud like me.

There was a slight lull in the action so I stand up. I get a good glimpse of myself in the wall length mirror, not bad for 37! I check my fit from head to toe. The leather pants were a good choice tonight. They hung just right on my 5'7" athletic frame. Not too tight, not too loose. My ass looked good in them. I was also glad I had worn the soft pack too. It filled out the front of the pants perfectly. I liked that you couldn't tell that I was packing unless you got really close. To ensure that some cutie would do just that, I wore my Black Kenneth Cole loafers and my tight black shirt. It was a little girlie, I had to admit, but it showed off my muscled arms nicely. I always added something feminine cuz the kinda girl I wanted to attract liked that. I was way over the stone butch/pillow Queen phase. I wanted a woman who would work for hers! I liked the way my brown face and bald head looked coming outta all that black. I look soft and hard at the same time. I think that's a hot combination. Then the voice in my head yells, "Enough already, damn!" Lord knows how I musta looked standing there ogling myself. Besides, the lull was over and the girlies were coming in again.

When I looked up, I saw this beautiful goddess-girl smiling at me. I was stunned momentarily by how incredibly gorgeous she was. Her mouth was amazing. It was the perfect combination of kissable lips and straight, white teeth. I was so attracted to her that I couldn't look at her directly. As she searched for her money, I suddenly felt goofy. But one look at those red spiked heels and my outer-butch got a chokehold on my inner geek enough to say, "Hey, beautiful. Put your money away. You are *my* guest tonight."

She looked at me still smiling with those pretty white teeth and said in a low sexy voice, "Why thank you. My name is Imani. And you are?"

Her voice made my clit vibrate. I was turned on cuz the soft pack had been banging around between my legs for about an hour already. I tried to squeeze my legs shut to calm myself but all that did was make the soft pack bulge out. I saw her eyes dart from my eyes to my crotch then back to my eyes, which only made things worse. My horniness made me a little surly, so I continued, "I am whoever you want me to be, as long as you save me a dance later."

Inside, I always crack up when I hear shit like that come out of my mouth. By nature, I am a dork. Luckily, I am usually a charming dork, especially when I am blind-sided by unadulterated deliciousness. She let my corny line slide with, "I'll bet you are. Be sure to find me and I'll pay what I owe you."

She then held the back of her hand out for the stamp. I

turned it over and planted a soft kiss on her palm. "That's your stamp for the night. Don't worry. There is no way in hell I would forget your face, gorgeous." She thanked me again and began to walk away. *Umph, umph, umph! God dayum! It's gonna be a good fuckin' night!*

As she threaded through the crowd, my eyes followed her like she was a snake charmer and I was a big ass cobra. Being the perpetual student that I am, I studied her hips as though I was cramming for a test. I took them in as they moved gently from side to side to the rhythm of the African drums that often thumped in my head. She looked like she had some Indian in her (as we say in the south) because of the red undertones in her brown skin, her chiseled chin, high cheek bones, and long dark hair. Her eyes were wide set and almond shaped. Her features were such a mix of cultures that I thought "island girl" or maybe I was just hoping cuz I am sucker for them.

Her tight low-rise jeans showed off her small body but I could see through her baby doll shirt that the ta-tas were full and banging! Her sexy hands looked graceful yet strong. Her nails were long and painted red and I couldn't help but imagine them raking deep red streaks up and down my back as we...

"Stop looking at that girl's ass and gimme the money, dammit!"

Uuuugh! Looking into Grace's face would make anybody's dick go limp. She looked like my old Uncle Ray, complete with moustache and beard. Her breath smelled like stale cigarettes and you could probably cut glass with that rock of wooly hair under her arms. I always wondered how the hell she got so many fine women. Good hygiene ain't a high priority for everyone, I guess. I gave her the money and melted into the crowd before she blew her breath on me again and singed my eyebrows off.

The club was dark, it was packed, the music was loud, and hot as hell. The crowd seemed to be smushed into one big jumble of sweaty arms and legs. Faces and bodies of all different shapes and sizes moved to the beat. Of course, some moved to their own music, but hey, all that mattered was that they seemed to be having a good time. I spotted Imani making her way toward the bar. I had just started in her direction when I felt my body being encircled in a big bear hug that damn near lifted me off my feet.

"Happy Birthday, Papi!" A high, tight voice whispered.

Oh Lord. It was Wanda and she had me in her death grip, smashed up against her huge 42 double Ds. I felt like I was gonna suffocate! Hell, there were definitely worse ways to die.

Wanda smelled like Jean Nate, that perfume that my mother used to wear and it kinda made me queasy. That smell also transported me back to the time when in a moment of weakness I had taken her home and fucked the shit outta her. *Damn my horny self during PMS! Damn me! Damn me!* Because of that incident, I hadn't been able to shake her since.

"Thanks, Wanda. You having fun?" I said wondering if she could hear me since the music was so loud and I was basically talking into her titties.

She responded, "Yes," while I pried her arms from around my waist and her hands from my ass.

"Well Papi, I got a nice birthday present for you. It's at my house and you can come get it anytime." She said with a wink and a sexy smile. I have to admit that I have a weakness for confident big girls and Wanda knew her shit was da bomb!

Still, once I was free, I began my retreat backwards, made the telephone sign with my thumb and pinky finger, and mouthed, "Call me." She seemed to be satisfied with that and turned in time to swallow up another unsuspecting butch in her breasts. I got to the bar just as the bartender was bringing my goddess-girl her order.

The bartender said, "$6.50, please." Imani didn't notice me standing right behind her. When she tried to pay, I made eye contact with the bartender who promptly pushed her money back at her. She looked a little puzzled then I breathed in her ear, "I told you, you belong to me tonight," and gave her waist a little squeeze.

She turned around and our faces were almost close enough to touch. She didn't move away. She looked me in the eyes and said, "Well thank you again. Are you this nice to all of your guests?"

I answered, "Trust me, not at all…just the incredible ones." *And she was incredible.*

Once more, I was caught off guard by her beauty. I observed bright flecks of amber in her brown eyes. Her gaze was a little guarded but steady. I stared for a moment longer, hoping I was looking sexy instead of how I was feeling, which was like she was a T-bone steak and I hadn't eaten in days. I leaned my body into hers without dropping our gaze.

She licked her lips.

I licked mine.

Her eyes said, "Kiss me."

Mine said, "OOOO-K!"

But just as I was close enough to kiss her, I changed my mind. Instead of slobbing her down, I picked up the glass of water that the bartender had left for me behind her and took a swallow.

"Enjoy the drink, luv. I'll be back for my dance later."

I loved the look of surprise and acceptance on her face. I didn't give her a chance to say anything before I was back in the crowd. But from that moment on, I knew she was as hungry for me as I was for her.

At about midnight, the DJ stopped the music and the whole club sang, "Happy Birthday" to me. The only present I asked for was kisses from cute girls, so that's what I got as I moved around people. Pretty femmes smooched me all over. Even a couple of icky butches took shots. When I caught myself in the mirror behind the bar, there was so much lipstick on my face that I looked like I had been on the losing end of a beat down. I turned to get a napkin but was surprised to find Imani standing there with a cloth going, "Lemme help you."

She put the tip of the cloth in her mouth and sucked, wetting it lightly with her spit. I imagined that that napkin was my clit and almost came right then and there! I leaned back against the bar. Imani positioned her body between my legs and began to wipe gently. She took her sweet time, especially around my mouth. I pulled her so close that I could feel her breath on my face.

She said, "There," when she was finished but she didn't move away.

"Where's my birthday kiss from you?" I said trying my luck.

She titled her face up slowly toward me. I titled mine down. She put her manicured fingers around my neck. I locked my fingers behind her back. My eyes said, "It's ooooon now!"

And just when I thought it was gonna really jump off, she put the cloth down and said, "I think you've had enough birthday kisses for one night."

As she unclasped my fingers from her back, I thought, *Daaaaaaang. She got me back!* I picked up the cloth cuz I noticed that I was drooling a little with excitement. I had to have her. She was about to walk off but I grabbed her hand and pulled her to me.

"I'd trade them all for one kiss from you, Mami."

She covered my hand with her other hand and said, "I'll bet you would," then slipped free and switched her cute ass into the mass of vibrating bodies.

"Thaaaat's right." I smiled with lust and admiration. "Tease me, goddammit, witcha fine ass." I couldn't wait to make my move.

On the dance floor, booties were bouncing everywhere. I saw Imani in the middle of the floor holding court. I slid up behind her close but not touching.

"May I have this dance?" I asked as I wrapped my arms around her waist again. Imani leaned her ass into me which I took as a yes. When her booty bumped my soft pack, I heard her catch her breath. My clit was jumping again so I pressed into her harder. My boxers were soaked. I was pleasantly surprised when she pressed back. *Man, was I glad I had packed!*

The music switched to dance hall, which made Imani move her hips in slow, steady circles. She tilted her butt back slightly so that she was almost dancing on my hips. I smelled amber as she reached up and wrapped her arms around my neck, opening her body to me, inviting me to touch her. I began to move my hands up and down her sides. I got even more turned on when I saw her nipples harden against her shirt. Those nipples were calling me like crack to a dope fiend. I let my hand brush them occasionally cuz when I did, she pushed her ass into me harder. Before the song was over, I turned her around so that we could do a little grinding, chest to chest, belly to belly. She let me feel her every curve. While still moving, the goddess-girl put her head on my shoulder. I reached down between her legs and pressed her clit hard with my fist. I felt her put her mouth on my neck, breathing me in, kissing softly. When she finally bit me, I knew she was ready. And so was I.

She said, "I gotta run to the little girl's room. I'll be right back."

I said, "How 'bout that? Me too! There's one in the office. Come with me. It's clean and there's no waiting."

She put her hand in mine without hesitation and we walked toward the back of the club. We stepped into the office and I shut the door. I thought I'd be chivalrous and let her go to the bathroom before I jumped on her but when I tried to step aside to let her pass, *Deliciosa* didn't let go of my hand. I didn't wanna get too excited but I could almost see the electricity between us. The goofy part of me was doing a happy dance in my head, chanting, "It's going dooooown, it's going doooooown!"

Then I looked at Imani and got myself together. She was truly breathtaking. Her lips looked delectable and I couldn't wait to feel my tongue in her mouth. Our eyes locked as I took a step closer to her. I wanted to slam her against the wall and ram my tongue down her throat but something told me to wait...to let the moment unfold. I am generally not patient but for once, I'm glad I waited. Imani took one red nail from her free hand and outlined my lips. Then she moved closer to me and said, "You have the sexiest mouth I've ever seen." The hunger in her eyes froze me to the spot. I noted that I was holding my breath and hoped to God that something happened quickly before I passed out. Finally she asked, "May I have this dance?" And before I could exhale, lil mama pushed *me* against the wall and rammed her tongue down *my* throat!

We kissed, licked, grabbed, and bit each other like the world was about to end: fast, furiously, hungrily, viciously. Imani undid my shirt and bra like a pro, while I ripped her clothes off. I felt her nails digging into my skin hard, leaving little cuts and marks. My clit felt like the plant in *The Little Shop of Horror*, needy, pulsing, and growing out of control. Her naked body was a religious experience and all I wanted to do was be her loyal worshiper for one night. Her breasts were a little smaller than I had imagined but they were perky and her nipples were huge. I pulled and squeezed them softly, then harder, until I heard her say, "Please suck them, Papi!" Baby tried to help by arching her back up. My mouth closed around the left one and ravaged it like a newborn. Her belly pressed against mine as she grabbed my head to keep me from moving. I took the hint and kneaded the right one. She whimpered like a puppy.

Imani reached for my pants but I stopped her. I love to get a little fuck juice on my leather; that way I can relive the episode as I wipe them down later. I slammed her against the office wall and shoved my thigh between her legs roughly. Goddammit, she was soaking wet! Her juices ran down my pants leg like a river. I gripped her hips tightly and thrust as she ground her pussy hard into my thigh. Our rhythm quickened. Her breath was like fire on my face, on my neck, in my ear. She mumbled incoherently. I didn't care what she was saying. She coulda been chanting incantations to the devil as long as she didn't stop. She hooked both arms underneath my shoulders and held on. Her tongue was all over me. My hands and tongue touched any part of her that I could reach. We were both moaning so loud that before I knew it, the coat check girl knocked angrily on the door, telling us to keep it down. At that moment, I made a mental note to fire her hater ass. But I put my hand in Imani's mouth anyway, not so much to muffle her screams, but more cuz I liked the way it felt to control her.

I lifted my gorgeous partner in crime up, carried her over to the chair and sat her on my lap, back to me. Her back was a gorgeous long, brown V, sloping gently into her heart-shaped ass. We both knew what she wanted. Her dripping pussy basically grabbed my soft dildo through my pants. The girl had skills. As Imani rubbed and bounced, I pulled a latex glove outta my drawer and slipped it on. I twisted three fingers together and pushed them into her hot wet pussy without missing a beat.

She moaned, "Give it to me, baby. I need it good. I need it like this." She rode my fingers and dildo like a stallion. After a few minutes, her moans deepened, her pace quickened, and her body began bucking like a wild bronco.

She screamed, "You're making me cum, baby! Baaaaaabbby!" I felt her nails dig into my legs as her orgasm lifted, twisted, and let her drop like a tornado. She slumped backward in a heap into my arms.

I was gonna be a gentleboi and hold her for a moment but my little island princess had plans of her own. I thought we would take a minute to catch our breath but she turned around, dropped to her knees in front of me, and began pulling my pants off like I had done hers. When they were down around my ankles, she lifted the dildo outta the way and said breathlessly, "Your scent is driving me crazy. I need to taste you." I tried to protest that I didn't have any more protection but before I could finish my sentence, she shoved both hands under each of my ass cheeks, lifted me to her mouth, and slammed her face into my pussy. I knew that she was literally trying to climb inside me cuz when I pulled her head back by her hair, even her forehead was wet. *Daaaammmm! Now that's what I call commitment!* I wanted to object more but her moist mouth encircled my clit (which felt like it was hanging down to my knees) and all I could do was make promises to God that if I didn't get an STD outta this, I'd...I'd...I'd....I just prayed not to get an STD.

Her tongue was lapping at my entire pussy, a finger on her right hand was playing with my asshole, and two fingers on her left hand were thrusting inside me. *God-damn!* Her expert multitasking had me wondering if she had extra mouths and hands that I hadn't noticed before. Then she hit that spot and all wondering ceased. I grabbed her head and held it where it was.

"Lick it, Mami. Fuck me. I'm gonna cum in your mouth. I'm cumin, baby!"

My body shook hard and I grabbed her tighter cuz I wanted her to feel my cum shooting down the back of her throat...thank God for female ejaculation. With that thought, I came in a warm stream in her mouth. She swallowed every drop and laid her head on my still throbbing pussy. Though I was tired, I couldn't stop there. I pushed her onto the floor, turned her over onto her belly, gathered some stray coats under her hips, and pushed my pussy almost into her asshole. I positioned my arms on either side of her ass cheeks and humped her 'til I came in a gush down the crack of that find round booty. Then I was done.

When the fog cleared, I could hear people banging on the door screaming. Apparently the strippers had arrived and needed the office to change. Imani and I dressed hurriedly, she helping me, me helping her, hooking, latching, and zipping. She looked at me and said, "Take these. I want you to remember me," then handed me her cute little thong panties. They were soaked through. I immediately crammed them into my mouth which made her laugh.

I said, "Thank you, Mami, but I'm sure I'll see you again. At least I hope I will."

She flashed those white teeth at me and switched out the door. I followed her outside but lost her almost right away because people were already pulling me outta the room and putting me in handcuffs. *The show was gonna be kinky.* Before I was completely shackled, I found Imani's hand one last time and said, "Hey, my name is Tory, just in case you were wondering."

She smiled with that beautiful mouth of hers and said, "Why yes, I certainly was wondering what you were calling yourself. Well nice to meet you, Tory. I love that name."

"I know you do," I said.

"Do you have bail money, just in case?" She asked.

"Hopefully I can talk these people outta pressing charges just because we borrowed their little office space for a moment or two of passion. They shouldn't be able to arrest people for making love." I said with a wink.

"Well, if they do, call me, and I'll get the lawyer. I'll get that nice white guy. He's used to our antics by now." Imani smiled that smile that always made my heart sing.

"F'sho, Boo-Boo. I'll call and let you know what's up once I know. Now scoot, luv."

Imani hugged me again and whispered in my ear, "By the way, Happy Birthday, baby! I love you."

I kissed her softly on her lips. "Thank you, my luv. I love you too."

About the Authors

RENAIR AMIN - wears many hats. A prolific author, her works have appeared in various publications including *GBF* (Gay Black Female) *Magazine*, *SABLE Magazine* (of which she is a board member) and *DEEP HUES* e-zine. She has also been featured on Nghosi Books, Femme Noir, Sistahs for Sistahs, and Soulful Pen Xpressions Web sites. As a spoken word artist, Renair has performed nationally, gracing the stage in cities including Rochester, NY, New York City, Los Angeles, CA, and her hometown of Philadelphia, PA. She is also active in her church's ministry. A member of Unity Fellowship in Brooklyn, N.Y., Renair is co-chair of the Performance Arts Ministry and chair of the David's Poetry Ministry. Recently, Renair Amin added entrepreneur to her list of talents by forming Pmyner, Ltd., a company created to provide services to the Lesbian, Gay, Bisexual, and Transgender literary community. The Web site includes an online community forum and a radio station, Invisible Verse Radio, on which she hosts Myne Myc, a talk show that showcases LGBT spoken word artists and musicians. She currently resides in Bronx, NY.

STEPHANI MAARI BOOKER - is a Black dyke Gemini mental sex fiend writer queen who lives in Minneapolis, MN. She is an editor at the African American newspaper *Minnesota Spokesman-Recorder* and holds an MFA from Hamline University of St. Paul, MN. Her work has been published most recently in *Blithe House Quarterly* and in *60 Seconds to Shine: 221 One-minute Monologues for Women*, edited by John Capecci and Irene Ziegler Aston (Smith & Kraus, 2006). Visit Stephani's Web site for more information about her work: http://members.iphouse.com/athenapm.

DAVITA D. BAKER - for this author, a penchant for writing developed at a very early age. As years went by, what also became evident was her love and affection for women. Having been labeled lesbian by societal imposed guidelines, she took her pen even deeper into heart and hand and began to tell a true story through poetry and spoken word performances. When asked where her ideas for writing poetry come from, she simply states, "I am my poetry." Her favorite poet is Audre Lorde. Future endeavors include cultivating her desire to compile and have published an anthology of poetry dedicated to Lesbian Emotions and to be recognized as one of the next great authors in the world. There are three projects in the works, two fiction novels and the aforementioned anthology. She currently resides in upstate New York with her two children.

LAURINDA D. BROWN - divine destiny is what motivates mother, daughter, and author, Laurinda D. Brown to do what she does --- write novels that portray real people in real life situations. Growing up in Memphis, TN and graduating from Howard University exposed her to diverse sides of human nature and gave her the opportunity to observe people and their situations. She wrote to work through her emotions, to find explanations for other people's circumstances, and to try to humanize idiosyncrasies. Writing expresses her take on the world.

TRISH CARTER - was born and raised in Far Rockaway, NY. She started her first career at the age of five with a top of the line Easy Bake Oven. Later she attended the prestigious Johnson & Wales University where she majored in Culinary and Pastry Arts. After finishing with two degrees, she then worked for some of the most noted hotels, restaurants, and bakeries in four cities, until she finally opened her own pastry shop in Philadelphia. After following her career passion, she decided to indulge into her deviant, erotic nature and wrote about it. So, if you read her stories, she asks that you read with an open mind, your panties or boxers off, and your hands away from your body. Presently, Trish is flying the friendly skies around the world as a Flight

Attendant for Continental Airlines. She is also working on her second novel, *Linger II, Passion is Inside* and other projects.

MUSEZETTE CHARLES - is an ethereal goddess currently inhabiting this terrestrial plane. Her purpose is to share her thoughts about love, spirituality, history, and culture with those seeking to explore the sublime. It is her sincere wish that fellow travelers on this journey who seek higher virtues will gain some degree of edification through the reading of her written works.

SUE HARMON - lives in a small town in Mississippi. After almost 15 years in the computer industry she returned to school as a full-time Psychology major at the University of Southern Mississippi. She is a single mother to her son Timothy. She enjoys computers, gaming, reading, cooking (a Food Network addict), road trips, biking, hiking, and sharing her esoteric experiences with others.

C.R. HILL - is a writer, teacher, drummer, dancer, transplanted east coaster from D.C., living in San Francisco, CA. Whether erotica, poetry, or drama, her characters help you see the humor in almost any situation. Her main project is writing Black Girl Stories for the Black girl in all of us.

TANAINE JENKINS - her editorial reviews say she "traps you with her words" and the hard facts seem to back up the implied claim of wisdom and experience that transcend Tanaine's style. In her mid twenties, Tanaine is responsible for an extremely hot new novel, *A Different Kinda Luv*. The novel, which she wrote over three years ago, blends diverse influences, including Homosexuality, Heterosexuality, and different forms of mental and physical abuse. The first month the book went on the market, it sold more than 100 copies. For a self-published novel that doesn't have much publicity that is unheard of. Around the time that *A Different Kinda Luv* was released, Tanaine was active in the spoken word circuit, making appearances at Boom Town and winning first place honors in the *2006 Mitz Sweetheart International Pageant* for her talent. She was also asked to speak a Convergy's third annual Black History program, where she wowed the audience with her spoken word talent. Where had she been before then? Her entire life, it seems, had been an accelerated learning experience, preparing for her writing career. A Jacksonville, FL native, her lyrical gifts became apparent when she was ten years old. As an Airman First Class in the United States Air Force, she further developed her education by attending the Community College of the Air Force and double majoring in creative writing and business management. Tanaine came into her own when she was introduced to a Nokturnal Escape at a local Jacksonville poetry club.

JEWELLS - began writing in early 2000. While working a boring job she felt a need for more in her life. One day she sat to a blank screen and her fingers introduced her to a new love, writing. Moving around her whole life, she has recently planted her feet in Charleston, South Carolina. She lives there with her family and two cats. She is fast at work on her debut novel. Check out her Myspace page at: www.myspace.com/the_literary_obstetrician for more on Jewells.

TASHA C. MILLER - is a poet and spoken word artist venturing into fiction and lesbian erotica. Her collections of poetry, *For Black Girls Who Feel Ebony And Essence Are Not Enough* (WCP February 2001); and *AssOut Incoherent Thoughts and Poems of an Unemployed Black Girl,* (WCP October 2002) are the first two installments in her *Black Girl* trilogy. Currently working on her first novel, Miller is a student at Harvard University.

CLAUDIA MOSS - writes full-time and resides in Atlanta, GA. Her writing has appeared in *The Hoot and Holler of the Owl, Catalyst, Labrys, Black Romance, Jive, Venus,* and *Black Issues*

Book Review Magazine. Moss is the author of the adolescent novel, *DOLLY: The Memoirs of a High School Graduate.* She is currently completing a second novel and collections of erotic short fiction and poetry.

NIK NICHOLSON - was born in E. St. Louis, IL, where she was raised until her family relocated to Las Vegas, NV at age 10. For the first time the world was not black and white. There she experienced a spectrum of people, cultures, and life styles. During this time period she became an avid reader and discovered her love for the arts and writing. Nik's appreciation of art and literature helped her find a voice. She began expressing herself on both paper and canvas. Her candid descriptions of life during her spoken word performances created an appreciation of her writing. Writing has allowed her a chance to explore other forms of art. She has played pivotal roles in poetry workshops, independent publications, and theatre. Currently she lives in Atlanta, GA, where she continues to pursue writing opportunities.

TONYA PARKER - multitasks in Maryland, DC as a writer/ trainer/educator/massage therapist/energy worker. She is studying to become a naturopath. Her work can also be found in Alyson Books' *Testimonies: Lesbian Coming Out Stories 3rd edition* and *Spirited: Affirming the Soul and Black Gay/Lesbian Identity.*

AIMEE PEARL - is the nom de plume of a kinky brown-skinned bisexual femme gender-fucker who currently resides in that sex-positive salad bowl known as San Francisco. She enjoys bossy Butches and adoring Daddies, but the softest spot in her heart belongs to her girlfriend, who is delightfully all of the above and more. *Bringing Up Daddy* was inspired by a couple of different ex-lovers, and Aimee thanks them both.

CHANDA RAE - is known by friends as C. Rae and the founder of Sistahs for Sistahs, one of the largest and most successful online dating communities for Lesbians of Color in the U.S. More than a Web site for dating, S4S is a community built by a woman with a vision of love. In October 2005 the site added an online discussion forum and recently celebrated their one-year anniversary with 387 forum members, over 20,000 posts, and 21 active forums! Her latest project has been S4S's own line of erotic lesbian photography, which is now one of the hottest selling items on the market. The project came to life after seeing a great need in the community of color for something new yet done with the same style and tastefulness of her Web site. As the tag line says, Sistahs for Sistahs is truly "Where Love Stories Begin." As another great addition to so many different projects, in late 2007, Chanda's book entitled *The Weekend* will be released.

NIKKI ROSE - makes her debut in Nghosi Books' *Longing, Lust, and Love: Black Lesbian Stories* with the skillfully written, *Heartfelt*. Residing in Indianapolis, IN, Nikki wrote stories in her youth as a relief from a busy household with seven other siblings. It was the initial spark where she found her niche for writing romance novels. With a double major in English and African-American Studies at Indiana University, Nikki wrote artist bios for the *I.U. Soul Revue*, a traveling band sponsored by the University. However, her interest in music led her to concentrate on writing poetry and lyrics, abandoning her novelistic skills until a move to Duluth, GA sparked her interest in writing about Lesbian Love. It was there that she found her niche for writing. Although she continues to write artist bios, press kits, and critiques music for the Karla Starr Band, she has taken an interest in writing short stories as well. Nikki has currently written two lesbian romance manuscripts, which she plans to have published to share with her eager audience in the near future.

C. RENEE STEPHENS - is a 44-year old native Philadelphian. Her writing reflects her experiences as a United States Naval

Academy midshipmen, a black belt in Uechi-Ryu karate, and a student of African/Asian spiritual systems. She is a history doctoral student, concentrating on Africa with an emphasis on women's organizations and agency. She is blessed with her experience as a lesbian --- the romance, sexuality, difficulties, and triumphs of a loving partnership between two African-American mothers.

S. STEPHENS - is originally from Miami, FL, but currently lives in Northern Virginia. S. Stephens has been living in the Northern Virginia area for about 14 years with her partner of 15 years and their 10 year-old daughter. S. Stephens has a Bachelor's Degree in Criminal Justice and is employed by the state where she works during the day and by night is an aspiring writer.

SUBMERGE - now a resident of Atlanta, GA is best known as Yvette Michelle Hall who debuted with *Unconventional Love* in March 2005. Her book featured three intriguing and intertwining storylines ending with an unexpected twist. True to her writing style, Yvette has produced *Once Bitten* which is determined to deliver an elevated page-turning absorption and sexual heat as *Unconventional Love*. Look for her future writings under the pen name Submerge and visit her Web site at www.submergebooks. com.

TAWANNA SULLIVAN - lives in New Jersey with her life partner/domestic partner. She is the webmaster for Kuma2.net, a Web site which encourages black lesbians to write and share erotica.

W.L. TRACY - resides in Atlanta, GA. She is a working professional with a passion for writing. She has recently had one piece of her literature published as the lyrics for one of the tracks on artist Dezz's debut CD, *Spend the Night*. These lyrics introduce the listener to Dezz's contemporary Jazz CD with the track, *Intro to Seduction*. W.L. Tracy's short story, *Titilayo* premieres in this anthology as well as her poem, *Longing, Lust, and Love*.

YAKIRI TRUTH - is a New Orleans native. She wrote her first poem at five years of age. Her writing career began at age 17 when she accepted an editorial position with *Excellence Magazine*. She has also worked as a Technical Writer for Topp Knotch Personnel, Inc., and other small businesses. Today, Yakiri works as a staff writer for *SABLE Magazine*. She is also working on her debut novel, entitled, *Until Death Do Us Part*.

DILLON WATSON - currently resides in the Southeast. She began writing fiction in the seventh grade and hasn't stopped since. Her story entitled *Too Late* will appear in *Erotic Interludes 4: Extreme Passions* by Bold Strokes Books. After her work day is over, her time spent writing runs neck in neck with her time spent reading. She is currently working on two romance novels and a couple of short stories.

About the Editor

SHONIA L. BROWN – lives in Atlanta, GA, as one of few remaining Atlanta natives. She is also one of the contributing writers in this anthology as well as the author of *A Deeper Love* (2002). Her fiction has appeared in the anthology, *Ma-Ka Diasporic Juks: Contemporary Writing by Queers of African Descent*. She is also a Technical Writer for a pharmaceutical software company and an entrepreneur who founded and maintains an arts and entertainment technology company designed to market and promote independent artists.

Through the original development of Nghosi Books.com's online artist forum, Shonia fed her need to share her creative talents (blessings) with other independent artists who also embraced the power and importance of giving and receiving. Through her four year development of Nghosi Books.com, Shonia has created a one-stop shop for news and reviews of emerging artists that includes a quarterly e-zine, *Nghosi Arts*, 24-hour Internet radio program, *CNOTES Radio*, artist profiles, e-commerce site, event planning and artist showcase platform, and the new addition of a small print press for African-American LGBT literature.

In the midst of the various projects and community services that she performs, Shonia is working on her second novel, *The Minister's Wife*, which will premiere in early 2008.

Printed in the United States
210766BV00002B/22/A